# The Light of the Lovers' Moon

Center Point
Large Print

Also by Marcia Lynn McClure and available from
Center Point Large Print:

*Dusty Britches*
*Weathered Too Young*
*The Windswept Flame*
*The Heavenly Surrender*

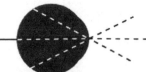

**This Large Print Book carries the
Seal of Approval of N.A.V.H.**

# The Light
## OF THE
# Lovers' Moon

Marcia Lynn McClure

CENTER POINT LARGE PRINT
THORNDIKE, MAINE

This Center Point Large Print edition
is published in the year 2017 by arrangement with
Distractions Ink.

The text of this Large Print edition is unabridged.
In other aspects, this book may vary
from the original edition.
Printed in the United States of America
on permanent paper.
Set in 16-point Times New Roman type.

ISBN: 978-1-68324-461-5

Library of Congress Cataloging-in-Publication Data

Names: McClure, Marcia Lynn, author.
Title: The light of the lovers' moon / Marcia Lynn McClure.
Description: Center Point Large Print edition. | Thorndike, Maine :
    Center Point Large Print, 2017.
Identifiers: LCCN 2017014429 | ISBN 9781683244615
    (hardcover : alk. paper)
Subjects: LCSH: Large type books. | GSAFD: Love stories.
Classification: LCC PS3613.C36 L54 2017 | DDC 813/.6—dc23
LC record available at https://lccn.loc.gov/2017014429t

To Jean, Jean, the Ten-Pin Queen!

For heartwarming friendship, for fantastic one-liners, and for a little story you once shared with me. As you know, I built this entire book around that little tale you told!

# CHAPTER ONE

Violet Fynne pressed her fingers to the dark scar in the bark of the old cottonwood tree. Gently she traced the heart carved there—each letter etched in its center. A warm breeze stirred the leaves overhead, causing radiant sunlight to speckle the grass beneath the tree. She smiled, suddenly bathed in whimsical sentiment. She fancied the dancing dapples of sunshine appeared more as frolicking fairies rather than as simple dollops of light.

Still, it was the carving in the tree's trunk that held Violet's attention captive—so old, so dark, lovingly etched many years before.

"S.W.," she whispered, the tips of her fingers lingering, caressing the letters over and over again. Had it truly been nearly ten years? Truly? At times it seemed it had been ten years; at times it seemed it had been a hundred. Yet here and there, it did not seem so long, as if only yesterday the bark of the cottonwood stood unmarred—as unmarred as her heart once was.

Violet closed her soft, hazel eyes. Slowly she inhaled, willing her mind and body—every one of her senses—to drink in the moment. There were meadowlarks some distance off, their familiar calls soothing, delightful. A shallow breeze toyed with a loose strand of her hair—whispered through the tree limbs and leaves, as if the wind had something to say but could not quite awaken to yawn or speak. The shade was cool where Violet sat, and she let one hand travel over the grass, the tender blades tickling her palm. Then, as if some invisible conductor of nature's sonata had raised his baton, the cicadas in the branches overhead began to sing.

All at once, Violet could nearly touch the past—nearly hear it, nearly smell it, nearly taste it. Her heart remembered delight then, even as it yet ached. She wondered if she could perhaps linger forever beneath the old cottonwood, where sunlight danced among the leaves, the scent of grass, bird nests, and flowers mingled with the meadowlark's call to lull the world to contentment.

"Yer trespassin', lady."

Violet stiffened—held her breath as she heard a rifle hammer cock. She opened her eyes and remained motionless, rigid with fear.

"I said, yer trespassin'," the man said again.

Slowly Violet stood, swallowing the fear in her throat. Turning, she saw the man standing behind her—the barrel of a Winchester rifle aimed at her head. The sun hung high at the stranger's back. She raised her hand to shade her eyes from the searing radiance. The man was large, in height and in stature. He wore a weathered hat, pulled so far down on his brow that even if the sun hadn't been merciless behind him, Violet could not have clearly seen his face.

"I-I'm sorry," Violet stammered, still facing the fatal end of the rifle. "I grew up here . . . in Rattler Rock. I've just returned a-and was taking a walk . . . to see a few places and things I remember as a child. Mr. Buddy used to let us—"

"Bud's dead," the stranger growled. "I own this land now . . . and I don't take to trespassers, no matter where they sprouted."

"Of course," Violet said. "Forgive me. I'll just be—"

"On yer way," the stranger finished for her.

Violet sighed, relieved when he lowered the barrel of the rifle.

"Yes," she said, nodding to the man, grateful he'd simply warned her instead of blowing a hole through her.

Quickly she made her way from the clearing surrounding the cottonwood tree and back to the road. As the scent of warm dirt and grass filled her lungs, she mumbled, "Mr. Buddy? Dead?"

It seemed impossible that Buddy Chisolm was dead, that anything could have killed him—man, beast, disease, or even old age. Buddy Chisolm couldn't die! As a child, Violet had been more certain of Buddy Chisolm's immortality than of almost anything else in life. Buddy Chisolm had lived through wars—broken and healed half the bones in his body. Certainly he'd been nearly seventy when Violet's family had left Rattler Rock. Yet she could not believe a mere eighty years had beaten Buddy Chisolm.

She sighed, melancholy over the knowledge Buddy Chisolm no longer walked the earth. It was hard to imagine him at rest—any kind of rest—but especially the heavenly sort. She gazed up into the clear, blue sky, wondering if old Buddy were causing chaos in heaven. Was he sitting on a cloud watching over Rattler Rock, grumbling about fences that needed fixing and horses needing to be broken? Was he telling tales to the angel-children in the clouds—tales of battle and adventure, the sort of tales he'd told to Violet and Stoney so many years ago? She could well imagine it. Violet giggled out loud at a vision of Buddy Chisolm sitting around a heavenly campfire, captivating the imaginations of little angel-children with stories of bear hunting and swimming faster than water moccasins.

Oh, how she and Stoney used to love to listen to his stories, sitting for hours, entirely enraptured by Buddy Chisolm's wild tales! She imagined the angel-children in heaven were no less enraptured. She adored the thought of those heavenly children being as delighted by crusty old Buddy Chisolm as she and Stoney had been all those years before.

*Stoney,* she thought then. *Stoney Wrenn.* Violet winced as her heart ached anew.

It was ever her heart ached at the thought of Stoney—for it was ever she was haunted by his memory. Dropping her gaze from the heavens above to the dirt of the road beneath her feet, the familiar guilt and agonizing that thoughts of Stoney Wrenn always bred wove through her. Oh, she understood it wasn't her fault, that there was nothing she could've done. She'd been a child, after all—and what could a child have done to help Stoney? Still, the guilt and regret haunted her—haunted her more miserably than the ghosts of the old abandoned house on Buddy Chisolm's property had haunted their last domain.

She hadn't inquired about Stoney, of course. She was hoping information regarding him would be presented in a more natural, less obvious manner. Yet no one had mentioned him. Still, she'd only been in town a day and a night—only seen a handful of people—and none of them had known her family when they had lived in Rattler Rock. Yet it was somewhat agonizing, not knowing whether Stoney Wrenn were even still alive. She feared the worst, of course—for she envisioned Stoney's father's violent rampages had most likely only increased once Violet's family had left Rattler Rock almost ten years before.

Violet paused in walking, closed her eyes, and

lifted her face toward the sun as memories began to wash over her. Oh, how she used to love to run, down the very road she now trod. How she and Stoney would run—barefoot and happy as any two larks in spring—racing down the road toward old Buddy's shack. She could almost feel the dirt between her toes, the tiny pebbles under her feet. She could almost hear Stoney's laughter—almost see the strange green-blue opalescence of his mesmerizing eyes.

Remaining still, Violet let the memory bathe her in melancholy, flood her senses with the joy of the past and with the pain reminiscing would inevitably bring. Yet she would remember—she could never forget—and she would welcome the memory—and the pain.

· · · · · · · · · ·

"I'll wallop ya good if I catch you, girl!" Stoney shouted.

"Well, you'll never catch me!" Violet called over her shoulder.

She giggled as she ran. Stoney Wrenn could never catch her; she was far too quick. "Like a danged rabbit," Stoney always said. Oh, once in a while, she'd let him win—just to make him feel better. Or let him catch her—just because she loved the feel of his arms going around her as they tumbled to the ground. Yet today—today she was impish, and she ran even faster as she saw old Buddy Chisolm's shack up ahead.

"I'll turn you over my knee, Violet Fynne!" Stoney shouted.

Violet shook her head as she ran, amused at Stoney's endless efforts to remind her he was thirteen and far more grown up than her mere eleven years.

"Come on then, old man!" Violet hollered. "Catch me if ya want me!"

He wouldn't catch her, but he wouldn't give up trying either, and her smile broadened at the knowledge.

Violet collapsed in a heap on the grass in front of Buddy Chisolm's shack. She lay back, placing a hand on her bosom to calm her pounding heart as she gazed up into the sky.

Moments later, Stoney collapsed beside her. "Yer a rotten little rat, Viola," Stoney panted.

"My name is Violet, and you're just mad 'cause I beat you . . . again," Violet breathed.

"Violet or Viola . . . my mama says they're the same thing," he teased.

"They are not the same thing," Violet argued.

"Are so," he said. "A dainty little flower . . . good for nothin' or nobody . . . except for old ladies who like to press 'em in books."

"Violets are a very beautiful flower! They're named for the lovely maidens in Greek mythology who—"

"Yeah, yeah, yeah," Stoney interrupted, rolling his eyes with such dramatic effect that Violet wondered if it hurt. "Them maidens were so beautiful that Cupid himself told Venus they was purtier than she was. And Venus got all fussy and jealous and beat them girls until they turned purple and turned into violets. I heard it a million times."

"And you'll hear it a million more if ya keep callin' me Viola," Violet giggled.

Stoney laughed, turned on his side, and studied Violet. He smiled and said, "Well, it's just that yer so much purtier than those girls Venus was beatin' on. I just like to call ya Viola . . . so's you'll remember yer purtier."

Violet giggled. She looked to Stoney—studied his handsome smile, the unusual green-blue of his eyes. She fancied they looked just like rare opals, all greenish-blue and shiny, like the ones set in the expensive earrings her Aunt Rana wore every Thanksgiving.

"Don't you be tryin' to woo me, Stoney Wrenn," she said. "I know your ways . . . even if all the other girls don't. You call me Viola to ruffle my feathers. So don't waste your time in flatterin' me. I'm immune to your charms."

"Immune?" he asked, raking fingers through his tousled brown hair. "Who uses that word?" He shook his head, still smiling. "You read too many books, Viola."

"Violet," she corrected. "And I do not." Violet pulled a long strand of hair from the loose braid

14

hanging down her back. Twisting the hair with her index finger, she said, "I just prefer stories . . . instead of wallerin' in the mud the way you and them other boys do."

"I like stories too," Stoney said. "That's why I come here . . . to ol' Bud's house. He tells the best stories I know. Better stories than the ones yer always readin' in them books of yers. What kind of a girly name is Cupid anyway?"

"Who's causin' all the racket out here?"

Violet looked to see Buddy Chisolm step out of his weathered old shack and into the sunlight. The frown at his aged brow only emphasized the deep wrinkles on his forehead. His white hair knew no order—simply stuck up this way and that as if he'd just rolled out of bed. Buddy pulled his suspenders up over his shoulders, and Violet smiled as they snapped into place.

"It's just us, Bud," Stoney said.

Buddy Chisolm's frown softened. He even grinned a little as he looked to Stoney and then Violet.

"Vi'let Fynne," he began, "yer mama will tan yer hide good if she sees you with yer skirts hitched up like that."

"Oh!" Violet exclaimed. It was true. She'd pulled the back of her skirt and petticoat between her legs and tucked them into her waistband at the front before she'd started racing Stoney to Bud's house. It wasn't proper to remain in such an indecorous state in the presence of a man. Quickly she tugged at the hem of her skirt and petticoats, smoothing them around her ankles as she sat up.

"Yer daddy give you a beatin' yet today, boy?" Bud asked Stoney.

As ever, Violet's stomach churned. Her heart ached at the thought of what Stoney endured at the hand of his violent father.

"Not today, Bud," Stoney said, smiling. "It's been near a week since he took out after me."

"Good. Good," Bud said, nodding. "He ain't takin' out after yer ma yet?"

"No. Just me."

"Well, if he does raise a hand to yer mama . . . you shoot that ol' son of a . . ." Bud paused, glancing at Violet. He cleared his throat and continued. "You shoot that ol' yeller skunk if he ever takes after her . . . right in the back if ya have to."

"Oh, I will," Stoney said.

Violet felt the frown puckering her brow soften as Stoney smiled at her. He winked, reached out, and pinched her cheek with affectionate reassurance.

"So," Bud sighed. Violet watched—couldn't help but smile—as the elderly man eased himself down onto the ground in front of them. "What kind of horse . . . manure . . . are you two shovelin' today?"

"Violet seen the light," Stoney said.

All at once, Violet's anxiety eased as she remembered the reason she and Stoney had sought out Bud's company.

"Well, praise be to the Lord, girl!" old Bud exclaimed. "But I thought yer folks already went to church and such."

Violet laughed. She glanced to Stoney. He was laughing too, and she thought his laughter was the most blessed sound on earth.

"No, no, Bud," Stoney chuckled. "She seen the light in yer old place . . . the lovers' light. There was a full moon last night, and I snuck her out of her house to go down there and watch for it. She didn't believe me before—said she had to see it for herself—so I snuck her out to yer old place, and she seen the light."

Buddy Chisolm smiled. "Oh! I see," he chuckled. "So, Miss Vi'let," he began, "you still think I'm a liar now?"

Violet shook her head. "I-I admit . . . I thought you were just pullin' everybody's leg about the ghosts in your old house, Mr. Chisolm."

"And now?" the old man prodded.

"I saw it for myself," Violet admitted. "There really are ghosts in that old house!"

"Yes, there are," Bud said. His eyes narrowed. He looked from Violet to Stoney. "You be careful sneakin' out like that, boy. If yer daddy catches you—"

"He won't catch me," Stoney interrupted. "But I want you to tell Viola the story, Bud. You tell it so much better than me."

Buddy Chisolm paused. He inhaled a deep breath—scratched the thick whiskers of his chin with the crooked fingers of one leathery hand.

"I don't know, Stoney," Buddy said. "Might be Miss Vi'let here would take to wakin' up screamin' in the night for the fright of knowin' the story. I can't have Graham Fynne knockin' down my door for scarin' the life outta his girl."

"I won't scream, Mr. Bud," Violet promised. "I swear I won't! No matter how scary the story is."

Buddy Chisolm winked at Stoney and chuckled. "Well, then . . . I guess it can't do too much harm to tell ya the tale, now can it?"

Violet shook her head with assurance, her insides swelling with delighted anticipation. "Look!" she exclaimed, holding one arm out for Stoney to inspect. "I'm so excited I got chicken skin!"

Stoney smiled, chuckled, and ran a hand over Violet's arms. Violet giggled when Stoney's touch caused the goose bumps on her arms to increase rather than to settle a bit.

"You ready then, kids?" Buddy Chisolm asked.

"Yes, sir!" Stoney said.

Violet nodded, drew her knees up to her chin, and waited. The grass was cool beneath her seat, the sun warm on her face, anticipation ripe in her young mind.

"Well, then, I guess I'll start by warnin' you. This ain't all around a happy story," Buddy began, "but it is a story to stay with ya all yer livin' days."

Violet smiled as Stoney sat up, crossed his legs, and leaned forward—already captivated by the old man's tale.

"That ol' house yonder, the one Stoney snuck you up to last night," Buddy said, pointing in the direction of the old house. "It was built before the war. Some ol' son of a . . . some ol' boy with a wagonload of money and no sense at all come out here from back east—from New York City, in fact. He hired him a bunch of fellers, and they built that house from the ground up. And it was a fine thing to see! Oh, indeed it was. A fine thing! Oh, it don't figure out here at all—not out west here where folks like their space, their horses, and their cattle. Still, folks said this ol' boy wanted to live in luxury and get away from the city all at the same time. Now, you and I know it can't be done. Either ya live for luxury or ya live for yer soul. Right?"

"Right!" Stoney said.

Violet wasn't quite sure what Buddy meant—but it didn't matter. She just wanted to hear the story of how the ghosts came to be in the old house.

"Anyhow," Buddy continued, "this rich feller built that house, filled it with his fancy belongin's, and tried to settle in. I say tried . . . 'cause he just couldn't seem to settle. Oh, he had his big house, and he had all his things of worth, but he didn't have nothin' else—no wife, no children, nothin' of importance. Folks said he just weren't happy, always wanderin' 'round town, lookin' like a lost pup."

"Poor little thing," Violet mumbled. She blushed when she heard Buddy and Stoney both chuckle.

"He was a grown-up man, Viola," Stoney reminded.

"I still feel sorry for him. He didn't know what was important at all," she said.

"That's right, girl. He didn't," Buddy agreed. "At least, not until he met her."

"Her?" Violet breathed, smiling with delight.

"That's right," Buddy chuckled. "Her—the purtiest gal he'd ever seen. Oh, she was a sight! Eyes as dark as the night and hair as bright as the sunshine! Everybody said she was a beauty. And it weren't just her face and figure that folks admired . . . but her kind heart and sweet soul."

Violet sighed, enchanted. Stoney poked an elbow at her rib, and she shoved at his shoulder.

"Yer so sappy, Viola," Stoney chuckled.

"Hush," she scolded. "Go on, Mr. Chisolm. Please go on."

Buddy smiled. "Well, folks say the very moment that rich man from New York City saw that purty girl from Rattler Rock . . . well, he knew what true wealth was then. He courted the girl and won her heart. Through and through, he won her heart . . . and she owned his like nobody had ever owned the heart of a lover before. They were married, right there in the old church outside of town. They moved into the house yonder 'cause . . . well, it was there. Didn't seem wise not to live in somethin' that was already built and waitin' . . . no matter how ridiculous it was for these parts."

Buddy Chisolm paused—stretched his bowed legs out before him as best as an old man could. "So they settled in, these two young lovers . . . and folks said they was happy. 'Blissful' is what folks said. They had themselves nine or ten kids—"

"Nine or ten?" Stoney exclaimed. "You said it was three or four when you told it to me."

Buddy chuckled and reached out to tousle Stoney's hair with one gnarled hand. "Oh, that's right. It was three or four," Bud said. "I was thinkin' of my own folks. I had me nine brothers and sisters—five brothers and four sisters."

"I knew that," Stoney said, pride beaming from his handsome face as he smiled at Violet.

"So they had themselves a few kids . . . and was happy as two people and their babies ever was,"

Buddy continued. "Oh, sure they was in that big ol' house. But it didn't make no nevermind. Love makes a home, whether it's a mansion or a shack. Ain't that right, Miss Vi'let?"

"Yes, sir!" Violet agreed.

Buddy Chisolm sighed; his smile faded a bit. "But then . . . then that ol' war broke out. That feller from New York City just couldn't sit still and watch his brothers go to fightin' without him. 'God means for the Union to survive,' he told his purty wife and his little children. 'How can I sit by and expect others to protect it if I ain't willin' to do the same?' His wife agreed; so did his young'uns. So he marched off to war, leavin' his family behind in that ol' house out yonder. Truth was he was a might old to go off to soldierin', already forty years to his name. But duty and freedom was callin' to him . . . so he went." Buddy paused—frowned a moment. "It was the consumption that got 'em. Wiped out near half the town . . . includin' the purty wife and the children livin' in the ol' house yonder. The war ended, and that ol' boy survived, in time to come on back to Rattler Rock and have his wife die in his arms, then bury every one of his three children. Folks say he never got over it. Folks say he never lived in the house again. No one ever know'd what become of the man who had the house built. Could be he died right there in it . . . just rotted away. Could be he moved—

couldn't take the pain of the loss of his family. Could be he went back to New York City and died there. That's why folks say it's the ghost of his purty wife roamin' in that house—that she's lookin' for her husband still. But I say different."

"What do you say, Mr. Chisolm?" Violet asked in a breathless whisper.

"I say it's both of 'em," Buddy answered. "I say it's the man from New York City and his purty wife both, just wanderin' through their home together. Maybe their kids are with 'em, though I only ever saw two lights at once and I only seen two lights together three times. Usually there's only one. Still, however and wherever the man died, I think he came back here—his spirit anyway. I think he came back here to search for his lover, and I think he found her. I think they're in that house together. That's what I think."

He looked to Violet. "Did you see one or two lights last night, girl?"

"Just the one," Violet said. "It was downstairs one moment, then upstairs the next." Again Violet felt the hair on the back of her neck prickle at the memory. "Do you think it was just one of them I saw?"

"Not necessarily," Buddy said.

"You can hear 'em wailin' or laughin' sometimes, late at night," Stoney said. He nodded at Violet. "I've heard 'em before. It's the scariest sound I ever knew!" He looked to Buddy and asked, "Ain't that right, Bud? Can't ya hear 'em sometimes?"

Buddy nodded. "Sometimes. But mostly it's the light that lets ya know they're wanderin' about . . . and only durin' a full moon. The light only comes durin' a full moon."

Violet sighed. "I think it is both of them, Mr. Chisolm—the two lovers, just like you say."

"But what if the feller never died?" Stoney asked. He frowned. "What if he's still alive? What if it's the purty wife just wanderin' around the ol' house waitin' for him? No one knows for sure he's dead."

"That's true. But it don't seem likely he really lived long after losin' so much. A man's heart can only take so much pain before it quits altogether," Buddy said. "Nope, I think his soul is right there, lingerin' in the ol' house yonder . . . with hers."

"I like to think they're together," Violet said.

"That's 'cause yer so sappy," Stoney said. "It's a lot more interestin' to think it's one ghost wanderin' about lookin' for another."

Violet stuck her tongue out at Stoney, and he laughed.

"Keep that tongue in yer mouth, Viola . . . else I'll yank it right outta yer head," Stoney threatened.

Buddy Chisolm chuckled and shook his head. "Boy, don't you know what that means?" Buddy asked. "When a girl sticks her tongue out at ya the way Vi'let done just now?"

"Yeah!" Stoney said. "It means she's askin' for trouble." Violet giggled as Stoney reached out and tickled her ribs with his fingers.

Buddy chuckled again. "It means she's a-wantin' ya to kiss her. That's what it means."

Violet gasped, blushed scarlet, and looked to Buddy Chisolm. "That ain't true!" she exclaimed. She was suddenly hot—embarrassed—felt shy.

"Oh, don't let yer mama hear you sayin' 'ain't' Viola," Stoney scolded. He wagged an index finger at her and shook his head. "She'll tan yer hide if she hears that," he teased.

"But it ain't true!" she squealed. "Is it?" For a moment, she wondered. Was that what it meant when a person stuck her tongue out at another person? Surely not! Her own mama stuck her tongue out at her daddy all the time!

"Why sure it is, Miss Vi'let," Buddy said. "And I'm sure Stoney here would be happy to oblige! Wouldn't ya, Stoney?"

Violet saw Buddy wink at Stoney.

"Yes, sir, I would," Stoney said.

Violet recognized the mischief gleaming in Stoney's eyes, and she started to scramble away.

"Oh, no you don't, Viola!" Stoney laughed, taking hold of her ankle. "If yer gonna stick yer tongue out at me . . . then I guess I better make good!"

"No! Don't you dare, Stoney Wrenn!" Violet squealed as Stoney rolled her on her back, straddled her waist, sat down hard on her legs, and pinned her wrists at the sides of her head. "Don't let him do it, Mr. Chisolm! Don't let him!"

But Buddy Chisolm only chuckled. "But you asked him to, girl! What's the boy to do? A gentleman always obliges a woman!"

"Kissy, kissy, Viola Fynne!" Stoney teased, leaning over until his face was only a few inches from her own. Violet continued to struggle as Stoney said, "How 'bout a good lickery one?"

Violet immediately ceased in wriggling and trying to escape. "What do you mean a 'lickery one'?" she asked.

Stoney chuckled. "You know, a big lickery kiss, like the one we seen Roy Gribbs lay to Ethel McCormick the other day when we was peekin' at them from the branches of that ol' cottonwood tree."

Violet gasped, horrified. "Stoney Wrenn, don't you dare!"

Buddy Chisolm laughed. "You get her good, Stoney. Don't you be lettin' her get away with disrespectin' you the likes she did!"

Violet squealed as Stoney kissed her cheek, then her forehead.

"Mmm-mmm! Viola, you taste just like sweet cream on berries," he teased. "Now, hold still so's I can kiss ya good."

"You let me up, Stoney! You let me up!" Violet squealed. She was giggling now, knowing full well Stoney was only teasing.

"Come on, let's have us a big lickery one, just like Roy Gribbs and Ethel McCormick," he laughed, wagging his tongue just above her mouth. He took hold of her face and chin, trying to keep her head from rolling back and forth in avoiding his kiss.

But Violet stuck her tongue out again, this time spitting and spraying Stoney's face with saliva.

Stoney shouted and immediately released Violet as he wiped his face on his shirt sleeve. "She spit on me!" he hollered.

Buddy Chisolm laughed and laughed, rocking back and forth, overcome with amusement.

Distracted by wiping his face, Stoney rolled off Violet to sit in the grass next to her. "You spit on me, Viola!" he hollered. "That ain't fair!"

"Well, don't hold me down! You know I hate to be held down," she told him, giggling as Buddy Chisolm winked at her.

"You two are a handful, I'll tell you that," the old man sighed. "A real handful!"

"He knows better than to hold me down," Violet said.

"I guess he does," Buddy chuckled.

"I coulda kissed ya if I'd really wanted to do it," Stoney grumbled. "But you ain't old enough."

Violet smiled as she studied him. Lands, he was

a handsome boy! Furthermore, he was her best friend. She couldn't imagine how dull life would be without him to get into mischief with.

"I'm sorry I spit on you," she told him.

Stoney grinned. "I'm sorry I held ya down," he said.

Violet heard Buddy Chisolm chuckle again. She looked to see him still smiling at her and Stoney.

"There's a dead coyote down by the crick. It's half rotted through if you two want to see it," Buddy said.

"Really?" Stoney asked. "Did you shoot it?"

Violet smiled, delighted by Stoney's ever morbid curiosity.

"Nope," Buddy said, shaking his head. "Looks like somethin' bigger took it down."

"Ya wanna go down there with me, Viola?" Stoney asked.

Violet giggled—for his green-blue opaline eyes fairly sparkled with excitement.

"All right," she said. "But I gotta be home before supper."

Stoney jumped to his feet and offered his hand to her. Violet took his hand, and he began pulling her in the direction of the stream.

"Thanks, Buddy!" Stoney called over his shoulder. "I'll be over tomorrow to help you with that fencin'."

"Thank you, Mr. Chisolm," Violet called as she

hurried to keep up with Stoney. "I really enjoyed the story!"

"Now don't you two go touchin' nothin' with yer bare hands," Buddy called. "Find a couple of sticks to poke around with."

"We will," Stoney hollered.

Violet giggled, delighted as Stoney Wrenn led her off to another adventure.

"I love dead animals!" Stoney said, glancing back at her and smiling.

"I know," Violet said. Then, sighing as Stoney squeezed her hand with excitement, Violet Fynne lowered her voice and whispered, "And I love you."

. . . . . . . . . .

Violet opened her eyes. The day was still bright, the air still fresh. Yet tears now stained her pretty, pink cheeks—tears wept for a boy she'd loved nearly a decade before, a boy she'd abandoned when he'd needed her most.

Inhaling a deep breath of resolve to buck up, Violet began to walk—walk away from the past and toward the little house the county school board had provided for her as part of her wages. It wouldn't be long before the house would be in sight. She'd make a little stew for herself for supper and then maybe go over her lessons for tomorrow—her first day of teaching at the Rattler Rock School.

She heard a rider approaching from behind.

Turning, she nodded as the rider reined in before her. The rhythm of her heart increased as hope began to rise in her.

"Howdy, miss," the man said.

Violet shaded her eyes and looked up at the man. He respectfully removed his hat. Quickly, Violet looked to his eyes. Blue eyes. He had blue eyes—not green-blue opalescent ones like Stoney's had been. A tiny twinge of painful disappointment pecked at her heart.

"Hello," Violet greeted.

"I'm Sheriff Fisher," the man said, offering a friendly smile.

Violet noted he was a very handsome man. She smiled in return.

"You must be Miss Fynne, the new teacher over at the school."

"Yes," Violet confirmed. "Violet Fynne."

"Well, I'm pleased to finally meet ya, Miss Fynne," Sheriff Fisher said. "Hope yer settlin' in all right."

"Yes, sir. Thank you," Violet said.

"Well, let me know if I can help ya in any way, miss," he said, touching the brim of his hat.

"Thank you," Violet said.

He nodded and rode off down the road.

Violet watched him go. "Fisher," she whispered. She didn't remember having known any Fishers when she'd lived in Rattler Rock before. "Hmm."

Another deep breath inhaled and Violet was off again toward her new home. She thought of the sweet rolls sitting on the kitchen table—the ones the parson's wife had dropped by for her that morning, an offering of welcome. She'd seemed a kind woman, another person new to Rattler Rock since Violet's family had left so many years before. For a moment, she wondered if there were any folks left in town she'd known before—if Stoney Wrenn were still in town or even alive. What if no one was left who knew what had become of him?

A large cloud moved in front of the sun. Violet thought it seemed foreboding, the fact the cloud had blotted out the light just as she had begun to wonder if Stoney's very existence had been blotted out somehow. Maybe he had never existed at all, she mused. Maybe she had only dreamed him up—a friend of her imagination with whom to pass the days when she had been lonely as a child.

Shaking her head, Violet straightened her posture as she walked. No. Stoney Wrenn had lived—lived in Rattler Rock ten years ago. Surely someone was left who would know what had become of him. She would discover his fate and at last lay to rest the wild haunting in her mind and heart. She would. She had to.

# CHAPTER TWO

"Good morning, boys and girls," Violet chirped with enthusiasm. "I'm Miss Fynne, your new teacher." She smiled, even for the rather skeptical group of young faces seated before her—and only fifteen skeptical faces. Yet she wasn't too disappointed in the numbers. It was to be expected the citizens of Rattler Rock would be wary of a new teacher. Furthermore, fewer students meant Violet would be able to nurture individual associations with her pupils. Thus, she was not disappointed and continued her greeting. "I hope to know each of you very well," she said. "And I hope you'll find school a thing you look forward to . . . instead of dreading."

One small girl, perhaps six years of age, giggled. Violet smiled and winked at the child. Violet knew the little girl, tawny-haired and bright-eyed, would fast become a joy to teach.

"Now, as I said, I do want to know each of you. Yet it does not quite seem fair that I would expect you to tell me all about yourselves without being willing to tell you all about me first, now does it?" Violet asked.

"No, ma'am," a young boy said.

Violet smiled when he blushed. It was apparent he hadn't meant to speak his thoughts.

"Therefore, we will take a few moments right now, and I will answer any questions you might have for me," she said. "Does that seem like a good start?"

Nods erupted, and Violet thought the children's faces looked like little pansies nodding in the spring breeze.

"Good!" she giggled. "Now, what questions do you have for me? And raise your hands please."

One older boy in the back of the room raised a hand. He sat slumped in his seat, a look of daring on his skeptical brow. "How old are ya, and how long you been teachin'?" he asked.

"I'll be twenty-one in September, I've had my certificate for four years, and I've been teaching for almost as long," Violet answered. "And, in return, may I ask your name, sir?"

The boy straightened at being called "sir." Violet knew older boys struggled with enduring school, yet it was so very important that they received as much education as possible. Therefore, she had learned to appeal to the young male ego often.

The boy grinned and said, "Dayton Fisher. The sheriff's my brother."

"Oh!" Violet exclaimed. "I met Sheriff Fisher yesterday. It's wonderful to meet you, Dayton. You're far as handsome as your older brother."

A broad smile spread across Dayton's face as he said, "Thank ya, ma'am!"

Violet silently congratulated herself: one pupil in her pocket, fourteen more to go. "Another question, please," she prodded.

A girl of perhaps seven or eight years, looking much in appearance like the small girl on the front row, raised a tentative hand.

"Yes?" Violet asked.

"My mama says you lived here when you were my age," the girl said. "Is that true? Are you really from Rattler Rock?"

"I am," Violet answered. "I was born in that little yellow house . . . the one just north of town. I lived here until I was almost twelve. Then my family moved back east. Perhaps I know your mother."

"My mama is Ethel Gribbs," the girl began.

"She's my mama too!" the small, tawny-haired girl on the front row erupted. The younger girl folded her arms across her chest, frowned, and began to pout.

"So you two girls must be sisters," Violet said. "We'll have to talk about that later . . . for I'm sure you have so much to tell me." This seemed to soothe the younger girl, and she smiled.

Violet returned her attention to the older girl. "Is . . . is Roy Gribbs your father then?"

The girl nodded and smiled, entirely delighted that Violet knew her father. A quick memory of Roy Gribbs and his girl, Ethel McCormick, sharing "lickery" kisses under Buddy Chisolm's old cottonwood tree lingered in Violet's mind. She giggled a little in her throat, delighted to know Roy and Ethel had wed.

"I remember your father and mother," Violet said. "And what did they name their two girls?"

"Three!" the younger Gribbs girl corrected.

"Remember to raise your hand before answering a question, all right, sweetie?" Violet taught.

The little girl nodded, wildly agreeable.

Violet nodded to the older sister, encouraging her response.

"I'm Hester, and she's Susan," the older Gribbs girl said.

"I'm glad to meet you," Violet said. "If I had taken a minute to gaze at you both a bit, I might have guessed Ethel was your mother. You both are quite as pretty as I remember her to be. Any other questions?" she asked.

An older girl timidly raised a hand. She had the blackest hair Violet had ever seen and beautiful blue eyes.

"Yes?" Violet urged.

"Have ya ever been married, Miss Fynne?" the girl asked.

"No," Violet answered. "I haven't."

"Why not?" the girl asked.

Violet paused. She laced her fingers, letting her hands hang in front of her. "Hmm. This is when I have to make a decision," she said aloud. "If I find the courage to tell you the truth, you might heckle me. If I don't choose to tell you why, you'll wonder if I'm keeping secrets . . . and then you might not trust me."

"Tell us the truth!" a boy on the back row called. "We won't heckle ya."

Violet smiled at the dark-haired beauty of a girl who had posed the question. She thought for a moment that this girl looked the way Violet had always dreamt of looking, mesmerizing in her beauty. Girls, or women, who owned great beauty had always intimidated Violet, no matter how hard she tried not to let them.

"Very well," Violet began, "I will tell you the truth." She inwardly smiled as she saw all fifteen sets of eyes widen with anticipation. "Though it's not a very interesting reason." She inhaled a deep breath of truth-telling resolve and answered, "I suppose it's not simply because I haven't found the right man. It's more likely for the fact I'm haunted by a love my heart cannot seem to release . . . for whatever reason. At least, not yet. I have had the opportunity to marry . . . but not the desire to wed those who have presented themselves, worthy though they may have been. Is that a good enough answer for you?"

The dark-haired girl nodded, smiled, and said, "I'm Maya Asbury, Miss Fynne. And thank you for being honest with me."

"You're welcome," Violet said. "I find that honesty is usually the best road to travel."

"Usually?" Dayton Fisher asked.

"Yes . . . usually. Another honest answer."

Another older boy, sitting in the back and next to Dayton, raised a callused hand.

Violet smiled and nodded at the young man. "Yes?"

"Is it true you knew Stoney Wrenn before he was a womanizin' ol' crank?" the boy asked.

"He ain't a womanizer!" Maya Asbury exclaimed. Turning around to glare at the boy, she added, "And he ain't an ol' crank!"

"He is too!" Dayton argued.

"No, he ain't!" another young woman said. "Yer just jealous 'cause yer sweet on Maya's sister and she's sweet on Stoney Wrenn instead of you!"

"That ain't true!" Dayton shouted. "Stoney Wrenn's a womanizin' ol' bastard, and you know it, Maya!"

A general gasp echoed through the room.

"Now . . . now children," Violet began—but the battling ranks were closing, boys on one side of the argument, girls on the other.

"Stoney Wrenn is the only true gentleman left in this town," Maya said. "And if that ain't obvious right this minute, I don't know what else is. He's a gentleman!"

"Like hell he is!" the older boy sitting next to Dayton hollered.

Violet put a thumb and an index finger to her mouth, her shrill whistle silencing the argument as all eyes turned to her once again.

"Now . . . boys," she began, "let's not use 'hell' in our schoolhouse . . . unless we're reading from the Bible, of course. Let's save that for other times. And . . . as far as Stoney Wrenn being a bastard . . . well, that's a very derogatory term cruelly used to describe those innocent children who are born into this world of a father who was not wed to the innocent child's mother at the time of the child's birth. I happen to know that Stoney Wrenn was born to a mother and a father who were married. Therefore, he is not a bastard—a term I do not approve of even when the circumstances may warrant it as fact. So I do not want to hear that word in our schoolhouse again either. Very well?"

"Yes, Miss Fynne," Dayton and his counterpart mumbled.

"Now, as for your question concerning my knowledge of Stoney Wrenn, I will be happy to answer it—as long as everyone agrees to keep their opinions and thoughts to themselves. All right?"

"Yes, Miss Fynne," the students chimed.

Violet's heart was hammering so hard within her bosom it was causing her ears to ring. Stoney Wrenn was alive! The knowledge caused a sensation of elation to well within her. Yet the argument—the boys hating the man Stoney Wrenn, the girls defending him—it was far more than merely disturbing.

She looked out to the waiting faces, the children waiting for her answer. She could not let her thoughts linger, nor lose her composure in front of her pupils. "I did know Stoney Wrenn when I lived here as a child," she began. "In truth, we were fast friends. He was a good, kind boy . . . and I sorely missed him when I was forced to leave Rattler Rock."

"I heard his pa beat on him somethin' terrible," Dayton said.

"Well, maybe he was all right as a boy . . . but he's a mean ol' thing now!" Dayton's friend said. "He'd as soon shoot ya for settin' foot on his property as look at ya."

Violet could see the fury in Maya Asbury's eyes, so she smiled at the girl—a smile of calming reassurance. "I believe I've answered your question, sir," Violet said to the boy next to Dayton. "Would you be so kind as to let me know your name in return?"

"Hagen Webster," the boy said.

"Thank you, Hagen," she said. Violet did not want to begin the lessons with her students at odds. Therefore, she knew other questions must be posed, questions that would settle the ruffled tempers of the older boys and girls.

"Another question, please," she offered, smiling

39

as if nothing at all had ruffled her own emotions.

A younger boy, sitting near Maya, raised his hand.

"Yes?"

"If'n you was born in Rattler Rock," the boy began, "did ya ever see the light?"

"I beg your pardon?" Violet asked, though her soul whispered that she already knew what he referred to.

"The light of the lovers' moon, out at the ol' Chisolm place, the one out there on Stoney Wrenn's property," the boy explained. "Did ya ever see that ghost light?"

Violet's mind was whirling! The old Chisolm place? Stoney Wrenn's property? The light? Inwardly she scolded herself for vowing to be so honest in answering the questions the children posed. Yet the lure of learning more about Stoney was too great to refuse.

"The old Chisolm property?" she asked. "Do . . . do you mean the fancy old house Mr. Buddy Chisolm owned? The one that was supposed to be haunted? Does Stoney Wrenn own that house now?"

"Yes, ma'am," the boy answered. "He owns all that property that old man used to own. That includes the ol' Chisolm place with the ghosts. Did ya ever see the light?"

Violet's thoughts were cast to the day before—to the moment she'd been kneeling under the old cottonwood tree on Buddy Chisolm's property. In her mind, she heard the click of the rifle hammer, heard the angry voice informing her she was trespassing. Had it been Stoney Wrenn himself who had thrown her off the place? Had she truly come so close to him—and not even known it?

"Well, did ya?" The young boy's question brought Violet's attention back to the school-room.

"Yes," she answered. "I did." The honest answer had escaped her mouth before she'd had time to stop it.

"You did?" the children gasped. Immediately Violet's pupils began whispering among themselves.

Violet sighed, knowing there would certainly be a price to pay for telling the truth this time. "Yes, I did," Violet repeated. "And now it's my turn, I believe. What is your name, young man?"

The boy who had asked the question about the light in the old Chisolm house sat mouth gaping open in astonishment. "Uh . . . Phelps Pierson, Miss Fynne," the boy answered.

"Phelps, is it?" Violet said, forcing a smile. "I like that name. I've never heard it as a first name before."

The boy smiled, and three more hands shot up.

"Before we continue," Violet began, "might I ask a question or two? I promise to answer yours again. But might you let me ask a few concerning

Rattler Rock—the way it may have changed since I lived here so long ago?"

The children nodded.

Violet inhaled deeply. She must be wary—ask questions that might glean information about Stoney without being obvious as to where her interest truly lay. "I had an old friend who lived here, someone I adored," she said. "From what I gather, I think he has passed on. Can anyone tell me exactly what happened to Mr. Chisolm?"

Dayton Fisher's hand was the first one up.

"Yes, Dayton?"

"He died. About four years ago," Dayton said. "That's why Stoney Wrenn owns all that property now. Old Buddy Chisolm left everything he owned in the world to Stoney Wrenn . . . for helpin' him out for so long, I guess."

Maya's hand rose.

"Maya?" Violet urged.

"Stoney Wrenn took care of Buddy Chisolm for a few years before Mr. Chisolm died," she explained. "He took care of his property and stock and the old man himself. That's why Mr. Chisolm left everything to Stoney. He didn't have any children of his own . . . just Stoney Wrenn."

"Thank you, Maya . . . Dayton," Violet said. Yet she wasn't finished—she wasn't finished in keeping the children's thoughts away from Stoney Wrenn. "Do any of you know how Mr. Chisolm died?"

Hagen raised his hand.

"Yes, Hagen," Violet said, nodding to the boy.

"Peaceful, in his sleep," Hagen answered. "My pa was out at the ol' Chisolm place helpin' Stoney Wrenn with some fencin'. They went into the ol' shack Buddy Chisolm lived in, and he was dead. He'd just gone to sleep and never woke up."

"That soothes my heart, Hagen. Thank you," Violet said, tears welling in her eyes.

Another girl—seated next to Maya—raised her hand.

"Yes," Violet said, nodding.

"So . . . you knew Buddy Chisolm?" the girl asked.

"I did," Violet answered. "He was a great friend to me. He used to buy pieces of hard butterscotch candy at Mr. Deavers's store—kept them in his pocket—and gave them to me whenever he saw me." The children giggled, and Violet decided they should know—know that Buddy Chisolm was a great man. She sighed and continued, "Mr. Chisolm used to tell the best stories I've ever heard—stories about the war, about battle . . ." She paused as the boys smiled. "And about love," she added and smiled as the girls all smiled. "He even told me the story of the light in the house on his property."

"He told you himself?" a little girl on the front row next to Susan Gribbs asked.

Violet nodded. "He did. And maybe I'll tell it to you one day . . . just the way he told it to me. Would you like that?"

The little girl nodded with delighted anticipation.

Violet turned her attention back to the girl who had originally asked her about Buddy. "And now . . . will you tell me your name? Now that I've told you about Buddy Chisolm?" she asked.

"Beth Deavers," the girl said, smiling. "That's my sister, Nina," she added, pointing to the little girl on the front row next to Susan. "Our grandpa owns the store, the one where Mr. Chisolm used to buy butterscotch!"

"How wonderful!" Violet exclaimed. "I feel I know you already."

Susan Gribbs raised her hand.

"Yes, Susan?" Violet couldn't help but smile at the little girl. She looked exactly like an angel.

"We ain't doin' no letters or numbers, Miss Fynne," Susan said.

"That's right, Susan," Violet said. "But I still have six more pupils who get to ask a question of me. So let's allow them their turn, and then we'll get to our lessons. Is that all right?"

Susan nodded, obviously delighted with Violet's answer.

A boy perhaps nine or ten years old raised his hand.

"Yes?" Violet smiled. The children were responding to her as she'd only dreamt they would.

"When will ya tell us about the time you seen the light of the lovers' moon?" he asked.

"Is that what they call the light at the old Chisolm place now?" Violet asked.

The boy nodded and said, "Yes, ma'am. And I'm Nate McGrath."

"Well, Nate," Violet said, "I'll tell you what—after we're done with questions, if we get our arithmetic finished before lunch, we'll go down to the creek, and I'll tell you all the story. Would that be all right?"

She giggled when the children nodded, again looking like a garden of pansy faces ruffled by the breeze. Violet found her heart felt light—yet heavy in the same moment. The children were wonderful! So many different personalities—such young, inquisitive, imaginative minds. Yet her thoughts lingered on what she'd learned of Stoney. A womanizing old crank? Surely not! Still, she remembered the angry man who told her to get off his property—the angry man who had held a Winchester rifle aimed at her head. From what the children had revealed, that man had been Stoney Wrenn himself, and that man was certainly not the boy she remembered. But how could it have been? Ten years could change anything—especially people.

Another girl raised her hand, and Violet nodded to her.

"Where did you live?" the girl asked. "After you left Rattler Rock?"

"Albany, New York," Violet said. "We moved to Albany. It's very far away." She frowned a moment. "Very far."

There had barely been enough time for the arithmetic lesson before lunch. In fact, Violet had shortened her planned lesson. She loathed arithmetic, and knowing she would have to see the lesson into the afternoon were she to present it in fullness, she shortened it rather than prolonging her own misery—and that of her pupils.

Lunch had given the children time to socialize, the older children choosing to sit near the creek and converse, the younger children running and playing nearby. Violet had eaten her meal on the schoolhouse steps, where she could watch the goings-on with clarity—clarity of vision, perhaps, but not of mind. Her mind was too alive with pondering what the children had told her of Stoney Wrenn. Had he indeed become a philanderer? A crank, as Hagen had termed it? The thought literally sickened Violet, and she vowed not to believe it. She chose to believe the girls' point of view—that Stoney Wrenn was a gentleman, that Dayton and Hagen were only envious of Maya's sister being "sweet" on

46

Stoney. She wondered then if perhaps Stoney was "sweet" on Maya's sister as well. This thought also sickened her, and she tossed the remains of her muffin to the ground where several ducks were waddling.

Violet opened the watch locket hanging at her bosom. It was time to begin lessons again. Standing, she took the handbell from its place in the small nook next to the schoolhouse door and rang it. Instantly, the children flocked to her— rosy-cheeked with refreshment.

"Should we head back to the crick, Miss Fynne?" Dayton asked.

Violet giggled. "You aren't about to let me get away without telling the story, are you, Dayton?"

"No, ma'am," he chuckled.

"Very well then," she said. "Everyone gather at the creek. But let's hope I don't have any angry parents arriving on my doorstep to scold me tonight."

"Scold you for what, Miss Fynne?" Susan Gribbs asked, taking hold of Violet's hand.

"For telling ghost stories instead of reading Dickens," Violet said.

"Who's Dickens?" Hagen asked.

"What?" Violet gasped with exaggerated dramatics. "Who is Dickens?" Violet smiled. "Oh, Sir Hagen, you have only just heightened my excitement for our studies. Especially when Christmas is near!"

• • •

When the children had settled—some on a fallen log that spanned the creek, others on the bank surrounding Violet—Violet began.

"I was eleven when I saw the light, the light of the lovers' moon as it seems you call it now," she began. She removed her shoes and stockings, letting her toes sink into the cool grass on the bank.

"I'm eleven!" Helen Little exclaimed.

"Me too," Nate McGrath added.

"So I was just the age Helen and Nate are now," Violet continued. "I had heard of the light in the old Chisolm house—many people in Rattler Rock had seen it—but I never had, probably because I was so young . . . and not in the habit of wandering about during a full moon."

The children giggled, and Violet leaned back. She loved the feel of the grass beneath her palms, of the fresh summer air and warm sunlight on her face.

"Well, Sto—my friend had sworn to me, sworn that he had seen the light in the old house on Buddy Chisolm's property," she said. "He swore to me he'd seen it more than once, but I didn't believe him. So, one night, when the moon was full, I heard a tapping at my window . . . a quiet, slow tapping—"

"Like a boney finger?" Phelps asked.

"Like a fleshy one," Violet said. She sighed as

Susan and Nina snuggled in closer to her. She knew someone's parents would raise Cain over her telling ghost stories during school. Yet it was far too late to reconsider now. She couldn't disappoint the children, not on her first day as their teacher.

"Who was it?" Beth asked.

"My friend, the one who had seen the light," Violet said. "He'd come to sneak me out of the house, to take me to the old Chisolm place to watch for it."

Dayton and Hagen both wore broad smiles, and Violet knew they liked her all the more for her admitted rebellion.

"Now, children. Do understand you should never sneak out of your safe homes at night," Violet said. "You should never do that. Do you understand?"

"Yes, Miss Fynne," the children said.

Maya, Dayton, and Hagen yet wore knowing smiles—and Violet winked at them.

"So, where were we? Ah, yes—the tap, tap, tap of a finger on my window. A fleshy finger, not a boney one," she explained to Susan and Nina. "I went to my window to find Sto—my friend there. He said if we went to the old Chisolm place, he knew we would see the light . . . the light of the ghosts who haunted it."

"I like this story!" Nate exclaimed.

Violet smiled. "I remember I cut my leg

climbing out my window, on the rose trellis, but I didn't care . . . for I was anxious to see the light. We hurried through the darkness, my friend and me. He'd brought a lantern, but because the moon was full, we didn't light it. We didn't want to be seen—didn't want the ghosts to know we were watching for them. The trees stood black and ominous against the starry sky. The moon hung with a sort of misty, gossamer shroud around it. All was quiet. Only the crickets and frogs were quietly conversing as on we trod on through the night, past the old oak on the border of Buddy Chisolm's property."

Violet paused, delighted by the widened eyes of the children. Even the older children had changed skeptic expressions for those of intrigued interest.

"Suddenly, there it was, looming up before us—the old Chisolm house, looming there, like something that had died and had its eyes poked out."

She heard Nina Deavers gulp and placed a reassuring arm around the child's shoulders.

"Sto—my friend led me to a place he said was best for waiting. He said the ghosts couldn't see us there but that we would still be able to see their light when they came. It was warm that night—a summer night, very like the one we knew last evening. All was quiet . . . and then all was silent . . . for the crickets suddenly stopped chirping . . . the frogs held their croaks in their throats . . .

and I thought I saw something. There . . ." Violet said, pointing toward a space beyond the creek. "There . . . on the bottom floor, in one of the windows, the furthest window to the right. There I saw it—a faint light at first, like a candle. It was small, and I thought perhaps it was a firefly. But my friend reminded me then . . ." Violet lowered her voice to a near whisper and continued, "We don't have fireflies in Rattler Rock, now do we?" All the children shook their heads yet made no sound.

"We watched—silent and still from our watching place—and I saw the light again, brighter this time, as if someone had indeed lit a candle and the wick loved the flame. It was in that lower window, for only a few moments, just long enough for me to breathe and count ten nervous breaths . . . and then it was gone." Violet paused—to let the goose bumps on the children's arms settle.

"I was scared—I remember being so scared—but my friend was with me, and I knew I was safe. I looked to him. His eyes seemed to hold the moonlight. They were bright with adventure and excitement, and he pointed to the house once more. 'Look!' he whispered. 'There . . . in the upper window.' I looked, and there it was again . . . the light of the lovers' moon, brighter this time, like an oil lamp turned down in the evening before bed. It moved from one room to the next

. . . seeming to pause before each window . . . as if someone stood there, looking out into the night, looking out toward where we sat hidden in the darkness. We watched the light roaming about the house for several minutes . . . watched it appear in one of the downstairs windows once more . . . watched it flicker, dim, and go out . . . as if it had never been there at all."

The children were quiet—silent for long moments.

"Did you hear the moanin'? Or the laughter?" Hagen asked at last. "Sometimes they say there's laughter, but I ain't ever heard it."

Violet smiled. "But you've seen the light, haven't you?"

Hagen nodded. "It's just like ya said, just like that. I seen it the same as you. More'n once. Me and Dayton, we both seen it. But we never heard the noises."

"I heard them once, just before my family moved," Violet said. "A low, breathy sound, like loud breathing, and then a quiet moaning followed by something akin to laughter. I heard it only once, but I did hear it."

"You all are tellin' tales! Surely, Miss Fynne," Maya exclaimed. "Ain't ya?"

"I can't speak for Dayton and Hagen, but I told you the truth of my own experience. Of course, that was many years ago."

"Well, I want to see it for myself," Maya said.

52

"Me too!" Phelps added.

"You all can't go there," Dayton said. "Stoney Wrenn would as soon shoot ya as look at ya if he caught ya out there. He guards his property like nobody I ever seen . . . just like a snarlin' ol' dog! You'd think he was hidin' a gold mine out there or somethin'. You best stay away, Maya . . . at least unless Hagen or me is with ya."

Violet smiled, noting the delighted blush rising to Maya's cheeks. Maya Asbury was sweet on Dayton Fisher; that's why she argued with him so.

"Someone's comin', Miss Fynne! We better hide!" Nate exclaimed in a whisper.

It wasn't until Violet was hunkered down on the creekbank—the other children hidden behind trees, rocks, and logs—that she even wondered why she had instantly taken the advice of a child.

"Why are we hiding, Nate?" she asked.

The boy was right next to her, eyes wide as he watched the road that passed by the schoolhouse. "Because we're supposed to be inside learnin' our letters and such, and we're out here tellin' ghost stories," he explained. "Don't ya see, Miss Fynne?"

"I do," Violet said, nodding. "I really do."

"Hush up!" Hagen called in a whisper. "There's a rider on the road."

"It's him!" Susan whispered.

"Who?" Violet asked.

"Stoney Wrenn!" Susan said. "That's his big bay! My pa says he wonders where Stoney Wrenn got so much money as to buy a horse like that."

"Stoney Wrenn," Violet breathed as she watched the rider approach.

The man riding the big bay horse sat tall in the saddle. His legs were long, weathered boots shoved in the stirrups. Violet strained to see him better, but the sun was too bright. Still, the weathered hat, pulled far down on his forehead—it was the same man that had thrown her off Buddy Chisolm's property the day before. Violet shook her head—felt her eyes fill with tears. Where was the body of the boy she'd loved so much? This man couldn't possibly be Stoney Wrenn! Stoney Wrenn was thirteen years old and ran around half-naked most of the time, careless of his shirt and shoes most any day.

"He's so big!" Violet breathed.

"Yeah, he is," Nate said. "I hope he runs that bay," the boy added, smiling with pure exhilaration. "Boy! It's somethin' to see."

"You think he'll run that bay?" Dayton asked, startling Violet as he and Hagen suddenly appeared beside her.

"I love to see that horse run," Hagen whispered. "He's reinin' in. I think he's gonna let him run."

Violet watched, breathless, as the man on the big bay horse reined the animal in. The horse stomped the ground several times, and the rider leaned forward, patting the bay on the neck.

Violet jumped as Stoney Wrenn hollered, "Ya!"

Dayton and Hagen leapt from their hiding places, whooping and hollering as the bay and its rider raced down the road at a speed that left Violet's mouth gaping open.

"Did you see that, Miss Fynne?" Dayton laughed when the horse and rider were no longer in sight. "Did you see that ol' boy race that pony?" Violet nodded, and Dayton said, "He may be a womanizin' bast . . . a womanizin' ol' crank . . . but that man can ride, and that bay can run!"

"Can we come out now?" Nina asked.

Violet smiled at the child still hiding on the creekbank next to her.

"Well, of course we can, Nina, you ninny," Susan scolded. "Them older boys made more noise than fryin' a flock of geese!"

"Should we wander on back to the schoolhouse, Miss Fynne?" Maya asked.

"Yes, Maya," Violet said, standing and smoothing her skirt. "We better get to our lessons."

Violet smiled as the grumbling began. As she retrieved her stockings and shoes, she watched the children head back to the schoolhouse.

"This is the best day I ever had at school, Miss Fynne," Hagen said, smiling and offering a hand to help her climb up the side of the creekbank.

Violet accepted his gallant assistance. "I'm

glad, Hagen," she giggled. "But you do realize they can't all be this way."

"I know," he said. "But I'm hopin' they sometimes are."

"Sometimes they will be. I promise," Violet said.

The children filed into the schoolhouse, and Violet began to follow. She paused however. Turning back to look down the road, she wondered—had Stoney Wrenn forgiven her? Had he? After she'd abandoned him ten years ago—had she lingered in his mind the way he'd lingered in her heart? Or had her unwilling betrayal cast her from his mind forever?

She could hear Dayton and Maya arguing once more inside the schoolhouse. Exhaling a heavy sigh, she turned and followed Phelps into the building.

"Now, settle down in here, boys and girls," she said. "Settle down. Let's see where everyone is in their readers, shall we?"

Violet glanced once more down the road— the road leading to Buddy Chisolm's place. The horse and rider were gone—even the dust was gone—just like old Buddy Chisolm was gone— and the past.

# CHAPTER THREE

Violet continued to frown as she braided her hair into a long, loose braid. Gazing into the looking glass, she did not see her reflection, for her mind wandered to other venues. She'd overslept—overslept for having endured a very fitful night of reminiscing. The day before— meeting the children, their innocent revelations concerning Stoney Wrenn—all of it had taxed Violet's mind and heart far worse than she had at first understood.

First, there was the fact Buddy Chisolm had willed everything to Stoney—the fact it had been Stoney himself who had threatened Violet when she'd been found beneath the old cottonwood tree. Hadn't he recognized her? Of course he hadn't! She hadn't recognized him; how could she expect he would recognize her? How could she expect he would even remember her?

Then there was seeing him on the road after she'd told the children the story of seeing the light in the old house. He'd been right there before her—tall and rather frightening and mounted on the finest bay she'd ever seen. She could not force the vision of him from her mind, and it haunted her, only adding to the ghosts of memory already mixing about in her soul.

Yet, most of all—most disturbing—were Dayton and Hagen's accusations that Stoney Wrenn was a philanderer! "A womanizing ol' crank," Hagen had called him. This piece of information caused great anxiety to boil in Violet's bosom. Surely it could not be true! Surely Maya was correct—that Dayton Fisher was sweet on Maya's sister and only jealous that Maya's sister was sweet on Stoney Wrenn. Surely the sweet boy Violet had known had not become so hardened and heartless as to have taken to toying with women.

All this plagued Violet's mind during the dark hours of night. She lay in her bed wondering if she were in fact insane! What kind of young woman obsessively advertised to gain the position of a schoolteacher in such a remote town as Rattler Rock, especially when so many far more favorable positions had been offered her in Albany? Still, for three years she'd advertised—written to the county school board every month inquiring—for Violet was desperate to sort out the pain she'd known, and caused, in the past—to keep a promise she'd made as a child—to return to Stoney Wrenn.

Indeed, Violet's family had wondered if she truly had her wits about her. Because for all their assurances that the past was the past, that nothing could be done, that she should let go of the memory of the boy in Rattler Rock and move forward with her life, Violet Fynne could not.

Thus, all the night long she'd tossed—slept little—and when she did sleep, she'd dreamt of a womanizing man on a bay horse, or of the past. The past is where her dreams lingered most. She'd dreamt of days spent on the banks of the creek when she was a child. She'd dreamt of catching frogs, picking flowers, and tossing rocks into the old abandoned well on Buddy Chisolm's place. She'd dreamt of running, climbing cottonwood trees, and hunting for treasure in the old caves near Rattler Rock. All these things—all these memories—were made of Stoney Wrenn too, and Violet awoke with a nearly sickening sense of melancholy.

In truth, it had been the last dream she'd had—the one that had awakened her—that caused her to cry out with tears streaming down her face. As if it had happened all over again, as if some devil of torture intended Violet Fynne should live the worst moment of her life over and over as penance for her cruelty, Violet had dreamed the memory of abandoning Stoney.

Now, as she sat before the looking glass, blind to her own reflection as the past continued to haunt her in the bright light of morning, she could not stop the memory from torturing her once more. It would never cease in torturing her: this she knew with all the certainty of her being.

"Yer pa's gonna get furious if ya don't get back," Stoney said.

"I can't leave you, Stoney," Violet sobbed.

"Ya have to. And I . . . I understand. Yer just a kid, Violet. Yer just a kid."

Violet brushed the tears from her cheeks. "I-I can't leave you, Stoney! I'll just die without you . . . a-and your daddy will beat you somethin' awful with me gone."

Violet watched as Stoney's eyes welled with tears. "He beats me somethin' awful when yer here. That won't be no worse with you gone." He forced a smile. "Besides . . . ol' Bud will look after me."

Violet buried her face in her hands and sobbed a moment more. Why did her daddy have to move the family back east? Weren't they all happy in Rattler Rock? Couldn't he just continue to be the schoolmaster in the small town Violet loved so much? Why did he have to go to a bigger school to teach? Why? She couldn't leave Stoney. She couldn't! Violet felt certain she'd die without him. What joy would life in New York hold without Stoney there to be with—to love?

"I wanna give ya somethin', Viola," Stoney said. "Now quit snifflin' and listen to me."

Violet gasped and angrily wiped more tears from her cheeks as she looked up to Stoney.

The green-blue of his eyes seemed dim; the

sparkle of delight in life even for hardship was gone. Still, he forced a smile at her. "You remember last fall when that feller came to town makin' photographs . . . and yer mama had him make mine?" he asked.

Violet nodded. "So you'd have somethin' to give to your mother for Christmas."

"That's right," he said. "Well, that feller give me two photographs of myself, and I did give one to Mama last Christmas. But I couldn't never figure what I'd ever do with the other one . . . 'til today."

Violet held her breath as Stoney reached into the back pocket of his trousers. Her tears only increased as he held the small, cardboard-mounted photograph toward her.

"I want you to have it, Viola. I want you to have it. That way I know you'll not forget me."

Violet didn't pause; rather, she quickly snatched the photograph from his hands, lovingly studying the image for a moment before pressing it to her bosom. "Thank you, Stoney," she breathed. "I . . . I thought about sneakin' into your house last night and stealin' the one you gave to your mama. I truly did! I didn't know you had this one!"

"You'll remember me, Viola. You will . . . won't you?" Stoney asked. He placed a hand on her shoulder and forced another smile, though his eyes were brimming with tears.

"You're my best friend, Stoney," Violet whispered. "I could never forget you. A-and I'll come back to you . . . I promise! One day . . . I'll come back to you and—"

Her words were silenced as Stoney's fingers pressed firmly to her lips. "Don't make me no promises, Viola," he said. "Don't make me no promises you might not be able to keep . . . even if ya did mean to."

"But I—" she began to argue.

"No," he said, shaking his head. "Just promise to remember me."

Violet choked back the argument rising in her throat. She would come back to him. She would! Then and there, standing near the old cottonwood tree, Violet Fynne silently vowed she would return to Rattler Rock one day—return to Stoney Wrenn.

"I . . . I got one more thing for ya," he said, taking her hand.

Violet clutched Stoney's photograph to her breast as he led her beneath the canopy of cottonwood limbs and leaves.

"He'll probably tan my hide for it . . . but I don't care. I done it anyway."

Stoney pointed to the trunk of the tree, and Violet gasped at what she saw. There, carved into the bark of Buddy Chisolm's old cottonwood, was a heart—a heart with S.W. and V.F.

"It's all I can give ya, Viola," Stoney mumbled.

"That silly photograph that feller made and this," he said, pointing to the carving in the tree. "I ain't got nothin' else."

Violet reached out—let her trembling fingers trace the fresh carving in the bark.

"It'll be here forever . . . won't it?" she whispered.

"Well . . . as long as the tree is here, it will," Stoney said.

"And this tree and the grass and the sky. The whole world will know we were here once, that we were friends, that we played and laughed . . . and . . . and . . ." Violet stammered. She stood, tears streaming down her face. "And that I love you . . . that I always will."

Stoney's head hung low for a moment. He brushed a tear from his cheek with the collar of his shirt before shoving his hands into the pockets of his worn trousers.

Violet reached into the pocket of her skirt. "I-I wrote a letter to you," she whispered, withdrawing a small envelope. "It ain't anything as grand as your carvin'," she said. "But . . . but maybe it'll help you remember me too." She smiled as he looked up, smiled, and accepted the letter from her. "And . . . and I stole the photograph that man made of me for my own mama last fall. I stole it out of one of her trunks after she packed it up. It's in with the letter."

Stoney laughed and wiped another tear from

his cheek. He looked up at her, eyes still moist, still dull and lifeless. Shaking his head, he said, "What'll I do, Viola? With you gone?"

"What'll I do without you?" Violet begged in a whisper.

Stoney shrugged. "Grow up . . . without me, I guess." His eyes narrowed as he looked at her. "You were meant for better than this anyhow, Viola. I can't begin to imagine what life holds for you."

"Violet! Violet Fynne!"

Violet looked to the road—to where her daddy was waiting in the wagon.

"We'll miss the stage!"

As she looked back to Stoney, a wave of pure desperation suddenly overwhelmed her. Throwing her arms around his neck, Violet clung to him—never wanting to let him go.

Though Stoney returned her embrace, he whispered, "You go on, Violet Fynne. You go on with yer family. Go be happy."

"I'll never forget you, Stoney," Violet whispered. "And I'll come back. I will . . . I promise!"

"Just promise to never forget me," he whispered. And then—in a much lower whisper, a whisper so quiet Violet could barely hear it—he breathed, "I love you too."

"Violet! Now!" her father hollered.

Violet kissed Stoney on the cheek as he released her. He forced a slight grin, shoved his hands into worn trouser pockets again, and nodded.

"Go on now, Viola . . . 'fore yer pa comes over here to get you," Stoney mumbled. "Draggin' it out won't change it."

"Will you come see the stage off in town?" Violet asked. "It leaves in an hour."

Stoney sighed. "Maybe," he said.

Violet nodded. She understood. He was right: dragging it out wouldn't change anything. "Goodbye, Stoney," Violet whispered, as her tears renewed their streaming over her cheeks.

" 'Bye, Viola," Stoney said.

Violet left him then—turned and went to her father waiting in the wagon. She climbed up onto the seat beside her father, and he brushed the tears from her cheeks, smiling with compassion.

Stoney raised a hand in farewell as Violet waved to him, and she watched him—let her gaze linger on Stoney Wrenn, standing there beneath Buddy Chisolm's cottonwood tree—until the road turned and the tree was out of sight.

She looked down at the photograph in her hand—at the image of the tall, handsome boy. She only wished he were smiling. Oh, she knew it wasn't appropriate to smile when a photograph was being taken. Still, she wished Stoney would've been smiling when the man had made the photo last fall, for she loved his smile—the light that leapt into his eyes when he did smile.

Letting her fingers gently caress the photograph

once more, Violet tucked the photograph of Stoney Wrenn into her skirt pocket. Her greatest treasure, that's what the photograph was, and ever it would remain so—she knew it.

· · · · · · · · ·

Violet fastened the cameo brooch to the lace of her collar at her throat. She closed her eyes a moment, trying to dispel the vision of Stoney Wrenn standing on the road at the edge of town waving as the stagecoach carrying Violet and her family left Rattler Rock. The vision yet haunted her. It ever would, for Mrs. Deavers had written to Violet's mother some weeks later. In her letter, she told Mrs. Fynne of Stoney's father's fury over finding out his son had been to town that day. Mr. Wrenn had beaten Stoney something awful, Mrs. Deavers had written. Violet had been beside herself with guilt and worry. For days she'd cried, telling her mother it was her fault Stoney was beaten, that the family must return to Rattler Rock to protect Stoney from his father.

Finally, Violet settled. She was not soothed—only settled—understanding that, at only twelve years of age and at the mercy of her family, there was nothing she could do to help Stoney Wrenn. It was then that Mr. and Mrs. Fynne decided to cease in corresponding with anyone from Rattler Rock—to leave the past in the past and move forward.

Violet did not write to Stoney, for she knew it

would only cause him trouble, and she would not be the cause of another beating. Therefore, the last memory Violet Fynne owned of her beloved childhood friend was the vision of him standing near the road, waving to her as the stage rattled away, and the knowledge he'd been badly beaten for it. Violet suspected Stoney knew what his father would do if he went to town to see the stage off, yet she had asked him to come—and he had, even knowing he would pay the painful price. In this, Violet's guilt worsened, and she could never forgive herself for being so selfish. Stoney had said his goodbyes under the cottonwood tree, but Violet—in selfish desperation—had not been content and had begged him to come to town to see the stage off. He had done as she asked, and, according to the details of Mrs. Deavers's letter (which Violet had taken from her mother's trunk some time later and read in full), Stoney had nearly paid with his life for Violet's selfishness. For this, Violet Fynne would never forgive herself.

The clock on the mantle chimed, and Violet gasped. "Oh, I'm late!" she breathed, brushing a tear from the corner of one eye.

She glanced in the mirror, hoping she was presentable enough. Picking up a stack of new readers and her lunch bucket, she hurried out of the little house.

As she rushed down the boardwalk, past the

general store and livery, she wondered if any of the children had related her story of the seeing the lovers' light to their parents. No one had appeared on her doorstep the evening before—no one intent on reprimanding the new schoolteacher for filling their children's minds with such fiffle. Violet knew she must be cautious however. She'd known many a fellow teacher who had lost their positions for far less than telling tales of ghosts.

Violet was suddenly aware of a discomforting feeling in her shoe. A pebble, perhaps? Irritated, she looked down to her feet, though she did not slow her pace.

The force of the collision did not unbalance her enough to knock her to the ground. Yet it did cause the lunch pail and readers she was carrying to tumble from her arms and clatter on the boardwalk.

"Oh, for crying in the bucket!" Violet sighed. "I'm so sorry," she said to whomever she had bumped into as she bent over to quickly gather the readers. She would be tardy for certain—and what would folks think of a teacher who could not be prompt?

"Let me help ya there, ma'am," a man's voice said.

"Thank you," Violet said, gathering several more readers into the crook of her arm. Standing erect once more, she began, "I guess I need watch where I'm—"

She gasped, however, rendered entirely breathless as she stared at the man before her. He held out her lunch pail, and Violet accepted it—even as her mouth gaped in astonishment.

The eyes! The face of the man before her, the remarkable stature, held little or no resemblance to the boy she'd once known. Yet the man's eyes—the unusual green-blue opalescence of his eyes—his eyes were unmistakable. The man standing before her was Stoney Wrenn!

"Th-thank you," she managed to breathe.

"My pleasure, ma'am," he said. He didn't smile—simply touched the brim of his hat and moved past her.

Dazed for only a moment more, Violet turned and watched him walk away. He was tall—so tall and vastly broad-shouldered! He wore a weathered pair of boots, worn trousers, a red shirt, and a brown hat. He hadn't recognized her, and she was somehow relieved he hadn't.

"Mornin', Stoney," Mr. Deavers greeted, stepping out of the general store and onto the boardwalk.

"Mornin' there, Alex," Stoney said.

The sound of his voice echoed in Violet's mind—deep in intonation, so very different from the way his voice had sounded as a boy. He paused to speak to Mr. Deavers, and Violet studied him quickly. He was so large—much more so than he'd seemed at a distance! She had expected he would have grown, knew he would most likely be bigger than he had been as a boy. Yet he was so very tall when viewed at close range, the breadth of his shoulders so wide. The sleeves of his shirt were rolled up to his elbows, and the defined muscles in his forearms were evidence of hard work and strength. Furthermore, he was extraordinarily handsome! Not just casually so, but mythically so. As he stood talking to Mr. Deavers, his profile was on perfect display. His nose was straight, his chin firm, his jaw squared and in slight need of shaving. His appearance seemed entirely altered. He'd been a handsome boy, yes. Still, as a man, he was so handsome as to merit pure ogling.

Violet closed her eyes just a moment. She tried to dispel the vision of those penetrating eyes, the same eyes that had mesmerized her as a child. Yet she could not, and she opened her own once more, still awed by his appearance.

A very pretty young woman approached. She was dark-haired—not so unlike Maya Asbury. Violet watched the way her eyes glanced briefly to Mr. Deavers yet lingered with admiration on Stoney Wrenn.

"Good mornin', Mr. Deavers . . . Mr. Wrenn," the young woman said.

"And good mornin' to you, Miss Asbury," Stoney said. The smile he offered the young woman in return was not only charming but entirely alluring. "My, my, my. Don't you look as sweet as summer honey? You'll sure have the bees buzzin' today, Miss Asbury . . . and the boys too, I reckon," Stoney said. He smiled at Maya's sister, and Violet felt the gape of her mouth widen.

"Mornin', Miss Fynne."

Violet startled, gasped, then closed her gaping mouth as she turned to see Sheriff Fisher standing behind her.

"On yer way to the school, I guess," the sheriff said.

"Uh . . . yes," Violet stammered. "Yes, indeed."

Sheriff Fisher grinned and glanced past Violet to where Stoney stood conversing with Mr. Deavers and Maya's sister. "I see Stoney's already got the girlies a-flutterin' this mornin'," he chuckled. "My brother says you used to know ol' Stoney . . . when ya lived in Rattler Rock before."

"Uh . . . yes . . . yes, I did," Violet said. "Way, way back . . . when I was just a little girl."

"Probably knew ol' Alex Deavers too, huh," he said.

"Yes, in fact. I did."

Sheriff Fisher shook his head. "That was a sad day for the whole town, the day Mrs. Deavers passed. Last Thanksgivin' it was. Sad day."

"Oh," Violet said, frowning. "I . . . I haven't

been into the store yet. I didn't know Mrs. Deavers had passed."

"Yep, she sure did." Sheriff Fisher smiled. "But I'm keepin' ya from yer path, aren't I? We can't have the schoolteacher arrivin' at the back end of the children, now can we?"

Violet smiled and shook her head. "We certainly cannot, Sheriff."

"You can call me Coby, Miss Fynne," Sheriff Fisher said. "I go by Coby . . . to purty ladies such as yerself."

Violet was surprised to feel a blush rise to her cheeks. Sheriff Fisher was very handsome—tall, dark-haired, and blue-eyed. He was unusually charming too, especially for a lawman. It was always nice to own a compliment from a handsome gentleman.

"You best be careful, Sheriff Coby Fisher," Violet said, smiling, "or you'll have the girlies all fluttering this morning too."

He laughed and touched the brim of his hat. "Oh, just one I hope, Miss Fynne. Just one. You have a nice day now."

Violet felt her smile broaden and her blush deepen as Sheriff Fisher nodded and walked past her. Still, as she looked again to where Stoney Wrenn stood smiling down at Maya Asbury's sister, her smile faded.

Regret, pain, and guilt washed over her, and she whispered, "What am I doing back here?"

"I beg yer pardon, ma'am?"

Violet looked up to see a young man standing next to her, a puzzled frown on her face. "Well, there certainly are a lot of folks coming and going in town this morning," Violet said, suddenly somewhat overwhelmed with having her path so constantly barred.

"I-I'm sorry, ma'am," the young man said. "I was only headin' over to the store. I didn't mean to get in yer way."

Violet inwardly scolded herself. Her own preoccupation with Stoney Wrenn, Sheriff Fisher being about his business—none of it was this boy's fault. "Oh, no," she said, forcing a smile. "I just don't remember town being so full of life before."

"Yer Violet Fynne," the boy said. He smiled, his dark brown eyes alive with light all at once. "Yer the new schoolteacher, ain't ya?"

"Yes," Violet said. "Are . . . are you coming in to school today?"

The boy dropped his gaze for a moment. He shook his head, causing his tawny hair to feather in the breeze. "No, ma'am. I ain't one for book learnin'. 'Sides, I got chores that need doin'."

"Well, what's your name?" Violet asked.

Something about the boy intrigued Violet. Something in her soul was drawn to the young man's obvious humility and kindness. He was already taller than she was, even for his apparent youth. Still, that wasn't saying too much; Violet Fynne was not tall.

"Jimmy Ritter, ma'am," he said.

"I'm pleased to meet you, Jimmy Ritter," Violet said. She moved the readers around in her arms, looped the lunch pail handle over one wrist, and offered a hand to Jimmy. She smiled when the young man took her hand.

"Can I . . . can I help ya haul them things over to the school, Miss Fynne?" he asked.

"Oh, would you?" Violet sighed. "I'm bound to be late as it is . . . and I don't want to find myself dropping these readers again, or I'll never make it over there. You sure you don't mind?"

"No, ma'am," Jimmy said, his handsome smile broadening. "I don't mind at all."

"Well, thank you, Jimmy," Violet giggled. "It's always nice to find a gentleman nearby."

"Yes, ma'am," Jimmy said, gathering the readers into his arms.

Violet glanced back to where Stoney Wrenn stood in conversation with Maya's sister and Mr. Deavers. Silently, she attempted to will him to glance at her—but he didn't. His attention seemed singularly arrested by Miss Asbury.

Swallowing a thick lump of disappointment that had gathered in her throat, Violet turned, smiled, and followed Jimmy Ritter as he crossed the street.

"He's much more grown up than Dayton or Hagen, that's for dang sure," Beth said.

"And much better lookin', if you ask me," Katie Mill said. Katie was one of Violet's older pupils—about the same age as Beth Deavers and Maya Asbury. "And more of a gentleman."

Violet felt somewhat guilty for eavesdropping, but it had happened quite by accident really. She'd been out under the willow tree enjoying the bread and apple butter she'd brought for lunch. The three older girls had simply chosen to eat their lunches nearby, and when Violet heard their conversation turn to the topic of boys— well, she didn't want the girls to be embarrassed by knowing she was there. So Violet had simply stayed. Besides, their chatter was delightful, insightful, and highly intriguing. She figured she'd pretend she'd fallen asleep beneath the willow—pretend she hadn't heard a word they'd said—if the girls happened to find her out. They were speaking of Jimmy Ritter now. It seemed Violet's older girl pupils preferred Jimmy to Dayton and Hagen. Violet liked the girls all the more for it. Dayton and Hagen were fine boys— handsome boys. But there was something special about Jimmy Ritter, although she couldn't quite put a name to it.

"He is a gentleman," Maya said. "At least . . . as close to a gentleman as we're likely to find in Rattler Rock. Did ya see how he helped Miss Fynne with her books and all this mornin'? Even though he don't come to school?"

"Too bad he's already eighteen," Katie said. "Otherwise, maybe he *would* come to school. Then we'd have somebody other than silly Dayton and Hagen to dream over."

The girls giggled, and Violet bit her lip to silence her amusement.

"Did Dayton go last night, Maya?" Beth asked. "Did he sneak out to the ol' Chisolm place and look at it for us?"

Violet listened more intently.

"He did," Maya said, lowering her voice. "And Hagen wasn't lyin'! Dayton says it's carved right there on that tree . . . just like Hagen said it was. Dayton says the initials are clear as day. S.W. and V.F., carved right in the middle of a big ol' heart."

Violet held her breath—covered her mouth with one hand.

"Ya don't think it's true . . . do ya, Maya?" Katie asked.

"I do think it's true!" Maya said. "What else could the initials mean? And Miss Fynne told us she knew Stoney Wrenn when she was a child. S.W. . . . Stoney Wrenn. V.F. . . . Violet Fynne. What else could it mean?"

"Do you think they were sweethearts once?" Beth giggled. "Stoney and Miss Fynne?"

"Miss Fynne couldn't have been more than

eleven when she moved, if she's tellin' the truth about her age," Katie said. "And Stoney Wrenn. He can't be too old if he's callin' on yer sister, Maya. No. They couldn't have been sweethearts. You can't have a sweetheart when yer only eleven."

"Well, my grandpa would know," Beth said. "He's run the general store for over twenty years. I'll ask him. Miss Fynne said she was friends with Stoney Wrenn. I'll ask grandpa how good of friends they were."

Again giggling. Violet did not giggle this time however. She could just imagine the tales Mr. Deavers might tell his granddaughter—about the mischief she and Stoney used to conjure up.

"Let's get back," Maya said. "Miss Fynne will be ringin' the bell soon."

"You just want another chance to catch Dayton's attention, Maya," Beth said. "Yer so sweet on him, and everybody can see it."

"I ain't sweet on Dayton Fisher," Maya argued—a little too emphatically.

"Well, I am!" Katie giggled. "So if yer not gonna claim him, Maya—"

"I'm not claimin' him," Maya argued as the girls stood and brushed at the seats of their skirts. "You can have him."

Once they'd gone, Violet made her way back to the school—by another path. She was unsettled about the curiosity of the older children where she and Stoney Wrenn were concerned. She silently scolded herself for being so forthright and honest in answering their questions the day before. Furthermore, she didn't want Dayton Fisher to find himself planted in the cemetery over ignorant curiosity. Hagen Webster swore Stoney Wrenn would as soon shoot someone for trespassing on his property as look at them. It hadn't been safe for Dayton to go to the old cottonwood tree.

Sighing, Violet knew she'd have to find a way to settle the curiosity of her pupils. She smiled as Nina Deavers appeared at her side, taking hold of her hand.

"Did you enjoy your lunch, Nina?" Violet asked.

"Yes, ma'am," Nina said.

"So you're fresh and ready to learn something new?"

Nina giggled. "Yes, Miss Fynne!"

"Where's Susan?" Violet asked. She frowned. Nina Deavers and Susan Gribbs seemed nearly inseparable. Violet was unsettled that they were not together.

"Oh, she's comin' along," Nina said. "She just had to visit the hitchin' post," Nina added in a lowered voice.

"The hitching post?" Violet asked.

"You know, Miss Fynne . . . the hitchin' post," Nina whispered. "I shore like you, Miss

Fynne. Yer so silly sometimes!" Nina giggled. Dropping Violet's hand, she ran ahead and into the schoolhouse.

Violet heard the outhouse door slam and glanced over to see Susan Gribbs hurrying away from it.

"Oh! The hitching post," Violet giggled. She'd forgotten—forgotten the term had been used to refer to the outhouse. Her smile faded, however, as Susan approached. The child was pale as snow—frowning.

"What's the matter, Susan?" Violet asked.

But Susan shook her head. "Oh, nothin'," she said. "I-I'm just fine."

Violet was certain Susan was not fine, however—especially when tears moistened her eyes occasionally through the remainder of the afternoon. Furthermore, Susan lingered after school. In fact, she didn't move to leave at all when the other children hurried from the schoolhouse. Nina lingered as well, a tiny arm resting comfortingly around her young friend's slight shoulders.

Violet waited until the other students were gone. Going to kneel before Susan and Nina, she took Susan's little hands in her own. "What's the matter, sweetheart?" she asked. "You've looked as glum as a hound since our lunchtime."

Instantly Susan burst into tears.

"Oh, honey! Don't cry," Violet soothed, gathering the child into her arms. "What's upsetting you so?"

"It's 'cause of her mama's brooch," Nina offered.

Violet nodded at Nina, encouraging her to explain.

"She wasn't supposed to touch it," Nina began as Susan continued to sob, "but it's so purty and all. It's got a real jewel in the center—a blue one—and it's worth a pile of silver." Nina paused, glanced to Susan, and lowered her voice as she continued. "But Susan took it—just to borrow, just to show me 'cause I didn't believe her mama owned somethin' like that."

Violet nodded. Gently taking Susan by the shoulders, she asked, "Did you bring the brooch to school today, Susan?" Susan nodded and wiped at the tears on her cheeks. "And did you lose it somewhere? Is that what the matter is?"

Susan's lower lip quivered—pushed so far out in a pout that Violet almost smiled. "I dropped it down by the crick," Susan confessed. "And we ain't supposed to go near the water. I dropped it, down where the bank is steep."

"Did you hear it go into the water?" Violet asked.

Nina and Susan both nodded, but it was Nina who answered. "I heard the splash. And we would've got all dirty if we'd tried to get it."

"You were right not to try," Violet said. "I don't want you younger children near the water. Sometimes the creek is flowing faster than it looks or deeper than you might think."

"But what am I gonna do, Miss Fynne? My mama will be so angry! It's her favorite treasure in the world!" Susan exclaimed, panic overtaking her. The fear on the child's face nearly caused Violet to burst into tears as well.

"Well, first of all," Violet began, "I'm sure that you're her favorite treasure in the world, Susan. A mama loves her children more than anything else."

"Even a fancy brooch?" Nina asked. Nina was crying too.

"Even a fancy brooch," Violet assured the girls. "Now, why don't we go down to the creek and you can show me where you think you dropped the brooch? Maybe I can reach it."

"Oh, Miss Fynne!" Susan cried, throwing her arms around Violet's neck. "You can find it! I know ya can!"

"I'll try, Susan," Violet said. "I really will try. But you listen now." Violet took Susan's face between her hands, wiping the tears from her cheeks with her thumbs. "If I do find it, you need to tell your mother that you took it. It isn't right to take things without permission."

"It's a sin!" Nina said. "Like it says in the Bible."

Susan began to cry once more, her lower lip pursing even further.

"Well, I think this might be something a little different, Nina," Violet said. "Susan's very young, and, well, I think she's learned a hard lesson today. Haven't you, sweetie?"

Susan nodded. "Please find my mama's brooch, Miss Fynne! Oh, please, please, please!" she begged.

"I'll try, sweetie. I'll try my best. All right?"

Susan nodded and forced a hopeful smile.

"Well, then, let's be on our way. Shall we?"

"Are you still watching for me, Nina?" Violet asked.

"Yes, Miss Fynne!" the youngster assured her.

"Let's hope no one decides to come fishing in this spot, Susan," Violet said as she placed her skirt, petticoat, and shirtwaist on the nearby log with her shoes and stockings. "You keep a sharp eye, Nina! Please, oh, please keep a sharp eye."

"I will!" Nina called.

Violet put her hands on her hips and studied the creek and the fallen log that spanned part of it.

"You girls shouldn't have been near this part of the creek," she scolded. "And you certainly shouldn't have been out on that log!"

"I know, Miss Fynne," Susan said. "I'm sorry.

We just didn't want anybody else to know I had the brooch."

Violet drew a deep breath of determination. She worried for Susan, and she didn't want Ethel Gribbs to lose the sapphire brooch.

"You stay right here, Susan," she ordered. "Do you understand? You stay right here." Susan nodded, and Violet looked up to where Nina stood on a higher part of the creekbank. "And you keep a sharp eye out, Nina."

"I will!" Nina called.

"All right then," Violet whispered.

The log spanning the creek was sturdy-looking but thin. There would be no walking on it; Violet knew she'd have to crawl out to the place where the girls claimed the brooch had fallen into the water. Violet stepped into the water and climbed onto the log. Straddling it, she leaned forward and began to inch out.

"Tell me when I get close, Susan," she said.

"It's a little farther out, Miss Fynne," the child explained.

Violet made her way out over the creek as quickly as possible. She certainly didn't need anyone passing by to find the new schoolteacher stripped down to her underthings and crawling on a log.

"Those're real nice bloomers yer wearin', Miss Fynne," Susan said from the bank. "And I never seen such a pretty camisole!"

"Thank you, Susan. Am I close?" Violet called.

"Yer almost there, Miss Fynne. Just a little further."

Violet paused—gazed down into the water below. She was relieved to find the creek wasn't deep where the log spanned it. She might be able to reach the brooch from her perch on the log. Perhaps she wouldn't have to go swimming for it.

"Right there, Miss Fynne! Right there!" Nina hollered.

"Watch the road, Nina!" Violet called. "Susan can help me."

"She's right, Miss Fynne! We were right there when I dropped it!" Susan exclaimed. Violet could hear the excitement and hope in the child's voice. "It's a silver brooch, Miss Fynne, with a pretty blue stone in the middle. Can ya see it?"

Violet frowned and searched the pebble-lined creekbed. She gasped, giggling with delight. "I see it! I do!" she said.

She heard the two little girls giggle with delight.

"Oh, thank ya, Miss Fynne! Thank ya!" Susan cried.

"I think I can reach it from here," Violet said.

Carefully—to keep the water as still as possible so as not to lose sight of the brooch—Violet reached into the cold creek water. She exhaled the breath she'd been holding as she closed her hand around the piece of jewelry and drew it from the water.

"I've got it!" she called to the girls, giggling herself as she heard the high squeals of delight from the bank. She sighed as she studied the brooch a moment. "Little girls and pretty things," she whispered, shaking her head.

"All right, girls. I'm coming back now." Violet called.

"Scootch back now, Miss Fynne," Susan encouraged. "Just scootch on back real careful. Don't drop it again!"

Violet was close. She was nearly to back to the creekbank. Ethel Gribbs would have her brooch returned, and Susan and Nina had learned a hard lesson—she hoped. Violet sat up on the log. She'd have to step back into the water to get to the bank.

"Well, well, well. Violet Fynne."

Violet held her breath—closed her eyes—winced.

"Hey there, Mr. Wrenn," she heard Susan say. "Hey there, Miss Fynne. Don't worry, it's just Mr. Wrenn, Miss Fynne," Susan called. "The one that Hagen and Dayton say is a womanizin' son of a—"

"Yes, Susan!" Violet interrupted. "Yes."

Violet brushed a loose strand of hair from her

cheek. She sat up on the log—inhaled deeply, and stepped into the water. There was no other course. She turned. There—standing on the creekbank, leaning up against an old tree—stood Stoney Wrenn.

# CHAPTER FOUR

He wasn't smiling—didn't appear at all astonished or amused to find the new schoolteacher straddling a fallen tree in her undergarments. He did study her a moment, however—studied her from head to toe and back again.

"Hello," Violet managed. She found every inch of her body was trembling, yet she could not determine whether she trembled because of her lack of attire, at her mortification at being caught in such a predicament, or simply because Stoney Wrenn stood blatantly studying her.

"We . . . we had an urgent situation," she stammered when he said nothing in response to her greeting.

"Mighty urgent, I'm guessin'," he said, his handsome face still void of any expression.

"Oh, give it to me, Miss Fynne!" Susan begged. "I promise I'll tell my mama what I done. Please just let me hold onto it. I won't drop it again. I promise I won't!"

Violet swallowed and looked to Susan and Nina. She held out her hand and offered the brooch to Susan.

The child instantly snatched it up, clasping it tight in both little hands. Drawing her hands to her bosom, Susan closed her eyes. "Oh, thank you, Miss Fynne! Thank you, thank you, thank you!" the child whispered.

"Y-you're welcome, Susan," Violet said. "Now . . . you and Nina run on home. But remember what we talked about. Promise?"

Both girls nodded. Susan threw her arms around Violet's waist in a grateful hug. "Oh, thank you, Miss Fynne!" she said.

"You're welcome . . . but let's keep this just between us. All right?" Violet whispered, stroking the little girl's hair with reassurance.

"All right, Miss Fynne," Susan whispered.

Stoney Wrenn still stood leaning against the tree, staring at her with green-blue eyes void of any emotion—even mirth.

"But Miss Fynne," Nina whispered, "we can't leave you here with that man, Miss Fynne. Stoney Wrenn is a womanizin' son of a—"

"It'll be fine, Nina," Violet interrupted. "I'll be fine. You girls get home . . . before someone gets worried and comes looking for you. Please."

Nina and Susan both glanced at Stoney Wrenn. He nodded, smiled just a little—displaying just a hint of the long, handsome dimples he owned— and winked at the two little girls. "I'll make sure yer teacher stays safe, ladies," he said. "Now you run on home like Miss Fynne says. Sound good?"

Both girls smiled, nodded, and giggled. Violet felt her eyebrows arch in astonishment as she saw their cheeks pink up with delighted blushes too.

"Yes, sir," Nina said.

"Thank you so much, Miss Fynne!" Susan called as she and Nina held hands and ran off in the direction of town.

Once the girls had disappeared, Stoney Wrenn looked back to Violet. The green-blue of his opaline eyes studying her once more caused Violet to shiver. She cleared her throat, straightened her camisole, and smoothed her hair. There was nothing to do but behave as if being found sprawling across a log in her undergarments was the most natural thing in the world.

"How have you been?" she asked as she walked to the nearby log and picked up her shirtwaist. Her hands trembled something awful as she slipped her arms into the sleeves. Was he not even gentleman enough to give her his back while she dressed? She wondered a moment if perhaps he still viewed her as a child—for as children, it was often they'd each stripped down to their undergarments to wade through the creek.

"Fine. Just fine," he answered. "I see you haven't changed much."

Violet swallowed, finished buttoning her shirtwaist, and said, "I suppose not." She snatched up her petticoat, stepping into it and fastening it at the back of her waist.

"You ran headlong into me in town this mornin'," he said. "Looked me right in the eye and didn't say a word of greetin'." He left his position of leaning against the tree and started toward her.

Violet startled slightly at his advance and quickly stepped into her walking skirt. "Oh, I'm sorry. I guess I didn't recognize you," Violet lied.

"I see you still can't lie worth a hill of beans," he said.

"And you still can't resist making the little girls blush," she countered, nodding in the direction that Susan and Nina had gone.

He smiled a little—enough for his charming dimples to begin dimpling but not enough to reveal them fully. Violet was far too aware of his nearness. It was almost as if he emanated some sort of alluring heat, for she fancied she was slightly perspiring.

"I came to ask a favor of ya, schoolteacher," he said.

Violet frowned. Was this to be it—an exchange of casual pleasantries and nothing else? For the first time, the reality of life washed over Violet like a bitter, cold cloudburst. Ten years had passed. There was no going back to a friendship that had caused so much pain to two children almost a decade before. Stoney Wrenn was a man, and whether or not Violet's heart still loved the boy he had once been, men were not held captive by sentimentality the way women were. The boy Stoney Wrenn was gone. In his place was an intimidating man who displayed no joy in an old friend's return—showed no regret at having lost her in the first place.

"A favor?" she asked, sitting down on the log and pulling on one stocking. What kind of a favor would he ask of her? Oh, her soul knew well enough that she owed him a favor—owed him a million favors for having abandoned him. Though she remained calm in appearance, inwardly she cried out—begged him to ask anything of her. She would grant him any favor, any recompense she could offer for having left him.

"I want ya to teach my boy to read," he said.

Violet paused in pulling on her second stocking. She near gulped with astonishment. She felt as if someone had plunged a knife into her bosom. Emotions she could neither explain nor manage whirled within her. "Y-you have a son?" she asked.

"Oh, hell no!" he growled. "Jimmy ain't my son. I found him."

Violet looked to him. She felt like screaming! Didn't he care that she'd come back for him? Didn't he care that she'd been told he was a philanderer? Didn't he cherish anything they'd shared in the past? How could he stand before her, calmly conversing—watching her get dressed, for pity's sake—as if they'd never meant anything to one another?

"You found him?" she managed to ask. "Wh-who?"

"Jimmy Ritter," he stated, frowning as if he couldn't fathom why she didn't understand him. "I found him in a cave, and I want ya to teach him to read. I'll pay ya for yer time."

"Jimmy Ritter? The young man I met this morning?" she asked.

"Yeah," he said. "He tells me he carried yer books to the schoolhouse for ya. Ain't that sweet?"

"You found him?" Even for all her emotions, Violet almost laughed—surprised by Stoney's matter-of-factness—as if it were the most normal thing in the world to find a boy.

Stoney nodded. "Sure. He run away from the orphan home in Valencia. I found him holed up in a cave right after Bud died." Stoney shrugged. "I had a lot that needed doin' on the place, so I hired him as my hand. That was two years back, and I figure he's about ready to move on. I can sense the itch in him."

Violet smiled as Stoney reached down and plucked a blade of foxtail grass. Breaking off the spiky foxtail tip, he flicked it away and took the remaining stalk between his teeth.

Stoney Wrenn had always chewed on foxtail grass—at least, as a child he had.

"I figure he ought to learn to read before he leaves. A person needs readin'. I tried to teach him myself, but we butt heads over it. He wouldn't have anything to do with the last two schoolteachers we had." He smiled at her then, the blade of foxtail grass still between his teeth. His dimpled smile nearly melted Violet into a puddle at his feet. Certainly dimples were always adorable on a child, and Stoney Wrenn had been no exception. However, the long, deep dimple that adorned his face as a man—well, Violet thought there could be no more attractive embellishment to such an already magnificent face. Furthermore, that same smile—the one from her memory, the one from her dreams—it caused her heart to suddenly leap within her bosom.

"I don't figure he'll butt heads with you though." He winked, and Violet was breathless with sudden delight. He leaned forward, lowering his voice. "I think he's kinda sweet on ya already."

Violet was somewhat mortified when she felt the heat of a blush rising to her cheeks. Even she was not immune to his attractive, flattering ways. "Of course I'll teach him to read," Violet said, reaching down to slip lace one boot. "He seems like a very nice boy. Just have him come to the school and—"

"He won't come to the school," he interrupted. "You'd have to meet with him another time. That's why I'm offerin' to pay you."

"Why?" she asked. "Surely it's not his age. The Fisher boy and the Webster boy are older, and they don't seem to mind."

"No, they don't," Stoney said. "But that's 'cause they'd rather be in school than workin' hard. Jimmy's not that way at all. He sees daylight as somethin' that shouldn't be wasted. He doesn't understand how important readin' and writin' are."

"I see," Violet said, lacing her other boot. "Well, would we have to wait until dark? Or do you think he'd be willin' to meet me just before suppertime maybe?"

"Oh, he'll meet ya whenever I tell him to meet ya," Stoney said. "I just didn't want to bully him too much. He's gettin' older; he's nearly his own man. He don't need me naggin' like I was his mama."

Violet couldn't help but smile. How handsome Stoney had grown up to be! Furthermore, his concern over Jimmy's future was admirable. Womanizing son of a gun or not, Stoney Wrenn was doing right by Jimmy Ritter.

"Then send him to my house at about five o'clock today," Violet said. "We'll start this evening."

"All righty then," Stoney said. "Do you want

me to pay ya after every lesson? Or just at the end of every week?"

Violet felt her smile fade. "You don't need to pay me," she said. "He's a member of this town . . . and thereby my pupil. The school board pays me. I wouldn't accept a wage even if they didn't."

"He's a handful," he said. "He can talk the feathers off a magpie. Are ya sure ya don't want—"

"No," Violet interrupted. "Just send him to me. I'm more than happy to teach him."

"All right then, Miss Fynne," Stoney said. "Just remember that I warned ya—that boy'll near talk yer ear off."

Violet nodded. She made the mistake of letting her gaze linger on Stoney's face for a moment. All at once she was nearly overcome with the desire to throw her arms around his neck and tell him she was sorry—sorry for abandoning him so many years before. Still, she sensed he wouldn't care, that he'd left the past far behind, even though Violet had never been able to.

"I'll be fine," she said, still unable to quit staring at him. "And I better get home . . . if I'm going to have Jimmy's first lesson prepared for him before he arrives."

"Why did ya come back?" he asked unexpectedly.

Violet felt her cheeks burn with a renewed

blush. She felt uncomfortable, overly warm. She certainly couldn't tell him the truth—that she'd come back for him. He'd think she was insane—surely he would!

"I-I always missed Rattler Rock," she began, "ever since Daddy moved us away. So when I was informed there was a teaching position open here—the one my own father occupied years ago, now that I think about it—I chose to come back."

Stoney Wrenn's green-blue eyes narrowed. He studied her for a moment, seemed to consider her answer, as if he didn't quite believe it to be the truth. "That's good," he said at last, " 'cause I sure hope ya didn't come back to check up on me."

Violet gulped—tried to appear unaffected. "Of course not," she lied. "You're fine. It's obvious you've made quite a success of life."

"I am fine," he said. "Oh, folks may say that I'm a—what was it that little Deavers girl said? A womanizing son of a—"

"Gun," Violet interrupted.

"Oh yeah," he chuckled. "I'm sure that was it." He chuckled again, and Violet smiled—delighted by the way his opaline eyes and dimples complemented his already wildly good-looking face. "But no matter what the folks in town think, I've done all right for myself. I guess I'm about as content as a man can be."

"Well . . . I'm . . . I'm very glad to know that," Violet said. She lowered her gaze for a moment—still haunted by the past, still needing further affirmation Stoney Wrenn had been all right after she'd abandoned him. "I admit, I worried for you. I worried that your father—"

"Oh, he eased up on me pretty soon after yer family left town," he said. "It was like somethin' just knocked some sense into him one day. And he didn't lay a hand on me again."

"Oh, good!" Violet breathed. She felt as if something had been resting on her shoulders and was suddenly lifted—slightly. "I'm glad to hear . . . to see you so happy."

His eyes narrowed as he looked at her and nodded. "And you don't seem to have suffered none for livin' in the big city," he said.

"I don't?" she asked.

"Well, yer still wadin' through cricks in yer underwear, savin' children from gettin' a lickin', and huntin' treasure."

Again Violet felt cheeks pink up. She couldn't believe he'd caught her in such a situation—in such a manner of undress! "Susan Gribbs took her mother's brooch without asking then dropped it in the creek when she was showing it to her friend," she explained.

Stoney nodded. "I'm thinkin' that would've been quite a lickin' then. Ol' Ethel Gribbs ain't as tenderhearted as she once was."

"She's not?"

Stoney shook his head. "Nope. But I guess that's the way with most of us. Ain't it?"

There was a deeper meaning to his words. Was it his way of letting her know he was no longer the kind, mischievous boy she'd once known?

"I don't know," she said.

He grinned, as if knowing her soul was confused and in torment. "I'll send Jimmy over this evenin'," he said. "You have a good afternoon, Miss Fynne."

"Thank you," she said as he tugged at the brim of his hat and turned to leave.

He paused. Turning back to her once more, he said, "Let's keep this little . . . situation here between just us two. All right? I don't need nobody thinkin' I had my way with the new schoolteacher or somethin'. Apparently folks already name me as a womanizin' son of a . . . gun. I don't want certain folks wonderin' if it's true. And you sure don't need folks wonderin' if yer a—"

"You mean you don't want Miss Asbury wondering if it's true," Violet said. She was angry! She didn't even know why, but she was. In fact, the fury that had suddenly risen in her bosom was entirely unfamiliar.

"That's right." His eyes narrowed. "And I don't want the sheriff on my heels neither."

"The sheriff?"

He grinned. "Oh, he's already staked his claim to you, Miss Fynne. And don't nobody buck Coby Fisher once he's got his mind set."

"But I don't—"

"You have a good afternoon," he interrupted, turning from her and striding away. "Hope Jimmy don't talk yer head clean off yer shoulders."

"Goodbye," Violet said.

She watched him go—watched him until he disappeared over the hill leading to the road. My, he was handsome. And so tall! The boy she'd played with as a child was gone. In his place was a man—a man who walked a path without the need of an old friend for company.

Sighing and awash with a sort of discouraged melancholy, Violet ambled along the creekbank toward town. Was this it? After ten years of worrying and guilt—after a decade of thinking of little else but returning to Rattler Rock in search of Stoney Wrenn—was this all there was meant to be? What had she expected? Had she expected Stoney would be so overjoyed to see her again that he'd take her hand and pull her off in search of a dead carcass to investigate or an old tree to climb? Those years were gone; those children were gone. Yet, admittedly, she had expected more than a simple, "Why did ya come back?" and "I want you to teach my boy to read." Surely their childhood friendship had meant more to Stoney Wrenn than that—hadn't it?

As Violet followed the creek back toward town, she wondered if it hadn't. Maybe Stoney had simply not valued Violet to the depths she had valued him. It wasn't fair! Violet was hurt—angry in thinking Stoney had swept memories of their friendship aside.

Yet perhaps—perhaps when his father had ceased in beating him, he'd moved on to a happier life, let go of everything that may have reminded him of more difficult times. How could she feel badly about his having done so? Still, her heart ached—ached differently when she thought of Stoney now. At least, bearing the burden of guilt and worry that she'd borne for nearly ten years—at least in that she still felt she owned a part of him somehow, held to a tether that could never strip him from her mind and heart. Now, however, her mind was muddled and her heart aching, for Stoney Wrenn had grown into a fine measure of a man, a man Violet suspected could have just as powerful a hold on her soul as the boy Stoney Wrenn had owned—more powerful in fact.

There would come no good of letting her mind linger on such thoughts. Violet straightened as her little house came into view. She had a new pupil. Jimmy Ritter would arrive in less than two hours. She must prepare. She had to bake a cake.

Smiling, Violet whispered, "Yes. A cake should

do for Jimmy." If there was one thing Violet Fynne had learned as a teacher, it was the benefits of making certain that learning to read and write made a child feel happy. If she baked a cake—allowed Jimmy to enjoy the delicious sensation a human being experienced while eating such a sweet thing—then he would begin to associate reading and writing with delight and, therefore, delight in reading and writing.

She determined then to push thoughts of Stoney Wrenn from her mind to settle her heart. She would think of Jimmy Ritter—of the kind young man who indeed should learn to read and write before he set out full into life.

A vision of Stoney Wrenn endeavored to linger in her mind—tall, handsome, dimple-cheeked. Violet shook her head as she climbed the steps of the front porch of her little schoolteacher's house.

"A cake for Jimmy. It should do fine," she whispered.

"You didn't have to go to all this trouble, Miss Fynne," Jimmy said as he sat on the front porch step devouring a piece of cake.

Violet smiled and rested one elbow on one knee, her chin in her hand. "It wasn't any trouble at all, Jimmy," she said. "I love cake. But can you imagine if I were to make a cake and have no one to share it with?"

"You'd more'n likely get a bellyache," Jimmy said.

"More than likely, yes," Violet giggled. She'd been thinking she'd grow as big as a bloated dead cow, but she thought Jimmy's response much kinder.

"Ya know," Jimmy began, "maybe readin' ain't gonna be as hard to learn as I've been thinkin' all this time."

Violet smiled as Jimmy shoveled another bite of cake into his mouth. "Well, I hope not," she said. "Reading is so important, Jimmy . . . and so wonderful. Oh, the adventures I've known through reading!"

"Mmm-hmm. Stoney says ya always had yer nose stuck in a book when the two of you were kids." He ate another bite of cake. "He says ya near scared yerself to death after readin' some book by a feller named Charlie. Somethin' about ghosts and Christmas."

Violet laughed and covered her mouth with one hand when she realized how loud she had laughed. What a delicious memory! "I don't suppose Stoney told you that he was frightened near out of his wits too, did he?" she asked.

"What do ya mean?"

"Stoney and I read that book together," Violet began, "a book titled *A Christmas Carol* by a man named Charles Dickens. We'd sit out there by the old house—the haunted one that Buddy Chisolm owned—"

"The ol' Chisolm place?" Jimmy asked.

Violet nodded. "Every evening for near to a week, we sat out there taking turns at reading *A Christmas Carol* out loud to each other." Violet smiled. "Oh, we thought we were a couple of brave souls, reading all about ghosts, waiting for the light of the lovers' moon to appear in the windows of the old house. But when we'd finished the book, we found ourselves anticipating that spirits would appear to us in our rooms at night. I slept with my lamp lit for near to a month." She paused—felt her eyes narrow as her mind lingered in the past. "Stoney didn't have that. He couldn't leave his lamp lit." Pulling her mind from the dismal memory of Stoney's cruel father, she forced a smile, looked at Jimmy, and said, "I guess he didn't tell you that he was so scared he slept under his bed for quite some time after we'd finished the book."

Jimmy chuckled, shook his head, and set his empty plate and fork down on the step. "No, ma'am, he did not," he chuckled. "I think I'd like to read that book, Miss Fynne," he said, smiling at her. "I think someday I'd like to read it."

"Maybe we can read it together," Violet said. "I think I have two copies. When you're a little further on, I could read out loud, and you could follow along until you feel comfortable reading too."

Jimmy's smile broadened. "I think I'd like that." He frowned a little, shook his head, and added, "I can't believe I'm thinkin' I might like to sit still and read a book one day."

Violet placed a hand on Jimmy's shoulder. "You will, Jimmy. I promise."

"Hey there, Jimmy Ritter!"

Violet looked up to see Maya Asbury and Beth Deavers walking past.

"Hello, ladies," Jimmy greeted. "Don't you both look lovely this evenin'."

Violet felt her eyebrows arch. Had Stoney Wrenn been teaching Jimmy Ritter a lesson or two of his own? Maya and Beth both blushed and giggled.

"Hello, Miss Fynne," Maya called.

"Hello, girls," Violet said. "Are you out for an evening stroll?"

Maya nodded. "Yes. We thought a little fresh air might be nice. It's been such a beautiful afternoon."

Violet glanced to Jimmy—noted the way his eyes lingered on Maya.

"Well, you two have fun," Violet called.

"Yes, Miss Fynne," Beth said.

" 'Bye, Jimmy," Maya added, tossing a shy wave in Jimmy's direction.

"Goodbye, ladies," Jimmy said.

Violet giggled as she watched Jimmy's gaze follow the girls as they disappeared down the road. "She's a very pretty young lady," she said.

"Who? Maya Asbury?" Jimmy asked.

"Yes."

"She sure is," he said. His smile faded a bit. "I guess Dayton Fisher oughta count himself as one lucky feller."

"Dayton Fisher?"

"Maya's sweet on Dayton," Jimmy said. "Everybody knows it."

"Things aren't always what they appear, Jimmy. Most of the time, people hide what they're really thinking and feeling."

"That's what Stoney says too," Jimmy said. "He says Maya Asbury's sweet after me . . . said her sister Layla told him so." Jimmy shook his head. "But I don't see it. She's far too purty and smart to look twice at a feller like me."

"Of all the boys I've met in Rattler Rock," Violet began, "you're the most handsome and the most gentlemanly and the hardest working and—"

Jimmy laughed. "Oh, yer a charmer, Miss Fynne. You are a charmer. No wonder you and Stoney was such good friends. He's a charmer too . . . and a heap more handsome than any other feller in town." He smiled. "Even me." He shook his head and chuckled. "Why, I've seen him charm just about anything out of just about anybody."

"Then he hasn't changed much," Violet mumbled.

Jimmy's smile faded. He paused, as if considering whether to say what was in his mind. "Ya know, Miss Fynne," he began, "Layla Asbury's awful sweet on Stoney. She's ripe for the pickin' as far as marryin' goes too."

All at once, Violet felt ill, hot, and angry. She didn't want to talk about Miss Layla Asbury and Stoney Wrenn. Furthermore, she was experiencing a sort of self-disgust. Why did it bother her so to hear about Stoney Wrenn and his girl? Hadn't she always held to the hope that Stoney had grown up to be happy? Certainly she had! Then why did it bother her that he might enjoy love and happiness with such a beautiful young woman?

Jimmy frowned and began, "Folks are sayin'—"

"Good evenin' there, Miss Fynne . . . Jimmy."

Violet looked up to see Sheriff Fisher rein in his horse. She hadn't heard him approach. She guessed she'd been too enthralled in remembering the past, in encouraging Jimmy toward reading, in feeling sickened at the thought of Stoney Wrenn being so sweet on Layla Asbury.

"Evenin', Sheriff," Jimmy said.

Violet nodded her greeting, and Sheriff Fisher smiled at her.

He dismounted and dropped his reins over the limb of the apple tree nearby. "You helpin'

Miss Fynne with somethin', Jimmy?" the sheriff asked.

"She's helpin' me," Jimmy answered. "Miss Fynne's gonna teach me to read."

"Well, I suppose that's what schoolteachers do best, after all," Sheriff Fisher said, smiling.

"I best be gettin' home, Miss Fynne," Jimmy said. He picked up his well-worn hat from the porch step, plopped it on his head, and offered a hand to her.

Violet forced a smile, accepting his hand.

"I guess I'll be by tomorrow about the same time."

"I'll look forward to it," Violet said.

"Evenin', Sheriff," Jimmy said as he headed past Sheriff Fisher and out onto the road.

"He's a fine young man," Sheriff Fisher said as he watched Jimmy Ritter head for home. "The other boys in this town would do good to look to that boy and learn somethin'—includin' my little brother."

Violet returned Sheriff Fisher's smile.

He propped one foot on the top step of the porch and leaned forward, resting one arm on his knee. "Dayton tells me you've seen the light of the lovers' moon," he said.

Violet inhaled deeply—exhaled. This was it: telling ghost stories in school had gotten her into trouble. "Is this my first reprimand then, Sheriff?" she asked.

"No, ma'am," Sheriff Fisher said, smiling. "And you need to start callin' me Coby, remember?"

Violet did remember then—remembered that Stoney Wrenn had implied Sheriff Fisher liked her. She smiled, for he was a very handsome man. His sky-blue eyes combined with his dark hair did give him quite the look of a scoundrel—the delicious sort of scoundrel women favored.

"I remember," she said. "So . . . you're not here to reprimand me for telling the children I've seen the light out at the old Chisolm place?"

Coby Fisher chuckled, smiled, and shook his head. "Of course not. After all, I've seen it too."

"You have?"

"Yep. Several times. I just told Dayton to be careful. Ol' Stoney Wrenn would as soon shoot anybody steppin' foot on that place as look at 'em. So I just told Dayton to keep a watchful eye out . . . if he ever does decide to go back and watch for the light."

Violet frowned a little. "Everyone keeps telling me that . . . that Stoney Wrenn would as soon shoot you as look at you. Has he ever truly shot anyone for trespassing?" Violet thought of her own encounter with trespassing on Stoney's property—the rifle he'd leveled at her head. Had Stoney Wrenn earned such a reputation because he'd actually shot someone for trespassing at some time?

Coby Fisher chuckled and shook his head. "He ain't actually shot anybody, but he's shot at 'em. We all figure it's just safer to think he missed on purpose those times in the past than to take a chance he's truly just a bad shot. Why? You plannin' on waitin' on the light? The moon's awful close to bein' full. Could be tonight. Could be a lovers' moon out tonight."

He winked, and Violet smiled. He was flirting with her—something merciless! Violet's insides churned; her emotions swung from sheer delight to pure disappointment. Sheriff Fisher was a terribly handsome man—terribly handsome! Yet her heart whispered, *But not as handsome as Stoney Wrenn.*

"Well, if I ever do go looking for the light again," Violet began, "I will be careful not to get shot by Stoney Wrenn."

Coby Fisher chuckled. He stood straight once more. "That'll ease my mind quite a piece, Miss Fynne," he said. "You have yerself a good evenin'."

"Thank you," Violet said. "You too."

The sheriff nodded, touched the brim of his hat, and strode back to his horse. He mounted and nodded before riding away.

Violet put a hand to her forehead and watched the sheriff ride back toward town. Turning, she gazed out in the direction Jimmy had taken, in the direction of the old Chisolm place. The moon had nearly been full the night before. Violet was certain that it would be a full moon that would rise in a few hours. She felt the familiar sensation of mischief stirring in her bosom. All at once, her desire to see the light of the lovers' moon was nearly insatiable.

Stoney Wrenn had never shot a trespasser. Oh, he may have shot at them. But Violet remembered Stoney's aim with a gun—any gun. If Stoney Wrenn ever truly meant to shoot anybody, he wouldn't miss. Besides, she'd make sure he never knew she was there.

Violet thought of old Buddy Chisolm—of the day he told her and Stoney the story of the ghost in the fancy old house outside of town. She wanted to see it again—wanted to know she hadn't simply dreamed seeing the light as a child.

Smiling, she turned and went into her little schoolteacher's house. The full moon would rise—a lovers' moon. She was sure of it, and she'd be ready. Furthermore, maybe it would be worth being threatened for trespassing again—if it meant seeing Stoney Wrenn again.

# CHAPTER FIVE

Violet settled on the old fallen tree. She tucked her feet under, smoothed out her skirt, and set aside the unlit lantern she'd brought. It had been a pleasant walk to the old Chisolm place. The night air was warm, and the full moon lit the road nicely. The stars were brilliant overhead, and Violet thought that even if she didn't see the light, her midnight meanderings had been pleasant.

The house was dark, a looming silhouette against the starry, moonlit sky. Violet shivered with nervous anticipation. Had she really seen the light of the lovers' moon as a child? She knew she had. Yet ten years had turned memory to doubt, and she longed to see it again. She remembered the first time Stoney Wrenn had brought her to the same place in the middle of the night. For hours they'd waited—whispering their conversation, waiting with delicious expectancy—until Stoney had hushed her and pointed to a window on the lower floor of the old house.

Violet still remembered the gasp she'd caused to echo through the night, the way Stoney had clamped his hand over her mouth and shushed her so that the ghosts wouldn't be frightened away. What an adventure they'd had that night! What a glorious, delightfully frightening adventure!

Violet sighed, pleased as a different memory began to play out in her mind. She smiled—could almost hear Stoney's voice reading the last few lines of a chapter in Dickens's *A Christmas Carol*. Goose bumps rippled over her arms, the effect of the memory of a feeling experienced so long ago.

. . . . . . . . . .

Stoney closed the book.

"It's gettin' too dark to read . . . even with the lantern," he said.

Violet nodded and rubbed at the goose bumps along her arms—goose bumps caused from listening to Stoney read of a ghost shrouded in a black hooded robe. She looked to Stoney, wondering if he really felt it was too dark to continue reading. Or had the description of the ghost in the book unsettled him as greatly as it had unsettled Violet?

Violet glanced about. Evening was falling fast. She knew the walk home would be terrifying for the sake of having just listened to Stoney read of the wandering spirits who walked the earth with Ebenezer Scrooge.

"I-I guess I'll start home then," Violet whispered.

"I'll take you," Stoney said.

"No, Stoney," she said. "I'll be fine. We don't need your pa wonderin' where ya are. He might get angry again."

Stoney smiled. He stood, taking hold of the

lantern handle in one hand and Violet's trembling hand in his other. "He won't miss me for a while," he said. He raised the lantern and peered toward the road. "Come on. Let's get ya home before we're both too yeller to move."

Violet smiled. Stoney was so thoughtful! She knew he was risking a beating by seeing her home, but as always, he cared more for her than he did for himself.

They stepped out onto the moonlit road, and Violet said, "Maybe we should've just finished the book. Maybe it had a happy ending and we wouldn't be scared right now."

"I don't see how it can end good," Stoney said. "Ol' Scrooge oughta be dead from fright by the end. I don't see how he's hung on this long—ghosts runnin' this way and that all the time."

"Well, no matter how it ends, I won't sleep a wink for a year after this!" Violet confessed.

"Me neither," Stoney mumbled. He frowned and looked to her as they walked hand in hand down the road toward town. "Viola, did you know this story was gonna give us the willies like this when ya started us readin' on it?"

Violet shook her head. "No," she said. "My daddy just said it was a wonderful book—a real adventure that made a person think about his own life."

"Well, more'n likely it'll keep me thinkin' about my own death," Stoney said. "I swear my heart's gonna pound itself right out of my chest!"

Violet nodded in agreement. She moved closer to Stoney—wrapped her arm around his strong one that held her other hand.

A sudden realization washed over her. "Oh, Stoney! You'll have to walk home all by yourself!" she exclaimed.

"I'll be all right," he said. "Let's just hurry so's I can have it over with."

Violet smiled. He always thought of her first—always. Though she did she feel guilty, knowing Stoney would have to walk home in the dark, visions of ghosts swimming in his mind, while she was safe in a warm-lighted house with her mother and father.

"Let's finish the book tomorrow so we don't have to be scared anymore," she told him.

"Fine by me," Stoney said. "And I get to choose what we read next. All right?"

Violet smiled at him. "All right."

They both startled, and Violet let out a frightened yelp as a bird took flight from the grasses at the side of the road.

"I'm definitely pickin' out the next book," Stoney chuckled, shaking his head. "And it won't have nothin' to do with ghosts."

. . . . . . . . . .

Violet squealed—startled from her thoughts as Stoney Wrenn stepped over the log from behind, sitting down next to her.

"Yer tresspassin', schoolteacher," he said.

Violet placed a hand to her bosom, attempting to calm the painful racing of her heart. "You nearly scared me to death, Stoney Wrenn!" she scolded.

"Well, I thought about shootin' ya . . . so count yer blessin's," he mumbled.

She looked to him. He wasn't smiling—not his mouth anyway. Yet she was sure the mischief shining in his green-blue opal eyes meant he was only teasing about having considered shooting her.

"Don't tell me yer out here waitin' on the ghosts," he said.

Violet shrugged. "Maybe I am. Or maybe I was just out for a stroll and stopped to rest on this old log."

His eyes narrowed. "Out for a stroll in the middle of the night?" he asked.

"Of course I'm waiting for the ghosts," she said. "The light of the lovers' moon. Isn't that what it's called now?"

"It is," he answered.

Violet frowned and tipped her head to one side as she studied the great, dark edifice before her. The house seemed so lifeless—so lonely. "When did it become that . . . the light of the lovers' moon?" she asked.

When she lived in Rattler Rock as a child— when she and Stoney had sat together on bygone occasions waiting to see the light—it had merely been referred to as "the ghost light out at Bud Chisolm's old place." Sometimes folks had called it "the ghost light." But never anything as fancy and romantic as "the light of the lovers' moon." She wondered how the phrase had come to be, who had first uttered the phrase.

Stoney shrugged. "I don't know," he answered. "Folks have been callin' it that since before ol' Bud passed." He looked at her, his gaze lingering on her face. "I always thought it sounded about like somethin' you woulda come up with."

"I suppose it does," Violet said. She smiled at him, and she fancied his expression softened. "I'm glad Mr. Chisolm left it to you." She looked from Stoney to the old house. "Anybody else wouldn't have cared about the old place."

"How do ya know I care about it?" he rather grumbled.

"You're here, aren't you? Threatening trespassers?" She nodded to the Winchester rifle he'd propped up against the log.

"I guess."

"Sheriff Fisher says you've never really shot anybody for trespassing though," she said. "He knows you're too good a shot to have accidentally missed."

"Sheriff Fisher don't know everything," Stoney said. "But I see he's got yer attention already."

Violet shrugged. "He stopped by this afternoon

while Jimmy and I were having our lesson. I think . . . I think he was reprimanding me for telling the children that I had seen the light out here. I think he was afraid it might cause them to get into mischief."

Reaching up, Violet pulled a length of hair free from the loose bun she'd swept it into that morning. Almost unconsciously, she began twisting the hair with her index finger.

Stoney nearly smiled. Violet Fynne still twisted her hair when she was nervous. He willed his expression to remain stoic—to reveal nothing akin to amusement or delight. Although some part of him was charmed to see she still owned the adorable habit of twisting her hair, the weathered man in him would not be softened.

"I guess he don't want to see his brother shot for trespassin'," Stoney said.

"Dayton?"

"Yep. He's out here every other month or so, waitin' on the light. I usually just keep a close eye on him," he explained. "He ain't the only one. I figure he'll be haulin' some sweet little filly out here one day, hopin' to find her in his arms once the light appears and frightens her." He grinned a bit and lowered his voice. "You'd be plum astonished if I told ya some of the goin's-on I've seen out here durin' a full moon."

Violet smiled and felt a delicious curiosity rise within her. "Goings-on?" she whispered. "What kind of goings-on?"

He paused, seeming to consider whether or not he should answer. "Some I can't mention, bein' that I do have a little bit of a gentleman left in me," he said.

Violet felt her eyes widen. "Really? Well . . . what can you tell me?"

He grinned. "Well, I can tell ya that Sam Capshaw—he works over at the livery with his pa—I can tell ya he and Mary Pierson are far more than just sweet on each other," he said.

Violet smiled, nodding with encouragement that he should continue.

"Mrs. Wilson, the widow lady who owns the dress shop? She's been keeping company with Mr. Deavers . . . since about three months after his wife passed."

Violet giggled, delighted with the secret sweethearts of Rattler Rock that Stoney was revealing. "Anyone else?" she prodded.

"That little girl in yer school, Katie Mill?" he began, "I reckon she got her first kiss just last month when Hagen Webster drug her out here in the middle of the night. They missed seein' the light though." He paused and smiled at her. "They were too wrapped up in other business. The light was here, but they missed seein' it."

Violet laughed, mercilessly twisting the strand

of her hair she'd been toying with. "If folks only knew what you've seen!" she giggled. "But they know you don't like trespassers. What do they think . . . that you just happen not to be here on the nights that they are?"

He shrugged and smiled, and Violet felt her heart flutter a little at the sight of the long dimples displayed in his cheeks.

"I'm guessin' they ain't too worried about who else might be around," he said. He looked at her, his dazzling smile broadening. "They're usually a little more interested in other things."

Violet giggled again. Somehow the knowledge that Stoney Wrenn knew such secrets enlivened her mind—thrilled her.

She glanced back to the house then and gasped when she saw the tiny flicker of light in one of the bottom floor windows. "I see it!" she breathed.

"Where?" Stoney asked in a whisper.

"Just there, in that lower window. Do you see it?" Violet's eyes widened; her heart began to beat with an anxious measure. The light— the light of the lovers' moon! She saw it! She watched as the tiny light grew until it looked very much like a candle flame.

"You do see it, don't you?" she whispered.

"Yes," Stoney answered.

Goose bumps raced over Violet's arms and legs; her mind burned with wonder. The light—

it was there! She was witnessing it again, just as she had so many years ago. She marveled at the fact that Stoney sat next to her now, just as he had on the other occasions she'd seen the light.

"It's moving," she whispered as she watched the light pass from one window to another.

"It'll climb the stairs now," Stoney whispered. "We won't see it again until it's at the top of the stairs."

Violet held her breath—waited. She smiled and clasped her hands together in delight as the light did appear in one of the upper windows. "What do you think they're doing?" she whispered. "What are they looking for? You do think there are two ghosts, don't you? Just like Buddy once told us?"

"I know there're two," Stoney said. "One light maybe . . . but I know they're two souls."

He sounded so certain—so sure. Violet forced her gaze from the light in the upper window of the old house to Stoney. He wasn't looking at the house or the light; he was looking at her. A heartache Violet could never have before fathomed gripped her all at once. Stoney Wrenn—how she'd missed him!

"How do you know?" she asked.

"Because . . . because I know who they are," he said.

"The rich man from New York City and his wife, yes. Buddy told us," she whispered.

"No, I mean I know exactly who they are. Buddy told me their names."

Violet gulped and felt goose bumps ripple over her arms. "He did?" she breathed. "Who? What were their names?"

Stoney's eyes narrowed. "I-I'm not sure I should—"

Violet shook her head. "I'm sorry. I shouldn't have asked."

It was wrong of her to intrude the way she had—intrude on whatever secrets Buddy had shared with Stoney before his death. Perhaps Buddy had made Stoney promise not to tell anyone the names of the ghosts. In that moment, Violet resented her father for taking her away from Rattler Rock. If she'd stayed, maybe Buddy Chisolm would've told her the names of the ghosts too. If she'd stayed, maybe Stoney Wrenn wouldn't be courting Miss Layla Asbury.

"But . . . it is proof, isn't it?" she whispered.

"What do ya mean?" he asked.

Violet watched the light in the house—watched it slowly move from room to room. "The ghosts in the old house," she said. "It's proof that . . . though people die, love never does. Why else would they be wandering together tonight?" She looked to him. "If they didn't still love each other, they wouldn't be here together . . . would they?"

"I guess not," Stoney said.

121

Violet's heart was pounding so wildly within her bosom that its rhythm was echoing in her head. Stoney Wrenn—how she'd missed him! How she'd loved him! How she feared she would always love him! Silently she told herself she didn't even know this man. She'd known the boy, yes. But the man was different—wasn't he? She could not have legitimate feelings for a man she'd never known.

Stoney looked back to the house. "It's gone," he said.

Violet looked to see that the house stood dark once more—empty and lifeless against the night sky. The light of the lovers' moon was gone, and now Stoney Wrenn would go too. She knew he would, and she must tell him before he left. It was the only way to ease her mind—at least, ease it a little.

"I lied to you yesterday," Violet whispered. "I didn't come back to Rattler Rock because I missed it . . . or because I wanted to teach here." She looked back to him—nearly couldn't speak when she saw the glowing opals of his eyes intently watching her, the deep frown puckering his brow. "I came back . . . because I once promised a boy I wouldn't forget him . . . that I'd come back and make certain he was all right."

"I figured that," he said. "You haven't changed all that much . . . and I figured guilt had been eatin' at ya . . . whether ya shoulda let it or not."

Violet glanced away—up into the sky—to the large ivory moon hanging overhead. "Were you all right, Stoney Wrenn?" she asked in a lowered voice, afraid of the answer he might give. "Have you had a good life? What happened to your parents?" She looked to him once more. "To your mother?"

Stoney inhaled a deep breath. "I don't know," he answered. "I left Rattler Rock for a time . . . and when I come back, my pa had packed up my mama and left. I never heard from them again."

Violet felt tears well in her eyes. Not only had she abandoned Stoney, but his parents had too. No matter what kind of a monster his father had been, Stoney's mother had loved him—and he had loved her.

"I'm so sorry," she whispered.

"Don't be," he said. "It ain't yer fault. And besides, me and ol' Buddy, we had a fine time." He smiled. "A real fine time. Oh, he worked me hard . . . indeed he did. But it was good for me. And durin' it all, we had a good time of it."

"I'm so sorry, Stoney," Violet began. "So sorry that—"

"I've been fine," he interrupted. "You didn't need to worry about me all this time . . . and ya certainly don't need to worry over me now. All right?" His eyes were warm and encouraging. His smile was beautiful—sincere.

Violet nodded, knowing her guilt and remorse

123

would never subside, no matter his assurances. She swallowed the lump of emotion in her throat and said, "You do seem to be just fine. And . . . and you've got your home and your property now . . . and your girl." She forced herself to look up at him, to smile. "All this time I guess I . . . I should've known you'd be fine."

He nodded. "You did know me purty well," he said. "So ya shoulda known I'd be just dandy. I feel bad that ya worried so much over it . . . when there weren't really nothin' to worry over. And I feel bad that yer stuck in Rattler Rock now because of it."

Violet shook her head and forced a smile. She stood up from the old log and smoothed her skirt. "I'm not stuck here," she said. "I really didn't like teaching in the city—not at all. The children here, they're far more interesting . . . far more willing to learn than others I've taught." She looked at him. "And I really do like Rattler Rock. I really did miss it." She felt a tear escape her eye and travel over her cheek as he stood up from the log too. "But I do want you to know . . . that boy I left . . . that boy who was my friend when I was just a silly schoolgirl myself? I did worry about him. I hoped he was all right, that his daddy quit beating on him, that he had good people in his life and grew up happy. I loved that boy," she whispered. She brushed the tear from her cheek and forced a smile.

She watched as Stoney's eyes narrowed, glowing opalescent in the moonlight. She saw his jaw clinch and lock tight as he mumbled, "That boy loved you."

More tears escaped Violet's eyes as she felt a new sort of heartache envelop her again. This was it: the moment when her soul would have to let go of the boy Stoney Wrenn—for good. That boy was gone, and in his place stood a man, a man who led a life vastly separate from hers.

"Thank you," she began, "for trying to ease my mind . . . for trying to soothe my guilt." She turned to him, reached out, and placed her hands on his shoulders as she raised herself on the tips of her toes and placed a lingering kiss to his left cheek. In that moment, she inhaled the scent of him—the scent of pine and cedar, of leather and grass. She felt the warmth of his whiskery cheek against her lips and wondered how she would ever purge such a man from her mind and heart. She must let go of him. She knew she must. After all, he'd let go of her a long time ago. Furthermore, it seemed he belonged to someone else now. Violet's stomach churned as she thought of Miss Layla Asbury—of Stoney's affection for the young woman in town.

Violet's musing was interrupted, however. She gasped as Stoney reached out, taking her cheek and chin in one hand.

"Don't worry. I'll just do this once," he

125

mumbled. "Just because I always wanted to . . . and never had the chance."

"D-do what?" Violet breathed.

"Kiss Viola Fynne," he whispered.

Breathless, Violet felt warmth flood her body as Stoney's lips pressed to hers in the softest of kisses. His powerful hand tightened at her chin and cheek as he kissed her a second time. Violet's heart was pounding with such wild ferocity she thought she might fly apart! She wanted to touch him—wanted his arms around her—to be held against the strong protection of his body. Yet he did not endeavor to embrace her—or even touch her in any manner other than holding her face in one hand as his third and fourth kisses to her lips lingered far, far longer than the first two had.

As their fourth kiss ended, Violet felt his grip on her face lessen. Yet as his mouth began to leave the vicinity of her own, Violet whispered, "Just once more. You know how I hate even numbers."

She heard him chuckle and mumble, "Oh, that's right," a moment before he kissed her a fifth time—kissed her more firmly than he had before, his lips slightly parted, the warm moisture of his mouth causing a second and third wave of goose bumps to cover her body.

"Now," he began as he dropped his hand from her face and straightened to his full, intimidating height, "no more luggin' guilt around over me.

I'm fine. I'm happy and . . ." He paused, smiling at her as his green-blue opal eyes sparkled in the moonlight. "And nobody's beatin' on me anymore. We were friends once. We'll stay friends now." His smile broadened. "We just won't go wadin' in the crick in our underwear." He chuckled and added, "Although, from what I seen earlier today, you haven't given that up. Let's just say we won't go wadin' in the crick in our underwear *together*."

Violet giggled, delighted by his teasing, still tingling from his kisses. It was a dream come true, being kissed by Stoney Wrenn. Violet had dreamt of it since she was a little, tenderhearted girl. Though she wondered how anything else in life could ever measure the thrill and pure pleasure she'd known when he'd kissed her, she was thankful it had happened.

"I'm just relieved it was you who found me that way . . . and not someone else," she told him. "Just imagine the mess if someone else had found me like that, right on the heels of my getting the children all stirred up with my own stories of this place." She turned from him, for somehow her heart was aching in looking at him. Looking to the old Chisolm place, now dark and lifeless once more, she added, "I'm bound to get myself in a pickle or two here."

"Well, as long as ya keep Coby Fisher eatin' out of yer hand, you'll be fine," Stoney said. He leaned over and picked up the Winchester he'd propped up against the log. "You best run on back to your little house, schoolteacher," he said, "before ol' womanizin' son of a . . . gun Stoney Wrenn . . . shoots ya for trespassin'."

Violet nodded, picked up her lantern, and sighed. "Good night," she said.

He only nodded, and she turned to make her way toward the road.

Stoney winced as he watched Violet Fynne make her way through the tall grass. She'd made him feel things. He swore to himself he would begrudge her the fact forever. The boy she'd known was dead; he'd died the day her father had taken her away. Yet the man he was mourned the boy—mourned the happiness he'd once known because of a girl named Violet—mourned the loss of the girl who might have made his life worth something.

He could still feel the softness of her kiss, still sense the sweet fragrance of her skin. His mouth watered in wanting to taste hers, and he closed his eyes against the vision of her walking away from him. Still, he worried for her—just as he always had. Quietly, he made his way to the row of young cottonwoods that ran alongside the road. He'd follow her home, make certain she arrived at her little house all safe and sound. Then he'd head back to his place and get some rest. At least the little schoolteacher's house was closer to his place than Violet's daddy's place had been all those years before.

Silent and unseen, he followed alongside the road, keeping to the trees and tall grasses. He couldn't help but smile when he heard Violet begin to hum. No doubt she was unsettled at walking home alone in the dark, especially after having seen the light in the old house. He knew the tune she was humming—a song they'd always sang as children, an old saloon song Buddy Chisolm had taught them. He wondered if Violet was even conscious of what melody she was humming. He couldn't help but whisper the words to the song as he followed her.

" 'How the fellers all loved that red petticoat, the one of sweet Maggie McGee's. How them ruffles would fly when she'd take to the stage and kick up her red-stockin'ed knees.' "

He chuckled quietly as he watched Violet climb the steps of her little house, open the door, and disappear inside. He felt bad—guilty for the fact she'd worried about him for so long. Yet something deep within him rested in knowing she'd kept the promise she'd made to him nearly ten years before. Violet Fynne had returned to Rattler Rock, and she'd returned to see that he was all right.

Stoney shook his head as he turned and headed back toward his own place. Part of him—the grown-up man he was—couldn't believe she'd actually kept her promise. Still, the boy, lost somewhere along the way, whispered to him— asked him why he was surprised to find her returned. After all, hadn't she promised him she would?

"Stoney!"

Jimmy's loud whisper startled Stoney from his thoughts of the past. Jimmy was panting—had been running.

"What is it, Jim?" Stoney asked.

"You was wrong this time," Jimmy explained. "Somebody is millin' around tonight. I guess knowin' the light might show up tonight didn't scare 'em off after all."

"Are they in the house?"

Jimmy nodded. "At least they was. They mighta left while I was trackin' you."

Rage roared inside Stoney's head; his breath came angry and labored. "I swear, I'll shoot 'em if I catch 'em, Jimmy," he growled.

"I know . . . and that's why I come to fetch ya."

Infuriated, Stoney turned, leading Jimmy back toward the old Chisolm place. He'd promised Buddy he wouldn't let the old place be ransacked or defiled in any way—and somebody was endeavoring to do it. Ever since Buddy had passed, someone had been trying to root through the old house, and Stoney knew why. Though he didn't know how they knew about Buddy Chisolm's treasure, he was certain somebody did know it existed.

"You seein' Miss Fynne home?" Jimmy asked as they hurried back toward the house.

"Yes . . . even though she's a might independent," Stoney said. "She was out to see the light tonight, and you know you should never let a woman walk home alone, Jimmy. Right?"

"Yes, sir. Even if they don't know yer walkin' 'em," Jimmy stated.

"That's right."

"Well . . . did she see it?" Jimmy asked. "Did she see the light of the lovers' moon?"

"Oh, yes. Yes, she did." Stoney smiled at Jimmy. "And so did I."

"I remember the first time I seen it," Jimmy said. "I 'bout couldn't sleep a wink for a month!"

Stoney smiled, remembering his own experience the very first time he'd seen the light of the ghosts in the old Chisolm place.

"I'm sure whoever's trespassin' will be gone by the time we get back there," Jimmy mumbled. "I thought about goin' in there after 'em myself . . . but I didn't have my rifle."

Stoney stopped and placed a hand on Jimmy's shoulder to stop him as well. "I don't want ya gettin' hurt, Jim," he said. "I don't want ya in the middle of all this."

Jimmy smiled and patted Stoney on the

shoulder. "I'm already in the middle, Stoney. You know that."

Stoney smiled and nodded. Jimmy Ritter was the little brother Stoney Wrenn had never had, and Stoney worried about him.

"I guess you are," Stoney chuckled.

"Then let's go," Jimmy said, heading out once again. "Who do ya think it is, Stoney? Who keeps messin' around in that old house? And why?"

"I don't know who it is, Jim," Stoney said. He didn't know who; it was the truth. Still, he did know why, but that was information he couldn't share—not even with Jimmy—not yet.

Violet sighed as she crawled into bed. Reaching over to the little table at her bedside, she turned the lamp down. She wanted to linger in the low light of the lamp for a moment longer, before she blew it out and went to sleep.

It was so very late. Violet knew she wouldn't feel rested when she left for the school in the morning. Yet she tried not to worry about being tired. The soothing music of the crickets outside calmed Violet's rather tattered nerves, and as she lay back on her pillow, she thought of Stoney— thrilled at the memory of his kiss. She thought of seeing the light of the lovers' moon too— happy in the knowledge she and Stoney hadn't just imagined seeing it when they were children. It really did exist!

"Stoney Wrenn," she breathed, closing her eyes for a moment. Feelings of elation mingled in her bosom with feelings of despair.

How wonderful it had been to learn he had not suffered so badly as she had feared in her absence. How wonderful to have felt his kiss, however final it had been. Yet to lose him now, to give up the friend she'd known as a child—it haunted her, made her feel alone and abandoned herself. Stoney's memory had always brought hope to her, even for the guilt it carried. She'd always had hope in perhaps seeing him again. Yet now she had seen him, made her peace with him. Still, somehow she felt more frightened and alone than ever.

Violet sat up, cupped a hand around the lamp chimney, and blew out the flame. Tomorrow. She would think about tomorrow—and the school. She would look forward to meeting with Jimmy after she'd taught the other children of Rattler Rock. She would look forward—try not to look back—only forward.

"Impossible," she whispered to herself. She'd never be able to forget her past with Stoney Wrenn—especially with him prancing around town with his girl every living day for the rest of her life.

Turning onto her side, Violet fluffed her pillow and lay down once more.

"At least the lovers in Mr. Chisolm's old house

are together," she whispered. "They may be dead . . . but at least they're together."

Something creaked in the darkness, and Violet closed her eyes tightly shut. All at once the memory of Ebenezer Scrooge lying in his bed awaiting the next ghost of Christmas to visit washed over her. In her mind she could see the light of the lovers' moon, slowly wandering through the old Chisolm place.

Wishing she wouldn't have blown out the lamp, Violet pulled the covers up over her head. Determined to keep her wits about her, she thought of Stoney once more.

"Viola," she whispered to herself, smiling with sudden, renewed delight. "He called me Viola."

# CHAPTER SIX

"My mama wants to know if you'll join us for supper tomorrow evenin', Miss Fynne," Maya asked.

Violet smiled—though the thought of sitting at the same table with Miss Layla Asbury churned her stomach. "I think that would be lovely, Maya," she said all the same. "Please, tell your mother I accept her thoughtful invitation."

Maya nodded. "I will. It'll be nice to have ya over to our house."

As the other children began to file past Maya into the schoolhouse, the girl paused. Violet waited, sensing the girl had something further to say.

Maya smiled at Dayton Fisher as he moved past her with a flirtatious wink her way. Once he'd stepped well into the room beyond, Maya spoke again. "Are . . . are ya teachin' Jimmy Ritter in the afternoons, Miss Fynne? I-I was wonderin' why he was sittin' with ya on yer front porch yesterday. Is he all right?"

Violet smiled. She adored being correct in her suspicions—and once again, she had been. Maya Asbury wasn't sweet on Dayton Fisher the way everybody else thought; she was sweet on Jimmy Ritter.

"Oh, Jimmy's just fine," Violet said. She smiled and lowered her voice. "And he paid you a very nice compliment yesterday, after you and Beth passed by my house."

Maya's cheeks pinked up like ripened cherries. "He did?" she asked, entirely delighted.

"Yes, he did."

"What did he say? Do ya think he likes me . . . even just a little?"

Violet was entirely amused. The girl seemed ready to burst. "Well, I wouldn't want to repeat something he didn't want me to," Violet began, "but I can tell you this. Why don't you give up pretending Dayton's caught your eye, Maya? You never know who might muster up the courage to talk to you a bit more often if he knows you're not Dayton Fisher's girl."

Maya inhaled. A tiny squeal of delight escaped her throat as she nodded with excitement. "All right, Miss Fynne," she said. "I won't flirt with Dayton no more."

"Anymore," Violet corrected. "Don't flirt with Dayton anymore . . . especially in front of Jimmy Ritter," she added in a whisper.

"Yes, Miss Fynne," Maya said. She hurried into the classroom and to her seat.

Violet smiled—she couldn't help herself! She liked Maya Asbury, and she liked Jimmy. Quickly, she thought about what Stoney had told her the night before, as they'd sat on the log near the old Chisolm place waiting for the light to appear. Katie Mill and Hagen Webster—sparking out under the stars? It was much more delightful to imagine Jimmy Ritter stealing a kiss from Maya Asbury.

"How romantic!" Violet sighed as she started toward the front of the room.

"What's romantic, Miss Fynne?" Beth Deavers asked.

"Hmm?" Violet asked, turning to face the smiling faces of her pupils.

"I heard ya too, Miss Fynne," Phelps Pierson said. "You said, 'How romantic.' "

"Oh!" Violet exclaimed, inwardly scolding herself for the dreadful habit she owned of muttering her thoughts aloud. "Um . . . how romantic?" she stammered. She glanced to Maya—saw the crimson blush of humiliation rising to her lovely face. "I . . . um . . . I was thinking of . . . of our literature lesson today. I . . . um . . . I thought I'd read to you a little bit from . . . um . . . the poetical works of Bryant Tisdale." Quickly she turned to her desk and retrieved a copy of Tisdale's *Beautiful Is the Night*.

"Poems?" Dayton Fisher exclaimed. "Yer gonna make us listen to poems? Romantic poems?"

As every boy in the room began to groan—as every girl in the room smiled—Violet said, "Yes.

And if you're wise, you'll learn one or two lines by heart . . . for such an occasion—when you're older, of course—for such an occasion as when you'd like to capture a girl's attention . . . really capture her attention."

"Miss Fynne," Hagen began, "you can't really mean for us boys to listen to love poems!"

"Oh, but there's more to a love story than descriptions of beauty and affection," Violet began as she opened the book.

"Like what?" Phelps asked.

"Murder, blood, battle . . . often a skeleton or two," Violet said.

"Really?" young Johnny Wethers asked.

"Of course," Violet said, flipping through pages. "Ah! Here is one of my very favorite poems from Tisdale's *Beautiful Is the Night*. It's called 'The Maiden of Conkle Crypt.' "

"You said this was a romantic poem, Miss Fynne," Hester Gribbs whined. "We got enough ghost stories around Rattler Rock."

"This is a romantic poem, Hester," Violet said. "It just happens that there is a musty, mysterious crypt in it." Violet giggled as she looked out across the waves of rather pouting faces. "Literature is important, boys and girls," she said. "So we will begin our day with a reading . . . a reading of Bryant Tisdale's 'The Maiden of Conkle Crypt.' " Clearing her throat to settle the groans emanating from the throats of her pupils, Violet began. " 'A murky, musty mist adorned the cavern walls . . . and bugs and blackened bones lay scattered in its halls.' " Violet smiled as she looked up to see the boys wide-eyed, the girls with noses wrinkled. She continued, " 'Yet streaming through a fracture—a fissure in the crypt, the sun betrayed the darkness and lit as lovers sipped.' "

"As lovers sipped what? Buttermilk?" Phelps called out. The boys laughed; the girls frowned.

"Phelps, hush now. Wait and see," Violet said. She paused, looking to Maya, who now wore a very relieved expression.

"Thank you," Maya mouthed.

Violet nodded in understanding. "Let me continue," Violet said. "Beginning here again, so that we don't lose the rhythm: 'Yet streaming through a fracture—a fissure in the crypt, the sun betrayed the darkness and lit as lovers sipped . . . sipped kisses shared in secret—for kisses were forbad—'tween royal men of Conkle and maidens common clad.' "

"They're kissin'? In a boneyard?" Johnny Wethers interrupted.

"In a cave, you ninny," Hester Gribbs mumbled.

"Very good, Johnny . . . and Hester!" Violet exclaimed. She was delighted that the children had somewhat understood the subjects of the poem to the extent that they did.

"It's a story of a prince and a poor girl," Beth offered.

"Then there's bound to be blood somewheres along the way," Phelps said, eyes wide with anticipation.

Violet giggled, entirely certain in that moment that she was the worst teacher to ever receive a certificate. Still, it was her opinion that if reading were made an interesting, intriguing task, then children would read and she—as their teacher—would not have to fight so in teaching them.

"Ya might as well go on, Miss Fynne," Hagen said. "The little kids will never settle down if ya don't finish it now."

"Of course," Violet said, knowing full well it was Hagen whose curiosity would not be satisfied were she to stop the reading. Turning the page, she gasped slightly, having momentarily forgotten what was written there—not by the poet, but by the hand of boy long ago. She let her fingers trace the words. *Stoney Wrenn vows never to kiss a girl while standing in a musty old crypt. You're strange for liking this poem, Viola.*

Smiling, Violet continued to read the poem to the children—though once again her mind had been hurled into the past, hurled toward Stoney Wrenn.

"Stoney says you saw the light last night, Miss Fynne," Jimmy said. He shoveled a bit of the cake Violet had baked the day before into his mouth.

"He told you?" she asked. She was surprised Stoney would mention the incident to Jimmy. "Wh-what did he tell you about it?"

Jimmy shrugged. "That you seen the light . . . that he did too. He followed ya home, ya know, to make sure ya got home all right. And I caught up to him, and he told me the two of you had seen the light."

"He followed me home?" Violet was delighted! Stoney had seen her home, just like he always had. Well, not just like he always had perhaps—but he had seen her home. She smiled, adoring the idea of Stoney Wrenn following her in the darkness.

"Yep. Stoney says a feller always sees a woman home . . . whether she knows he's seein' her home or not," Jimmy answered as he ate the last bite of his second piece of cake.

Violet frowned a little. "What were you doing out and about so late? Were you watching for the light too?" Violet was suddenly a little unsettled. Stoney had told her about all the "goings-on" he'd seen while trying to keep trespassers away from the old Chisolm place. Had Jimmy seen the goings-on between her and Stoney?

"No, ma'am. I was helpin' watch for trespassers. I wasn't watchin' for the light last night," he said.

"Hello, Miss Fynne . . . Jimmy."

Violet looked up to see Maya on the road. It

141

seemed she was returning to town from picking peaches, for she pulled a small wagon behind her very heavy-laden with the pretty, ripe fruit.

"Hello, Miss Asbury," Jimmy greeted.

Violet smiled when she saw him gulp nervously.

"Mama sent me over to the Wethers's orchard for some peaches. They certainly are heavy," Maya said.

"Are we done here, Miss Fynne?" Jimmy asked, eyes bright with excitement.

"We are, Jimmy," Violet said. "Maya," she called then, "I bet Jimmy would be more than happy to haul that wagon home for you."

Maya blushed. "Would ya mind, Jimmy?"

"No, ma'am," Jimmy said, fairly leaping to his feet.

Violet giggled as she watched Jimmy saunter over to Maya, take the wagon handle from her hand, and offer her his other arm.

Maya's smile broadened as she placed her hand in the crook of Jimmy's arm.

"Bye-bye, Miss Fynne," Maya called. "Mama says we'll see you at five for supper tomorrow night."

"Thank you," Violet said, tossing a wave and winking at Maya.

Violet watched Jimmy and Maya walk up the road and around the corner into town. Though she was delighted in their young infatuation, she was again saddened. What if she had never had to leave Rattler Rock? Would she and Stoney have enjoyed such easy flirtations—arm-in-arm strolls in the warm light of evening?

She glanced away from the young couple. She had to find a way to keep her mind from wandering to Stoney Wrenn every living minute of the day. Glancing toward town, she suddenly thought of the fact she had not been into the general store. Mr. Deavers still owned the general store; she'd seen him talking to Stoney and Miss Layla Asbury. Mr. Deavers. Yes! Surely there were a few supplies she could gather from Mr. Deavers. The minister's wife had brought over a few necessities—several potatoes, a dozen eggs, a small sack of flour, sugar, some fresh milk—but if Violet were going to keep the hook baited with sweets for Jimmy Ritter, there were other things she needed. Furthermore, she wanted to get a look at Mrs. Wilson, the widow who seemed to be keeping Mr. Deavers company on occasion now that his dear wife had passed. Perhaps Mrs. Wilson would be there.

Drawing a deep breath, Violet set out. The schoolhouse was just on the other side of the town of Rattler Rock. Violet walked the board-walk of Rattler Rock every morning on her way to teach the children. Still, she realized as she walked it now how terribly unobservant she'd been. Stoney's tale of Sam Capshaw, who worked at the livery with his father, sparking with Mary

Pierson intrigued her. Thus, she paused before the livery, peering inside. A young man was grooming a horse. He smiled and waved, and Violet waved back.

"Sam Capshaw," she mumbled. She smiled and wondered what other goings-on Stoney had witnessed in the dead of night out near the old Chisolm place.

"Hello, Mr. Deavers," Violet greeted as she entered the general store. "Do you remember me?" she asked as the older man looked up from the columned pages of the book before him on the counter.

Mr. Deavers frowned a moment, studying Violet from head to toe. Violet smiled as she saw a grin of recognition begin to spread across the man's face.

"Why, Violet Fynne!" the man chuckled, hurrying around the counter with one hand out-stretched in welcome. "Little Violet! I wondered when you'd be in to see me. Whatcha been eatin'? Dirt?"

Violet accepted Mr. Deavers's hand, and he firmly shook hers. "Mrs. Abrams brought a wel-coming basket to the house the day I arrived. I've been eating more than dirt."

"Well, that's good to know," Mr. Deavers chuckled. "My grandchildren sure do like you. You must be a wonderful teacher. Every night at supper it's 'Miss Fynne said this' and 'Miss

Fynne said that.' You sure have got the Deavers girls in your posse."

"Oh, thank you!" Violet said. "It's nice to hear that. I've been a little nervous about it all."

"Well, don't ya worry none anymore," he said. "Rattler Rock is happy to have you back."

Violet glanced to the countertop, to the jar filled with amber-colored butterscotch pieces. Something pinched her heart, and she spoke her thoughts aloud. "I can't believe ol' Mr. Chisolm is gone."

Mr. Deavers shook his head. "Yep. We all felt that loss right through to our bones."

"But you still keep butterscotch in the store," Violet said. "Mr. Chisolm always had butterscotch in his pockets. Many were the times Stoney and I ate ourselves nearly ill from Mr. Chisolm feeding us butterscotch from his pockets." She giggled. "I remember how he had to sort them out from his pocket lint and coins sometimes."

Mr. Deavers smiled. "That's probably why most of the butterscotch I do sell since ol' Buddy passed is to Stoney Wrenn. I reckon he's linin' his pockets with it the way ol' Buddy used to."

"Really?" Violet asked, entirely delighted.

"Oh, yes. I seen him give my granddaughter Nina a piece from his pocket not half an hour ago."

"How sweet," Violet whispered. She glanced

over her shoulder to the boardwalk outside the store. Perhaps Stoney was still in town; perhaps she'd catch a glimpse of him if she were watchful.

"Stoney's a nice feller," Mr. Deavers said. "Oh, he's got hisself a little reputation of bein' somewhat of a womanizer . . . but it ain't his fault Layla Asbury prefers Stoney to Sheriff Fisher."

"What do you mean?" Violet instantly looked back to Mr. Deavers. Her curiosity had been triggered.

"Oh, I shouldn't go on about such things," Mr. Deavers said. He wore an expression of guilt, as if he'd accidentally revealed secret information. "Don't want folks thinkin' I'm an old gossip like them ladies over at the quiltin' society."

Violet smiled. She wouldn't press him. He was a kind man, and she wouldn't give him cause to be eaten up with guilt.

"Have ya run into Stoney yet?" he asked.

"Yes," Violet admitted. "We've spoken."

Mr. Deavers laughed; his eyes filled with the mirth of amusing memory. "I remember the mischief the two of you used to get into," he said. "Seems Stoney Wrenn and Violet Fynne were always causin' some kind of commotion."

"I guess so," Violet said. "But that was so long ago. I'm sure folks hardly remember it."

"Well, I remember it," Mr. Deavers said. "Now . . . what can I get for ya?"

• • •

Fifteen minutes later, Violet was ambling back toward her little house. She'd found a dime book in Mr. Deavers's store and had purchased a sweet potato and five pieces of wrapped butterscotch from the butterscotch jar too.

"Well, hello, Miss Fynne," Sheriff Fisher said as she approached the jailhouse. She'd seen him sitting on a chair outside the jailhouse as she'd walked along the boardwalk.

"Hello, Sheriff," she greeted.

"Coby," he said, flashing a dazzling smile.

"Coby, then," Violet said, giggling a little at his flirtation.

"I see you've been in to talk with Alex Deavers. What'd he talk ya into buyin' today?" Coby asked. He rose from his chair to stand tall and handsome before Violet.

"Just a few things," Violet said. "How's your business going today?" She teasingly glanced past him into the empty jailhouse.

"Quiet . . . just the way I like it," Coby said.

"Would you like a piece of butterscotch?" Violet asked. She opened her hand, offering a piece of the candy.

"Why thank you, Miss Fynne. Don't mind if I do," he said, taking a butterscotch from her palm.

"Violet," Violet said.

Coby Fisher smiled and winked at Violet as

he unwrapped the candy and put it in his mouth. "Why thank ya, Violet."

"Well, I'm glad to see there's no fuss in Rattler Rock where the law is concerned," Violet said.

"Oh, there's fuss enough," he said. "Stoney Wrenn was in here not more'n an hour ago, hollerin' at me about trespassers out at the ol' Chisolm place."

"Trespassers?" Violet asked. She swallowed the strange guilt rising in her throat.

"Oh, he's in here at least once a week goin' on and on about his property and how he don't want nobody 'round that old house."

"Did he . . . did he tell you who it was?" Perhaps Stoney was angry with her for trespassing. Surely they'd spoken in a friendly enough manner. He'd even kissed her. But maybe he'd considered on it more thoroughly and was angry at her now.

Coby Fisher shrugged broad shoulders. "He never gets close enough to see who it is. Just knows someone's tryin' to mess with that ol' house . . . and it gets Stoney's temper to sizzlin'."

"I see," Violet said, nervously removing the paper from a piece of the butterscotch candy and placing it in her mouth.

Coby frowned a moment and then smiled. "Stoney Wrenn's always got butterscotch in his pockets too. Is that somethin' that went on in Rattler Rock before I was here?"

Violet nodded. "Mr. Chisolm used to give us . . .

used to give children pieces of butterscotch all the time. I remember he'd reach into his pocket and offer you a piece. It always tasted a little bit like leather."

"Did you ride over to the house, Coby?"

It was Stoney's voice. Violet gasped at hearing it so unexpectedly as he suddenly stepped up to stand beside her, and in gasping, the hard piece of butterscotch lodged in the back of her throat. She tried to cough—but couldn't. She couldn't even draw breath.

"Are ya all right, Violet?" Coby asked.

Stoney Wrenn's strong hand brutally pounded her back, forcing the piece of candy out of her throat. Violet watched as the amber-colored confection leapt from her mouth and rolled across the boardwalk.

"You all right?" Stoney asked.

She turned to look up to see him frowning—his green-blue eyes narrow with irritation. "Yes. I'm sorry. Thank you," she mumbled. She felt the hot blush of humiliation rise to her cheeks. Choking on the butterscotch in front of the two men? How embarrassing!

"Are ya sure yer all right?" Coby asked, taking her hand.

"Yes. I'm fine," Violet said.

"Did ya ride over to the house?" Stoney asked. It was obvious he was angry—about something.

Violet watched as Stoney, still glaring at Sheriff

149

Fisher, reached into his front trouser pocket and pulled out a wrapped piece of butterscotch like the one Violet had just spit out onto the boardwalk.

"I haven't gotten over there yet, Stoney," Coby said. His voice held irritation now too. "I'm waitin' for Sam Capshaw. My horse threw a shoe this mornin'. I told you that."

Stoney inhaled a deep breath. Violet watched as he fumbled with the piece of wrapped candy in his hand. He shook his head and said, "It won't do no good if ya wait on it, Coby. It'll be dark soon and—"

"I'll get over there when I can, Stoney," Coby interrupted firmly. "I said I would, and I will."

Stoney finished removing the paper from the piece of candy. "Open up," he said to Violet.

For some reason, Violet did what he commanded—opened her mouth slightly. Stoney Wrenn then placed the piece of butterscotch in Violet's mouth, shoving the candy paper in his pocket as he looked back to Coby Fisher and said, "You gotta help me out with this, Coby. I know ya don't think much of me, but yer the sheriff in this town, and I got a problem with trespassers."

"Why do you even worry about it, Stoney?" Coby asked then. "It's just an empty ol' shell of a house. Nobody's lived in it for years. You don't look much like yer ever plannin' to. Why not clean it out and let the raccoons and the trespassers have their way?"

Violet had glanced at Sheriff Fisher, but now she looked back to Stoney. His eyes narrowed; his jaw clinched.

"Because I made a promise to Buddy Chisolm, Coby . . . and some of us in Rattler Rock keep our promises," Stoney said.

Violet lowered her head and sucked on the butterscotch candy lying on her tongue. Somehow the piece Stoney had put in her mouth tasted sweeter than the one she'd spit out.

The two men stood firm, broad chests rising and falling with the labored breathing of anger.

"Well, I guess I better get back to the house and fix myself some supper," Violet said.

"I'll walk a ways with ya," Stoney grumbled. He glared at the sheriff. "Do you want somebody to get shot, Coby?" he asked.

"Of course not," Coby said.

"Then help me find out who's messin' around in Buddy's ol' house," Stoney growled. Stoney shook his head and took hold of Violet's arm. "Let's go. I'll see ya on home."

"You have a good evening, Coby," Violet said to Sheriff Fisher as Stoney led her away.

"Thank ya, Violet," Coby said, touching the brim of his hat as he watched her follow Stoney down the boardwalk.

"He don't understand, Viola," Stoney said as they walked. "I promised Buddy I wouldn't let nobody set foot in that house."

"Why didn't he want anyone inside?" she asked. He'd let go of her arm, and she wished he hadn't. She liked for him to touch her. "Why didn't he let somebody live in it or—"

"He did," he interrupted. "He let me live in it for a time."

Violet felt her eyes widen. "You? You lived in Buddy Chisolm's old haunted house?"

He chuckled. The sight of his smile caused a mad fluttering to rise in Violet's stomach. "I did," he said.

"With the ghosts and everything?"

"I didn't never see the ghosts," he said. "But the light was there."

Violet stopped cold and shook her head. "I cannot believe you didn't tell me this!" She turned to face him. She poked his chest with an index finger and said, "You lived in Buddy Chisolm's old haunted house and you didn't tell me?"

Stoney frowned. "You been back for less than a week, Viola," he said. "I've only seen ya a few times . . . and only one of those times was in private."

Violet settled her indignation. She felt her eyes widen, and a smile spread across her face as she asked, "What's it like inside? Is it all cobwebby and dusty? Does it smell funny? Is it empty, or are there things in there? Things other than ghosts, I mean."

His smile broadened. "I swear, you haven't changed a lick."

Violet frowned. "You're not going to tell me about it?"

Stoney looked past Violet for a moment, smiled, and tugged on the brim of his hat. "Evenin', Mrs. Wilson," he said.

Violet turned to see an older woman approaching.

"Evenin', Stoney," the woman said.

"This is Violet Fynne, Mrs. Wilson," Stoney said, "the new schoolteacher."

Mrs. Wilson's eyes suddenly filled with merriment. "How do?" the woman said, offering a hand to Violet. "I'm Velma Wilson, and it's so nice to finally meet you."

Violet accepted her hand and smiled. So this was the Widow Wilson. Violet smiled, delighted at imagining this woman and Mr. Deavers out sparking near the old Chisolm place.

"And it's so nice to meet you, Mrs. Wilson," Violet chirped. "My! What a lovely hat!" The truth was Violet had nearly giggled out loud when she'd glanced up to Mrs. Wilson's hat— so large and entirely covered in blue and yellow feathers.

"Why thank you, Miss Fynne," Mrs. Wilson

said. The woman looked to Stoney—studied him from head to toe. "I see you've already met our local sugar-darlin', Stoney Wrenn."

"Actually, I knew Stoney when I lived here as a child," Violet said. She was irritated, angry that the woman had instantly assumed Stoney was trying to woo the new schoolteacher.

"Oh, really?" Mrs. Wilson said. Violet fancied the woman seemed somewhat relieved. "Well, ain't that nice."

"You have a lovely evenin', Mrs. Wilson," Stoney said, tugging at the brim of his hat as he took hold of Violet's arm and began leading her away once more.

"It was so nice to meet you," Violet called as Stoney pulled her along.

"Sugar-darling?" Violet asked as they walked.

"I won't tell you a thing about that ol' house if you start into teasin' me about her callin' me that," he growled.

"All right," Violet said. "But do tell me about the old house, Stoney. You know how badly I always wanted to go in there. You lived in it?"

Stoney let go of her arm as they continued to walk. Violet looked up, disappointed to see they were almost to her little house.

"Only in the summers," he said. "Buddy had me live in it to try and keep trespassers out. But I swear I never seen one soul try to get in 'til about six months ago." He shook his head.

"Now . . . now it's near three or four times a week that I'm chasin' somebody away."

"Well, what changed?" she asked. "Did anyone new move to town that might be curious?"

He shook his head. "No. And even though I keep thinkin' that somehow somebody's lookin' for—" He paused, his brow deeply furrowed in a frown. "But that can't be."

"Looking for what?" she asked. "The ghosts?"

He was keeping something from her, she knew he was. Yet she wondered what. She wouldn't press him however. She wouldn't. There were times he would've told her everything on his mind—even things she maybe didn't want to know. But that was the past. He owned secrets now; she could see that. Secrets he wasn't willing to share—at least, not with her.

"This is a nice little house," he said as they stopped before Violet's house.

Violet frowned. She wanted to know more about the old Chisolm house, not this one. Still, she couldn't expect him to trust her, not after she'd abandoned him for ten long years.

She followed his gaze and said, "Yes. It's perfect." She smiled, for she did like the little house. "It sits just far back enough off the road that it's private . . . .but close enough to town that I don't feel too isolated."

"Did they ever get that piece of the roof fixed?" he said.

Violet followed him as he strode around one side of the house to the back.

He frowned and looked up to the roof. "We had a terrible wind last November. It took part of the roof right off the Gribbs's place. Damaged this one back here. Just there. See?" He pointed to a place on the roof where Violet could now see it had been repaired.

"Must've been some wind," she said.

"Oh, it was," he mumbled.

"You're avoiding telling me about the old house," she said. "Aren't you?"

Stoney looked to her then, sighed, and shook his head. "You ain't gonna let this go . . . are ya?" he asked.

"All I want to know is what it's like in there," she giggled. "I always dreamed of being able to go in. Remember how we used to peek through the windows . . . hoping to see the ghosts?" She sighed and looked down the road that led to Buddy Chisolm's old place. "It still had furniture in it then. I remember paintings still hanging on the walls, as if somebody still lived there and had just stepped out to go to town for a while."

"It looks the same as it did when we were pressin' our noses up against the windows," he said.

"And you never saw one ghost while you were living there?" she asked.

"I hate to break yer heart, Miss Fynne . . . but I truthfully never did see one ghost in that ol' Chisolm place."

As Violet sighed with disappointment, Stoney laughed. "It don't mean they're not there, Viola," he began, "just that I didn't see 'em." He inhaled quickly, as if he had planned to say something and then changed his mind.

"What?" she asked. "Tell me."

"You know," he began, "that old house . . . it ain't exactly . . ." He paused, and Violet could tell he'd changed his mind about telling her whatever he'd begun to.

"Thanks for seeing me home," she said. She could see the restlessness in him.

"My pleasure," he said. "And besides . . . if I woulda lingered one more minute with that lazy Coby Fisher . . . well, me and him have swapped fists before."

"You have?" Violet said. She felt her eyebrows arch in surprise.

"I'll bid you good evenin', Miss Fynne," he said, smiling and tugging at the brim of his hat.

Violet smiled and gazed into the mesmerizing green-blue light of his eyes. Something whispered to her mind then—a secret she'd only just become aware of.

"You knew the roof had been patched," she said. "You just didn't want anyone seeing you with me."

His smile faded. "We ain't kids anymore, Miss Fynne," he said. "And if you hadn't of told Mrs. Wilson that we knew each other as children . . . by tomorrow mornin' she woulda had this town buzzin' like you can't imagine."

"And your Miss Layla Asbury would've wondered—"

"It ain't that," he said, shaking his head. "For reasons I can't understand, I've got myself a reputation as a womanizer . . . and I can't change that. Sometimes folks think what they want, no matter what the truth is. But you . . . yer the new teacher. Folks gotta trust you, and they won't if they think yer foolin' with me."

"Are you a womanizer?" she asked. Part of her feared he might answer truthfully with a yes. Still, most of her doubted the fact.

He grinned. "Well . . . you've been alone with me exactly once since you've been back. And that one time you were alone with me, I kissed you. So what do you think?"

Violet smiled. "I think you're better at it now than you were when we were kids."

Stoney Wrenn laughed—the honest, heartfelt laughter of pure amusement. Violet giggled too, pleased that she had caused him to be happy.

"Well, thank you for the compliment, Miss Fynne," he said. Then, frowning a bit, he added, "Anyway, I think it was a compliment."

"It was," Violet said.

"Well then, you have a nice night," he said, tugging at the brim of his hat once more.

"You too."

Violet sighed as she watched him walk away. He didn't return to the road; rather, he walked down the small incline behind her house following the creekbank back toward town.

Violet went into the little house. Thoughts and visions of Stoney Wrenn dominated every corner and every pathway of her mind. She smiled as she went about fixing her supper—smiled when she thought of the way he'd knocked the piece of butterscotch out of her mouth. She marveled at the way he'd unwrapped a new piece of candy from his own pocket and popped it right into her mouth, in just the manner he often had so many years ago. In that one moment, it had seemed as if they'd never been apart.

Once her solitary supper was finished and her arithmetic lessons ready for the next day, Violet crawled into her bed. She sighed as she picked up the copy of *A Christmas Carol* sitting on the small table next to her bed. She'd decided to read it again—ensure it wasn't too morbid and frightening to read aloud to the children just before Christmas.

Opening the book, she smiled as she saw familiar eyes gazing out at her from the photograph she'd always kept inside the front book cover. Lifting the photograph from its haven, she studied the familiar face of the boy Stoney Wrenn. She shook her head, marveling at how different he looked as a man. With the exception of his eyes, Violet wasn't certain she would've recognized him in simple passing. She wondered for a moment if she looked as different, though she feared she did not. No doubt she looked just as ridiculous and plain as she always had.

She placed the photograph back in the book, closed the book, and closed her eyes. She could not keep thinking of him. The past was over! He had a life without her now—a life that included Layla Asbury.

Violet grumbled, "Layla Asbury. Oh, why did I accept that invitation to supper?"

With a heavy sigh, she determined not to read. She'd stayed up far too late the night before—had far too taxing a day. She needed rest, especially if she were to feel fresh and friendly for supper with Maya's family.

She wondered if Stoney was out protecting the old Chisolm place from trespassers. She thought of the mirth shining in his eyes when she'd teased him about being better at kissing now than he had been as a boy.

That night, Violet dreamt of opals—beautiful, fascinating opals. She dreamt of Thanksgiving and her Aunt Rana's opal earrings. She dreamt of a ring she'd once seen on the finger of a wealthy patron of the opera in New York City. But most of all, she dreamt of green-blue opals—the unusual opaline of Stoney Wrenn's alluring eyes.

# CHAPTER SEVEN

"Good evenin', Miss Fynne," Maya greeted as she opened the door. "Come on in. Supper's almost on the table."

"Thank you, Maya," Violet said as she crossed the threshold into the Asbury home. It was a bright, cheerful-looking little house from the outside, and as Violet stepped into the parlor, she fancied it was as bright and cheerful on the inside. "I have to confess to being a little nervous. I'm not very good with meeting new people," Violet told Maya.

Maya giggled, took Violet's hand, and began leading her into another room. "Oh, that just can't be true, Miss Fynne," the girl said. "And anyway, it's just my family. There's no reason you shouldn't feel as comfortable as a kitten in a mitten."

Violet smiled. She felt more comfortable already.

"Mama," Maya began as they stepped into the kitchen, "this is Miss Fynne. Miss Fynne, this is my mama."

Mrs. Asbury dried her hands on her apron. Smiling at Violet, she offered a hand in welcome. Violet accepted her hand, and Mrs. Asbury said, "I am so delighted to finally meet you, Miss

Fynne. Thank you for acceptin' our invitation for supper."

"Thank you for having me," Violet said. She was somewhat puzzled. Maya looked nothing like her mother. Mrs. Asbury had golden, straw-colored hair and the brownest of brown eyes. She was a lovely woman but so very opposite in appearance to her daughters that Violet stared at her for a moment.

Mrs. Asbury giggled. "Maya looks like her daddy," she said.

Violet smiled and blushed. "I'm sorry, Mrs. Asbury. I didn't mean to—"

"Oh, do call me Emeline . . . and it's all right. Everyone is always so surprised when they see the girls and me together for the first time. But once ya see my Tony, you'll realize they look just like him."

"Daddy's grandparents came from Italy," Maya explained. "That's where Layla and I get our dark hair."

"We're just so glad to have ya, Miss Fynne," Emeline said. "Maya can't seem to say enough good things about you."

"Come on, Miss Fynne," Maya said, taking Violet's hand again. "I want ya to meet Layla."

Violet nodded—though the last thing she felt like doing in that moment was meeting Stoney Wrenn's girl.

"Thank you again for inviting me, Mrs. Asbury," Violet said.

"Emeline. And it's our pleasure," Maya's mother said. "You tell Layla to be at the table in five minutes, Maya."

"Yes, Mama," Maya said, rolling her eyes with exasperation.

Violet couldn't help but giggle a little at Maya's irritation.

"Come on, Miss Fynne. Layla's been askin' me all kinds of questions about you. I figure it's time she met ya for herself."

Anxiety rose in Violet's chest as Maya led her through the dining room, past a table set with lovely china and silver.

"She's out back," she explained, "on the porch swing."

Before she'd even realized it, Maya had pulled Violet through a door leading to a back porch. She gasped—felt as if she might indeed empty the contents of her stomach with retching—as she saw Layla Asbury sitting on the porch swing with Stoney Wrenn.

"This is Miss Fynne, Layla," Maya said.

Violet's eyes lingered on Stoney a moment. He seemed entirely unaffected—but why shouldn't he? Layla Asbury was his girl, after all. Violet was the stranger here.

"Well, I am so pleased to finally meet you, Miss Fynne," Layla said, rising from her seat next to

Stoney and offering a dainty hand. "Maya has nearly talked my ears off about you."

"Really?" Violet asked, accepting the girl's hand.

At the first touch of Layla Asbury's handshake, Violet's skin crawled with animosity. She didn't like this girl—not one bit. Maya was sweet, kind, and sincere; Layla Asbury was not.

"You already know Mr. Wrenn," Maya said.

"Evenin', Miss Fynne," Stoney said. He smiled a little, and the sight of his adorable dimples and bright eyes caused Violet's heart to pinch.

"So . . . now . . . ya need to meet my daddy," Maya added. Taking Violet's arm, Maya turned her around. A very handsome man sat in a rocker just behind them. He rose to his feet and offered a hand to Violet.

"Tony Asbury, Miss Fynne," the man said. "It's a pleasure to finally meet you. A real pleasure."

"Thank you, Mr. Asbury," Violet managed as he shook her hand.

She felt somewhat relieved that Stoney and Layla had a chaperone. Still, the situation was making her stomach feel more and more as if it would rid itself of any contents.

"Mama says we need to get to the table," Maya said.

"Then we better get," Mr. Asbury said.

"Come on, Miss Fynne," Maya chirped. "You get to sit by me!"

Violet forced a smile. It wasn't Maya's fault that Violet's father had taken her from Rattler Rock, that Stoney Wrenn was finding happiness in the company of a beautiful young woman instead of in the company of a girl he'd only known as a child.

"Mama used her good china—the plates and such we usually only use for Thanksgiving and Christmas," Maya whispered as they approached the table.

"Allow me, Miss Fynne," Mr. Asbury said. He pulled Violet's chair out for her and helped her to be seated.

Violet tried to ignore the way Stoney did the same for Layla.

"Maya!" Mrs. Asbury called from the kitchen. "Come help me."

"I'll be right back," Maya said softly to Violet.

Violet nodded, her stomach churning into knots. She could feel the color had drained from her face. Why was she so affected? For pity's sake!

"Maya tells us yer the best teacher in the world," Layla said.

Violet forced a smile—forced herself to look at the young woman. "Maya's very sweet to me," she said. "I think she's a jewel. I'm sure I'm far, far, far from being the teacher I should be."

"Oh, surely not!" Layla exclaimed. "I know I never had a teacher who would tell me ghost stories or read morbid poetry to the class."

"Morbid poetry?" Mr. Asbury said.

"Oh, um . . . just Tisdale, Mr. Asbury," Violet said. "Bryant Tisdale. Are you familiar with him?"

"No. Can't say that I am," Mr. Asbury said. "And . . . and this poetry . . . it's morbid, you say, Layla?"

"Maya says it gives her goose bumps all over," Layla said.

"Really," Mr. Asbury mumbled.

Violet could see Mr. Asbury's disapproval. Her innards began to quiver, for she could sense a reprimand.

" 'The Maiden of Conkle Crypt,' " Stoney said.

Violet looked to him. Would he put the last nail in her coffin himself?

"What's that, Stoney?" Mr. Asbury asked.

"I'm guessin' the poem Miss Fynne read to the children is 'The Maiden of Conkle Crypt.' Is that right, Miss Fynne?" he asked.

"Yes," she managed to breathe.

"It's very famous. I read somewhere that it's required readin' at many a college these days," he said. "Is that right, Miss Fynne?"

"Yes," Violet answered.

Layla giggled. "Oh, Stoney Wrenn! Do you mean to be tellin' Daddy that you know anything about this morbid poem Miss Fynne's been readin' to the children?"

Violet felt emotion rising in her throat—felt

167

tears threatening to well in her eyes. Mr. Asbury was disapproving of Violet's teaching methods, and it was clear Layla Asbury meant to feed her father's doubt. Stoney had tried to champion her as best he could—that fact warmed her heart. Still, she could see it would take more than that to convince Mr. Asbury that Violet had done nothing wrong.

"I learned that same poem when I was boy," Stoney said.

Violet grinned at him. She knew her father had never taught Tisdale's "The Maiden of Conkle Crypt" to the children in Rattler Rock when he had been the teacher at the schoolhouse. Stoney and Violet had discovered the poem on their own, after hearing Violet's father talking about it to someone on the county school board.

"You did not, Stoney Wrenn!" Layla exclaimed.

" 'A murky, musty mist adorned the cavern walls,' " Stoney began.

Violet smiled, warmed by his championing her and his memory of the poem they'd loved as children.

" 'And bugs and blackened bones lay scattered in its halls,' " he continued. " 'Yet streamin' through a fracture—a fissure in the crypt, the sun betrayed the darkness and lit as lovers sipped . . . sipped kisses shared in secret—for kisses were forbad—'tween royal men of Conkle and maidens common clad.' "

"You know it, Mr. Wrenn?" Maya said, appearing from the kitchen and placing a bowl of mashed potatoes on the table. "You know the poem Miss Fynne's been readin' to us at school?"

"Of course," Stoney said. "Like I was tellin' yer daddy, Maya, 'The Maiden of Conkle Crypt' is a very renowned work. It proves what a good teacher Rattler Rock has . . . and that you boys and girls are gonna get a far better education than ya woulda had with someone else."

Violet dared not thank Stoney—not with the look of pure indignation plain on Layla Asbury's face at that moment. Instead, she looked to Mr. Asbury. "It's not so morbid as you might think, Mr. Asbury," she ventured. "I-I could send it home with Maya . . . for your review, if you like."

"It sounds like a fine poem to me, Miss Fynne," Mr. Asbury said. "I'm glad to know Maya is bein' taught more'n just how to add apples and pears."

"Thank you," Violet said.

"Layla's just a yeller bug, Miss Fynne," Maya said. "She's scared of everything."

"And you, Stoney," Mr. Asbury said, patting Stoney firmly one shoulder. "I had no idea you were so book smart."

Stoney winced a little as Mr. Asbury patted his shoulder again. "I guess I'm just full of surprises," Stoney said.

"Yes, you are, Stoney Wrenn," Layla said.

As Mrs. Asbury arrived with a ham, Violet wondered how she would ever eat. Sitting across from a lovesick Layla Asbury and a far too handsome Stoney Wrenn, she was sure that anything she tried to force down her throat would come right back up.

"Maya," Mr. Asbury began, "would you please bless the food?"

"Yes, Daddy," Maya said.

A moment before Violet closed her eyes in reverence, she glanced across the table to Stoney. He was looking at her, winked with encouragement, and then closed his own eyes. Maya blessed the food, and Mr. Asbury served everyone a slice of ham.

"We're so glad to have you to supper too, Stoney," Mrs. Asbury said. "It's always nice to have you at the table."

"Thank ya, ma'am," Stoney said.

Violet studied him quickly. He wasn't wearing a hat. She realized it was the first time since returning to Rattler Rock that she hadn't seen him with a hat. She couldn't help but smile, adoring the way his hair rebelled and fell across his forehead. She remembered the way he'd constantly raked his fingers through his hair as a boy, to keep it from falling across his forehead the way it did now. She wondered for a moment if his hair still felt as soft as it

170

had when he was a boy. She wanted to reach across the table and run her fingers through his hair.

"So," Mr. Asbury began, "what's goin' on out at that place of yers, Stoney? Coby says yer havin' trouble with trespassers."

"Yes," Stoney said. "A bit."

Mr. Asbury shook his head. "Folks just don't have no respect for a man's privacy. Coby says you took a shot at somebody again last night. He says they took a shot at you."

Violet dropped her fork, suddenly horrified by the thought of someone shooting at Stoney. The fork clattered to her plate, drawing everyone's attention.

"I'm sorry," she apologized. "I can be so clumsy sometimes."

"It wasn't anything so interestin' as that, Mr. Asbury," Stoney said. "I assure you."

"Well, I hope not," Mr. Asbury said, patting Stoney on the shoulder once more. "I'd hate to see you get hurt."

"Mr. Wrenn!" Maya exclaimed then. "Yer bleedin'!"

Violet gasped as she looked up to see the dark crimson of fresh blood beginning to soak Stoney's shirt at his shoulder where Mr. Asbury had just patted him.

Stoney glanced at his shoulder. "Oh, that ain't nothin', Maya," he said. "I just . . . I just cut myself on a nail that was stickin' out of the barn door this mornin'. It's just a scratch."

"That's no scratch, Stoney Wrenn!" Layla exclaimed.

Rising from her seat, Violet's mouth gaped in astonishment as the girl went about unbuttoning Stoney's shirt.

"Layla!" Mrs. Asbury exclaimed as Stoney gently took hold of Layla's hands.

"It's just a scratch, Layla," he said. "I'm fine." Still, the blood soaking Stoney's shirt was spreading. Whatever the wound was, it was far worse than he was letting on.

"Mama! Make him take his shirt off so you can look at his shoulder!" Layla demanded.

"Layla Asbury!" Mrs. Asbury scolded in a whisper.

"She'll never settle down unless you let us have a look at it, son," Mr. Asbury said.

Violet's eyes narrowed. It was becoming very clear that Mr. Asbury favored Layla—that Layla Asbury probably got anything she wanted if she simply asked her daddy for it.

Violet looked at Stoney. His eyes blazed with irritation, and his jaw was tightly clinched. His broad chest rose and fell with anger. Yet he quickly unbuttoned his shirt, pulled one side open, and removed one arm from its sleeve.

Violet felt herself gulp at the sight of Stoney's bare torso. He was incredibly brawny, every muscle intensely defined. She felt her cheeks pink—felt overly warm and uncomfortable.

"Let me see that, Stoney," Mrs. Asbury said. She rose from her seat and went to Stoney. A bandage, a length of cotton now somewhat saturated with blood, was wrapped under Stoney's arm and up around his shoulder. Violet watched as Mrs. Asbury gently pushed the cotton aside.

"Well, Doc Coppell did a terrible job of bandagin' this up, Stoney," she exclaimed. "A terrible job!"

"The doc didn't bandage it," Stoney mumbled. "I did. And it ain't anything to worry about."

"Of course it's somethin' to worry about!" Mrs. Asbury said. "You come on in the kitchen, and I'll change this bandage, Stoney."

Mr. Asbury leaned over as he stood up and looked at the wound.

"Nail, huh?" he said. "Looks more like you got grazed by a bullet there, Stoney."

"A bullet?" Violet said aloud.

"It ain't nothin'," Stoney grumbled, putting his arm back through the sleeve of his shirt. "It'll quit oozin' in a minute." He fastened the buttons of his shirt.

"He's right," Mr. Asbury said. "You girls quit fussin' over him. Let the man eat."

"But Pa!" Layla began to argue.

"He's fine, Layla. Isn't he, Emeline?"

Emeline forced a reassuring smile to her daughter. "Yes. Yes, he's fine."

"I guess there's more truth to what Coby Fisher told me today than I thought," Mr. Asbury said.

"Just the same ol' thing," Stoney said. "Somebody don't know well enough to stay away from Buddy Chisolm's old place."

"You are gonna get yerself killed over that stupid house, Stoney Wrenn!" Layla scolded.

Stoney glanced to Violet. Her heart was hammering so hard with fear for Stoney's safety she could hardly breathe! Still, the smoldering green-blue of his eyes told her he did not want to talk about it anymore. "Do ya like that little house the school board set up for ya, Miss Fynne?" Stoney asked.

"Um . . . yes," Violet stammered. "It's perfect." For a moment, she wondered why he asked her a question he already knew the answer to. Then she realized—he was trying to take the Asbury's attention off his wound. "I-it's just right for me . . . so close to town and the school."

Mrs. Asbury laughed. "Well, Miss Fynne, I'm sure Stoney's mighty glad to hear you call that little house 'perfect' . . . bein' that he built it himself."

"What?" Violet breathed.

"Mr. Wrenn built that house you live in, Miss Fynne," Maya said. "Isn't that right, Mr. Wrenn?"

"Ol' Buddy thought I had too much time on my

hands and too many worries on my mind a few years back," Stoney said. "So he put me to work buildin' that little house. Took me near to a year to finish it."

Violet was stunned into silence. Stoney had built the house she lived in? Suddenly she loved the little house more than she already did!

"Well . . . well, it's lovely," Violet stammered. "I was so grateful the school board offered it as part of my wages. I was afraid I'd have to take a room at the inn. The house is much, much nicer. Did Buddy sell it to the board or something?"

Layla giggled. "Oh, Miss Fynne! I swear, sometimes I wonder at how you ever got a teaching certificate."

Violet blushed under Layla's masked insult.

"Stoney owns that house himself. Mr. Chisolm left it to him in his will." Layla frowned a little. "You are aware that Stoney is quite a wealthy property owner around these parts, aren't ya? I guess ya could say Stoney Wrenn's yer landlord. Isn't that right, Stoney?"

"I guess so," Stoney said. The opalescence of his eyes smoldered as he looked at Violet.

Violet wanted to scream. She hated Layla Asbury—purely hated her in that moment! What was Stoney doing courting a girl with such arrogant vanity?

"Is the ham all right, Miss Fynne?" Maya asked.

"Y-yes, Maya," Violet stammered. "It's delicious."

Maya smiled. "Mama let me bake it . . . even though I know she was scared I'd burn it and ruin supper."

"It's wonderful," Violet said.

"Did ya hear Sam Capshaw asked Mr. Pierson for permission to start courtin' Mary, Daddy?" Layla said.

"No. I didn't hear that," Mr. Asbury said.

"Sam just now asked Mary's pa if he could court her?" Stoney asked.

"Yes. Why?" Layla answered.

Stoney looked at Violet, a knowing twinkle lighting his eyes. Violet bit her lip to keep from smiling. Stoney had seen Sam Capshaw and Mary Pierson involved in goings-on out by the old Chisolm place. Violet all too well understood his amusement at the secret he owned—that Sam Capshaw and Mary Pierson were already far beyond the simple beginnings of courting.

"No reason," Stoney said. He winked at Violet. "No reason at all."

"It's one of my favorite days of the year!" Maya exclaimed as the Asbury family and their supper guests sat in the parlor. "Didn't they have the Founders' Day picnic when ya lived in Rattler Rock before, Miss Fynne?"

Violet nodded. "Yes. They did. It was always great fun."

"Well, it's next Saturday," Mrs. Asbury said. "I can't believe the children haven't already told you about it."

"Mama wins the pie contest every year," Maya said.

"And Stoney wins every contest he enters," Layla chirped.

"Will you enter any contests, Miss Fynne?" Maya asked. "There's still plenty of time to enter things. The judgin' don't start 'til that mornin'."

"Well, I . . . I don't really—" Violet stammered.

"Miss Fynne used to be able to outrun any boy in school," Stoney said.

Maya giggled. "Really, Miss Fynne?"

"Well, I don't know about that," Violet said.

"Do ya still run fast, Miss Fynne?" Mr. Asbury asked.

"Well I . . . I . . ." Violet stammered.

"I'd give anything to see somebody beat Hagen Webster this year," Maya said. "He's the fastest runner in school, and nobody's beat him at the Founders' Day footrace in three years."

"Well, I'm certain that even if it would be proper for me to enter the footrace . . . I'm sure Hagen is much faster than I am," Violet said. Yet something deep in her rather wanted to try the race. She'd always liked to run—still did. Nothing invigorated her mind and body like running barefoot as fast as she could. She glanced to Stoney—thought of the kiss he'd given her out under the full moon. *Almost* nothing invigorated her like running did.

"He ain't that fast," Stoney said. "Everybody else who enters is just slow as an old turtle."

"Anybody can enter the footrace, Miss Fynne," Maya said. "I'm entered in it. So is Beth Deavers. Katie Mill too."

"I can't believe yer lettin' her run in that race, Daddy," Layla said. "It's so unladylike."

Mr. Asbury smiled. "Oh, all the girls do it, Layla. And besides, Maya's different than you are. She don't care so awful much about how she looks and such."

Violet glanced to Maya—saw the hurt on her face. "How old are you, Maya?" Violet asked.

"I'll . . . I'll be seventeen at Christmas," Maya answered—red-faced and ashamed.

"Don't feel badly, Miss Fynne. Maya looks much younger," Layla said. "Maya was sickly last year. She missed a spell of school, and Daddy wants to make sure she gets as much learnin' in as she can. Rattler Rock's last teacher didn't know Maya was too old to be in school either."

"She's not too old to be in school," Violet said. "Nobody's ever too old to be in school. And anyway, I'm sure Maya is one of the only reasons those older boys are still willing to come to school and learn. And anything, or anyone, that keeps children coming to school . . . well, they'll find themselves at the top of my list of favorite things."

Maya smiled at Violet—a grateful smile. Still, Violet could no longer tolerate Mr. Asbury or his favorite daughter, Layla. As desperately as she wished to linger in Stoney's presence, she couldn't watch Layla flirting with him any longer either.

Turning to Mrs. Asbury, she said, "Emeline, that was a wonderful meal! Thank you so much for inviting me to supper. It was a delight."

"Are ya leavin' so soon, Miss Fynne?" Maya asked.

Violet looked at Maya—studied her for a moment. Now she understood why she'd felt so drawn to Maya all along. Maya was nearly seventeen, only three years younger than Violet. What Violet had sensed in Maya was the potential of friendship. She determined then and there that she would begin treating Maya Asbury as an equal instead of as just a student.

"I think you need to call me Violet, Maya," Violet said. "At least when we're not in school."

Maya smiled. "All right, Violet. Do ya have to leave? It's still early."

Violet smiled as well. "I need to get home before it gets too dark."

"Tony can see ya home, Miss Fynne," Emeline suggested.

"Oh, no! No . . . I enjoy the walk," Violet said. She had no desire to spend any time at all with Tony Asbury—especially alone in his company.

"I best be on my own way," Stoney said, rising to his feet.

"Oh, Stoney! No!" Layla whined. "You never stay past six."

"Don't want to wear out my welcome," Stoney said.

Mr. Asbury stood and shook Stoney's hand. "You come back as often as ya want, son," he said.

Violet felt angry—furious with the way Mr. Asbury referred to Stoney as "son."

"It was such a pleasure to meet you, Miss Fynne," Mrs. Asbury said. "Thank you for comin'."

"Thank you again for having me," Violet said.

"Are ya sure ya don't want Daddy to see ya home, Miss Fynne?" Layla asked.

"I'll see her on home," Stoney answered. "I'm goin' that way. I wanna stop in at the jailhouse and talk to Coby."

Violet tried not to smile at the indignant expression that owned Layla's face then. The black-haired beauty didn't want her beau walking another woman home. Sinful though it was, Violet let herself bathe in knowing Layla would most likely seethe for the rest of the evening over Stoney seeing the schoolteacher home.

"I left my horse tied out back, Miss Fynne," Stoney said. "I'll meet ya 'round the front."

"Thank you, Mr. Wrenn," Violet said.

"Good night, Stoney," Layla rather spat. Turning, Layla stormed from the room.

Violet glanced to Maya, who seemed unable to keep a smile of delight from spreading across her face.

"Thank you, Mrs. Asbury," Stoney said. "It was a fine meal."

"You're welcome, Stoney. You have a good evenin'," Emeline Asbury said.

"I'll see Violet out, Mama," Maya said. Taking hold of Violet's hand, Maya led her to the front door and out onto the porch.

"I'm meeting Jimmy Ritter again after school tomorrow," she whispered. "Oh, I've liked him so much for so very, very long. I thought he didn't even know who I was . . . but he does!"

Violet giggled. "I'm so glad. I think Jimmy's wonderful!"

"Oh, he is! He really is!"

"Miss Fynne?" Stoney said, appearing from one side of the house. The beautiful bay horse Dayton and Hagen admired slowly followed behind him. "You ready to get home?" Stoney stood holding the bridle reins in one hand and raked his other hand through his hair.

"Yes, of course," Violet said. "Thank you, Maya."

"Thank *you*, Violet," Maya said.

Violet fell into step beside Stoney. She loved the sound of the horse slowly plodding along behind them, the cricket noise of early evening. A warm breeze caressed her face.

"Who shot you?" she asked. Ever since the incident at supper—ever since she'd become aware that Stoney had been injured—she'd been unable to really think of anything else.

"Nobody," he said. "Somebody shot at me. There's a difference, Viola."

Violet felt goose bumps race over her arms. Simply because he had called her Viola, she was now covered in goose bumps.

"Another inch or two and there wouldn't have been a difference," she told him.

Stoney chuckled. "You were always so dramatic."

"It's true!" she argued. "There's more going on out at that old house than you're telling me."

He frowned. "Maybe."

They walked in silence for long minutes, past the schoolhouse and into town. Violet determined not to press him about what was really going on at the old Chisolm place, but it was difficult. Why was Stoney so upset about trespassers? Why was a trespasser so determined to trespass that he would go up against the likes of Stoney Wrenn?

Finally the silence grew too uncomfortable.

"She's very beautiful," she said.

"Who?" Stoney asked.

Violet looked to him. Was he in earnest? He truly appeared as if he had no idea who she was referring to. "Your girl . . . Layla Asbury," she said.

"She is pretty," Stoney said. "I'll give her that. Layla Asbury ain't my girl." He chuckled and added, "That there's just another consequence of gossip."

"What do you mean?" Violet asked, a strange, unfamiliar hope leaping to her bosom.

"I won't say I ain't been thinkin' about it. Been thinkin' maybe I oughta do like Sam Capshaw and talk to her daddy about courtin' her official." Violet frowned as a painful ache began in her heart. "But I ain't talked to him yet. Folks just assume that I'm courtin' her . . . 'cause her folks have me over to supper so often."

"But . . . but you want to court her?" Violet asked.

"That mess with Coby Fisher don't help none either."

"What mess with Coby Fisher?" Violet remembered Stoney telling her he and Coby had swapped fists before. What did Stoney's involvement with Layla have to do with the sheriff?

"I've been thinkin'," he began, " 'bout what you said about always wantin' to see inside Buddy's old house."

"You're changing the subject," Violet said.

He smiled. "What if I were to let ya in there?"

"You're just trying to keep from asking about—"

"I'm serious, Viola," he said, stopping in the middle of the street. "Do you still want to go into that old house?"

He was distracting her; she knew he was. Yet the bait of the possibility of going into the old Chisolm place was too delicious for Violet to resist.

"Of course I do. You know I've wanted to go in there," she said. "You're just teasing me. And I don't want you shooting me for trespassing anyway."

He smiled, and Violet couldn't help the sigh that escaped her at the sight of it.

"I'll make ya a deal," he began.

"Oh, no you don't!" she exclaimed, walking on. "I know what your deals are like, Mr. Stoney Wrenn!"

"What do you mean?" he asked, catching up to her.

"The last time you said to me, 'I'll make you a deal,' I ended up runnin' for my life!"

"I didn't know that ol' bull of Bud's was in that pasture, Viola," Stoney said. "You know that! You know I woulda never asked ya to see if my pa was home yet if I'd known that bull was there."

When Violet kept walking, Stoney reached out and took hold of her arm, stopping her. "You do know that, right?" he asked.

Violet could see he was truly worried that she didn't believe him. She couldn't let him worry any longer. "I know," she said. "But even so . . . any time you start a sentence with 'I'll make you a deal,' there's always some mischief involved."

"Don't ya think I've changed a bit since you left?" he asked. "In ten years, don't you think I—"

"No," Violet interrupted. "I don't."

He smiled, displaying charismatic dimples. He laughed and started walking once more. "All right, all right," he said. "But ain't you just a little bit curious about the deal I was gonna make? After all, it did involve you finally gettin' a peek inside that old house."

Violet glanced over as they passed the livery. She wondered if Sam Capshaw and Mary Pierson were out sparking somewhere. "What then?" she asked. "What's the deal?"

Stoney chuckled. "You enter that footrace next Saturday. You enter that race, and I'll take ya through Bud's old house out there. Day or night, full moon or none—you choose. You beat that Hagen boy and I'll let ya wander around in there as long as yer curious little mind wants to."

"You won't let me go in just because we used to

be friends and you know how badly I've always wanted to see inside?" she asked.

"Oh, probably," he grumbled. "But this would be more fun . . . for me anyway."

"What if I can't run fast anymore?" she said.

Stoney's eyes narrowed as he looked at her. "I remember how much you liked to run. I figure you still do. I figure you more than just like it. I figure you run whenever you get the chance and that yer just as fast as you ever was."

"That's a lot of figuring," Violet said as they rounded the corner and her little house came into view. She gasped as she saw the house, for something struck her memory just then.

"You knew that roof had been fixed when you asked me," she said. "You probably fixed it yourself."

Stoney shrugged. "Maybe. Now will you enter that race?"

Violet kept walking—instinctively walked around to the back of her little house—even though she knew it was unlikely that anyone would pass by and see her talking to the womanizing Stoney Wrenn at that time of evening. Somehow, she just wanted to be secluded with him—alone, without the Asbury family, Sheriff Fisher, the Widow Wilson, or anyone else.

Violet paused, folded her arms across her chest, and leaned back against the house. Stoney dropped his horse's reins as the animal lowered its head and began to graze on the grass.

"So if I enter this race . . . do I have to win to go into Mr. Chisolm's old house?" she asked.

Stoney smiled. "No. You just have to enter . . . and run it, of course."

"Why?" she asked, frowning. "Why can't you just let me go in? Why are you making me earn it?"

Stoney's smile softened; his beautiful green-blue opal eyes narrowed. "You know I'll let you go in that house no matter what you do, Viola," he said. His voice was low, laced with some sort of sentimental emotion. The intonation of it had a rather hypnotic effect on Violet. She felt as if he'd cast some sort of spell over her, a spell that would cause her to agree to anything he asked in that moment. "But it would be fun to see you whip that Hagen boy at the Founders' Day picnic. I could beat him myself—I know I could. And yer a might faster than me."

"I used to be faster than you," she reminded him.

"Oh, I'm sure I'd still have a hard time catchin' you," he said.

Violet smiled. How she still loved to play with Stoney Wrenn!

"And you'll let me go through the house . . . and you'll tell me about all this trespassing nonsense?"

Stoney chuckled. "I promise."

Violet began wringing her hands. "What will people think?"

"It don't matter," he said. "Will ya do it?"

Violet frowned—worried over what the folks in Rattler Rock would think of their schoolteacher running in a footrace. Still, as she gazed up into Stoney's handsome face—as she glanced at the blood soaking his shirt at one shoulder—she was reminded of just how badly she wanted to please him, how badly she wanted to know his secrets concerning the old Chisolm place.

"All right," she said. "I'll do it."

Stoney clapped his hands together with excitement, tossed his head back for a moment, and laughed.

"But you have to promise to tell me everything . . . show me everything inside," she said, wagging an index finger at him.

"I will," he said. "I promise."

He reached out, taking her face and chin in one hand and quickly kissing her square on the mouth. He kissed her again—forcing her lips to part—mingling the moisture of his mouth with her own. He broke the seal of their lips briefly—long enough to whisper, "It's gonna be great!" He kissed her a third time and then pulled away to look at her.

"It's time someone fed that Hagen boy a piece of humble pie," he said as Violet struggled to catch her breath. "He's too careless with the tender hearts of the girls around here. Maybe this'll slow him down a bit."

"Wh-what do you mean?" Violet asked, thinking Stoney Wrenn wasn't too awfully careful with tender hearts either. Stoney still held her face in his hand; his head was still bent toward hers. She could feel his breath on her mouth as he spoke. She wanted to throw her arms around his neck and taste his kiss again—the kiss that had left such a delicious flavor in her mouth—a flavor she still savored.

"If Rattler Rock thinks I'm a womanizer . . . well, this town ain't seen nothin' 'til it knows what Hagen Webster's been up to," he said, releasing her face and stepping back from her. "He's coaxed about every girl between the age of fourteen and twenty out there to the old Chisolm place for some sparkin'. Every girl except Maya Asbury . . . least the way I count it."

Violet gasped. "Really?"

"Yep," Stoney said, still smiling. "And I can't wait to see him cut down a length or two."

"But what if I can't beat him in the race?" she asked, her mouth watering for want of another kiss from him. Her heart still hammered, but he looked completely unaffected. He'd kissed her because he'd been glad she'd agreed to enter the race. Yet his kiss had been so intimate—so consuming—even for its brevity. Violet didn't know whether to be happy or miserable over such a kiss.

Stoney shrugged. "At least with you runnin' against him, there's hope." She must've frowned, for he asked, "What's the matter? You all right?"

"I'm fine," she lied. "I was just thinking that . . . that . . ."

"That what?"

"That it would be gratifying to win," she lied. She'd really been thinking that she was insane—insane because she had such thoroughly obsessive feelings toward a man she'd known less than a week.

"You'll win," he said. He whistled, and the bay raised its head and started toward its master. "And then I'll tell you all about that damn house. I promise."

Violet nodded and watched him mount the bay.

He smiled at her, his eyes flashing in the falling darkness. "We had us some fun . . . didn't we, Viola?" he asked.

"Yes. We did," she said.

"You have yerself a good day, Miss Fynne."

"Thank you," was all she could manage as response.

"Get on, boy!" Stoney said.

Violet watched the horse and rider disappear in a cloud of dust. She placed trembling fingers to her lips, for they still tingled with the sense of Stoney Wrenn's kiss. She hadn't struggled when he'd tried to kiss her, and although she had been astonished by the intimate nature of his kiss, she hadn't denied herself the pleasure of returning it. Frowning, Violet tried not to cry.

If Stoney Wrenn was a womanizer, then what was she?

# CHAPTER EIGHT

As Violet's first week back in Rattler Rock waned, she found herself greatly unsettled. She startled easily—felt a frown puckering her brow more often than she would've liked. Although she wore a happy countenance when teaching the children or Jimmy Ritter, her innards were constantly stirred.

At first, she thought it was the anxious anticipation of the Founders' Day picnic and the footrace she'd promised Stoney Wrenn she'd enter. Then she wondered if her lack of serenity was the fact that she now viewed Hagen Webster with curious disapproval. She was so very aware of things she had not been aware of before in regard to him. As Violet observed Hagen more closely, she found that the older girls did indeed seem to own some sort of delight mingled with scorn where he was concerned. Also, there was the way Dayton tended to listen to whatever Hagen suggested—to act on his friend's decisions instead of his own—as if he owned some secret admiration of Hagen. Maya seemed immune to Hagen's charm and prowess where flirting was concerned. Violet liked her all the more for it too.

Still, in the end, and in the truthful depths of her heart, Violet knew exactly why her innards were forever stirred—why she felt jittery and unsettled. Each time she would consider her state of unrest—no matter what excuses her mind tried to offer her heart—she knew Stoney Wrenn was the reason. Her very core was in a state of chaos, and it was all for the sake of Stoney Wrenn.

Violet spent hours in painful, confused contemplation. She'd loved Stoney when they were children; she'd always known she had loved him. Certainly she knew her young heart had owned an intense adoration, a loving sense far beyond mere infatuation. In this, she even understood why she should even yet adore him. Still, the feelings so powerful and alive in her now moved far beyond adoration and infatuation, and Violet could find nothing rational in them. She was in love with Stoney Wrenn—truly in love with him—as a woman loved and obsessed over a lover or husband. Yet how could she be in love with him? She'd been back in Rattler Rock less than two weeks, and in this she felt it was impossible to be so thoroughly and painfully in love—with anyone! But when she was being fully honest with herself, when she was alone in her little house near town, she knew she was in love with him.

She came to realize that her love for Stoney Wrenn was the thing keeping her so terribly unsettled. She thought of nothing else, even while teaching or reading or walking or eating. Always

Stoney Wrenn dominated her thoughts and emotions. Once she even blushed while sitting at her desk in the schoolroom. The children had been going over their individual reading lessons in silence while she worked on future lessons for them. Sitting at her desk, the sudden memory—the actual sensational effect—of Stoney Wrenn's last kiss set her cheeks to pinking. Susan Gribbs had noticed and asked aloud if Violet were feeling all right, for her cheeks were "as red as the tomatoes in my mama's garden," Susan had said.

Each time Violet thought of Stoney—of his warm, moist, and demanding kiss—she felt her cheeks pink—felt overly warm and as if a swarm of butterflies were fluttering about in her stomach. None of this could Violet seem to settle in her mind. Her mature, lucid self was constantly reminding her that no woman could love a man she'd only known for a week. Yet her heart told her she'd known Stoney Wrenn much longer. Whether or not they'd been parted for nearly half their lives, she had known him the full length of hers.

Thus, Violet remained in a constant state of unrest all through the week preceding the Founders' Day picnic. She thought she hid her silent turbulence well. Stoney Wrenn himself did not seem to sense it on the few occasions Violet saw him during the week. They'd spoken for quite some time standing outside the jailhouse, having met when Stoney was arriving to talk with Coby Fisher and Violet just passing on her way home after school. Violet saw him riding home one evening. He'd reined in before her little house and spoken with her—asked if she were still enjoying the children at school now that she'd been teaching them for more than a week. He had not tried to kiss her again, however. Of course, there had been no opportunity, for each time they met, it was in some place with other people milling around in some manner. How she longed to be alone with him, talk with him, just linger in his presence. Yet there came no opportunity, and the second week waned.

It was Friday afternoon, and Jimmy Ritter sat on the porch steps of Violet's house enjoying the cookies Violet had just taken from the oven. It was in this moment that Violet—having thought no one was aware of the preoccupation of her mind and heart—discovered she was wrong.

"I cannot believe how fast you're progressing, Jimmy," Violet said—and it was true. In a mere two weeks, Jimmy had thoroughly absorbed so many concepts of reading. Violet was amazed at his ability to retain the lessons.

Jimmy smiled and shrugged. "Well, once I put my mind to somethin', I like to get it done and move on to the next chore," he said.

Violet smiled. "Well, that's a good piece to have in your character."

"Stoney taught me that," he said.

"Then he's a better teacher than I am," Violet said. She sighed. "I tend to be easily distracted. I get tired of one thing and simply move on to the next. I can't tell you how many things I've left unfinished."

"But ya didn't leave Stoney unfinished . . . did ya, Miss Fynne?"

Violet felt her heart begin to pound. What did Jimmy mean? What did he know?

"What do you mean, Jimmy?" she asked.

He seemed to pause—brushed the cookie crumbs from the front of his shirt. "It was before you come back," he began. "A year or so ago . . . while me and Stoney was sittin' around a fire after brandin'. We'd finished with the heifers a little earlier than we expected, so we was just sittin' around talkin' about life. That was when Stoney told me about his pa beatin' on him. He told me everything—about his pa, about Mr. Chisolm . . . and about you."

"What did he tell you about me?" Violet asked. Her heart hammered with some sort of strange anxiety. A deep sense of foreboding began to wash over her, yet she waited. She wanted to know what Stoney had told Jimmy—she needed to know.

Jimmy looked at her, his gaze rather severe.

"He told me what great friends the two of you were," he answered. "He told me all about the trouble ya used to find together. He said the two of you thought nothin' could keep ya apart . . . that all ya ever wanted was to grow up together . . . be together yer whole lives."

Violet winced, for it was true. Unspoken perhaps, but it was the way she'd always felt then—that the only thing she wanted in life was to be with Stoney forever. "It's true," she whispered.

"That's what Stoney said," Jimmy continued. "He said he thought he'd drop dead when you moved . . . whether from his pa's beatin's or from a broken heart. He thought sure he'd drop dead. But he didn't. He didn't because you'd promised him you'd come back one day. Oh, he didn't really believe it. He knew you was a kid and didn't have yer own means and such. But he said it was the hope you'd find a way that kept him goin' for them first few years while his pa was still beatin' on him and all."

Somehow Violet managed to will her tears to stay in her eyes—kept them from escaping to trail over her cheeks. Yet Jimmy's story was not the same one Stoney had told her.

"Stoney told me he was fine," she said. "He told me his daddy quit beatin' on him right after my family left Rattler Rock. He said he was all right."

Jimmy paused and seemed to be considering whether or not he should continue. Then he said, "He weren't all right, Miss Fynne."

"What do you mean, Jimmy?" she asked. A strong sense of foreboding, a fear of owning Jimmy's knowledge, began to sift through her.

"His pa beat him somethin' awful," Jimmy answered.

"I remember," she said. "I remember, and it pains me every day of my life. But . . . but at least he stopped when—"

"His pa never stopped beatin' him, Miss Violet," Jimmy interrupted. "Stoney ran away."

"What?" Violet breathed. "But he said—"

"Stoney says a lot of things . . . when he don't want people diggin' in his business." Jimmy shrugged and continued. "I figure it's how he keeps calm and still, ya know? Instead of gettin' all tore up or hurt, he just don't tell folks things. He'd probably give me a hollerin' if he knew I was tellin' you."

"Give you a hollering?" Violet asked.

Jimmy nodded. "He'd never lay a hand on me—never did and never will, no matter what kind of trouble I get into," he said. "But he can sure raise his voice."

"You say he ran away," Violet began. "When?"

"When he was, oh, sixteen, I guess," Jimmy said. "His pa had at him good . . . and Stoney decided he was old enough to go. So he run off. Cowboyed for about two, three years. Then he come back and went to work for ol' Buddy Chisolm. He even lived in the ol' Chisolm place awhile. Old Bud let Stoney live there—ghosts and all—fer free, providin' he looked after the place and didn't bother the ghosts none. Then when Buddy Chisolm passed, a fancy lawyer from over in Texas showed up. Said Bud had left a will, left everything to Stoney. Bud never had no kids of his own. Guess he got to thinkin' of Stoney as his boy instead . . . and that's how Stoney got hold of all of that land and them houses, including the haunted one." Violet watched as Jimmy ate another cookie. "He's done good by it too. Made himself a wagonload of money off crops and stock and such."

"He told me his daddy quit beatin' on him," Violet said.

"Why would he tell ya different?" Jimmy asked. "It wouldn't do nothin' but make ya feel bad again for leavin'."

"I-I guess you're right," Violet whispered. Renewed guilt washed over her disappointment in herself—disappointment that she hadn't seen through Stoney's keeping the truth from her. She should've seen it.

"He keeps yer photograph, ya know."

"What?" Violet asked.

Jimmy nodded. "I seen it in his drawer. He keeps it there . . . and there's a letter with it. I always figured the letter was from you, bein' it's with yer photograph and all."

Violet felt the tears increasing in her eyes. Part of her heart experienced joy—comfort in the knowledge Stoney truly hadn't forgotten her as easily as she'd thought. Yet another part of her heart—the deepest, most tender part—felt worse than ever.

"Why are you telling me this, Jimmy?" Violet asked. "It's . . . it's not something a person starts talking about for the sake of conversation."

Jimmy dropped his gaze to the ground and nodded. "I'm tellin' you because Stoney Wrenn has been the only father I ever knew . . . or at least the only big brother I ever knew," he said. "He took care of me when nobody else woulda wanted to. He taught me a mountain about life and a lick or two about stock and land and hard work." He paused, his eyes narrowing as he looked to Violet. "And I want to see him rewarded with a good life . . . with knowin' he's a good man."

"Well, surely he knows he's a good man," Violet said. "Everyone in town likes him. Every woman in town nearly swoons when he passes. How can he not know he's a good man?"

"Oh, but you already know why, don't ya, Miss Fynne?" Jimmy asked. He grinned a little. "You know Stoney Wrenn better than anybody—even me—don't ya? Don't matter how much I respect him, don't matter how much ol' Buddy Chisolm told Stoney he was a great feller, Stoney Wrenn don't think it's so. Maybe he's just awful humble. Maybe he's just plain ignorant. But, you and me, we both know it's probably 'cause his pa was such a mean ol' son of a . . . gun. And the fact people gossip somethin' awful about him . . . callin' him a womanizer and all. It's the only reason he's even thinkin' on Layla Asbury. He told me that settlin' in with her might stop all the talkin'."

Violet brushed a tear from her cheek. She placed a hand to calm the sickened feeling in her stomach, the sensation of nausea that had begun to churn when Jimmy spoke of Stoney's considering settling with Layla Asbury.

"I still don't understand why you're telling me—"

"Yes, ya do, Miss Fynne," he interrupted. "You know exactly why I'm tellin' you. I'm tellin' you because you can turn Stoney's head."

"What?" Violet asked. Her heart was beating faster, for her heart began to understand. Yet her sense of reason could not accept.

"Stoney's thinkin' about nailin' himself down to that Asbury girl," Jimmy said. "You know it . . . and I know it . . . and we both know it ain't right."

Violet paused—uncertain as to how much of her own thoughts she should reveal to the boy.

"He's very handsome . . . and he's owns a great deal of property," Violet mumbled. "He's the sort most girls would do anything to end up with."

Jimmy smiled. "Ya see? I know ya knew it. I think Stoney knows it too. It's just that everyone in town has been naggin' him to settle down for so long and all . . ." Jimmy paused and grinned at Violet again. "But you could turn his head. Fact, you already done it."

"I haven't done anything, Jimmy," Violet sighed, discouraged. "I've done nothing but remind him of how miserable his childhood was. When he looks at me, he sees the past . . . and everything bad that he finally managed to put behind him."

Jimmy shook his head. "Nope. No, he don't. I think he sees the only thing that ever made him happy."

Violet shook her head. "I caused him pain," she whispered. "Maybe we were happy together as children. But for ten long years, I've only caused him pain."

Violet gasped as Jimmy reached out and took hold of her shoulders.

"Ain't you been listenin' to a word I've been sayin', girl?" he growled. "The dream of you comin' back . . . that's the only thing that saved that man!"

Violet sat astonished—awed into silence at the way Jimmy Ritter suddenly seemed her equal instead of her student.

"So keep savin' him," Jimmy said. "You want him, Miss Fynne. I seen the way yer eyes sparkle when anybody even mentions his name. Maya says you was plum agitated the other night when you was over at her house for supper. She says the attraction 'tween you and Stoney was thicker than pea soup. Layla knew it too and went on and on and on to her daddy about it after you and Stoney left." He paused and brushed a tear from her cheek with the back of his hand. "Stoney told me yer plannin' on enterin' the footrace tomorrow . . . so's you can whip that weasel Hagen Webster." He studied Violet from head to toe for a moment. "You gonna sit there and tell me you woulda agreed to enter a footrace if anybody else in the world besides Stoney Wrenn woulda asked ya to?"

Violet straightened her posture and tried to regain the feeling of teacher and pupil she'd owned where Jimmy was concerned before. Such feelings had vanished however. She saw Jimmy Ritter as a man in that moment—an equal—and one who had a frightening insight.

"You're sweet on Maya Asbury, aren't you, Jimmy?" she asked.

"Of course," he said. "But that don't have nothin' to do—"

"What do you think of Layla? She's beautiful, refined . . ."

"Oh, I ain't even gonna listen to ya if yer gonna

start in on how she'd be better for Stoney," he grumbled. "Yer just yeller, and you know it. Layla Asbury would make Stoney's life a hangin' of misery. Yer scared—scared he don't feel the same as you. But he does. I know he does. You just gotta find the strength to save him. Ain't that what you always planned on anyway? All these years you've been thinkin' on Stoney Wrenn, thinkin' you had to keep yer promise and come back for him. I know that, else you wouldn't be sittin' here with me right now. So what did you plan on doin' when you come back?"

"I-I just wanted to make sure he was all right . . . that he'd been happy," Violet stammered.

"Like hell you did," Jimmy said. "You wanted to come back and find him just the way ya did find him—strong, a man who survived a harsh upbringing, a man who weren't married yet."

Violet leapt to her feet. She shook her head emphatically, brushed the tears from her cheeks, and said, "You're wrong. You're wrong. We were just children when I was taken away. Stoney and I . . . we were friends . . . children who were friends."

"I was only fourteen when I first laid eyes on Maya Asbury," Jimmy said, rising as well. "I weren't much older than Stoney was when you left Rattler Rock. But I've been in love with her ever since. I'd marry her tomorrow if I thought she'd have me and her pa would allow it. It's why I agreed to learn to read when Stoney asked me to meet with you. I finally wised up—figured I need to be the best man I can be if I ever hope to have her. So don't tell me true love can't grow from a seed that's planted in a child's heart."

Violet shook her head. "You don't understand, Jimmy," she said. "Men are different than women. They—"

"Hey," he interrupted. His eyes narrowed. "Say what you want; I'll say what I think. In the end, it's up to you. I can only tell ya what I know . . . what I see in my friend, Stoney Wrenn. He's yer friend too, Violet. So what do you see?"

Jimmy reached down and picked up the reader Violet had asked him to study at home. "I'll see ya tomorrow, Miss Fynne," he said. He forced an understanding smile. "I sure hope you whip that Webster boy."

Violet watched him go. She brushed the tears from her cheeks, but more simply escaped her eyes. He'd lied to her! Stoney had lied to her. He'd told her his daddy had quit beating him, that he'd been just fine. Why had he lied to her? They never lied to each other as children—never! Still, they weren't children anymore—and Violet had been gone for ten years.

Such a turmoil rose within her, a turmoil she hadn't known since her family had left Rattler Rock and moved to New York. Violet was sure she would burst apart from the feelings fighting within her.

Without thinking, she left the porch of her little house and started down the road to Buddy Chisolm's old place. She had to walk—needed to find peace. She angrily wiped at the tears still streaming down her face. Who was Jimmy Ritter to tell her anything anyway? He didn't know her. What gave him the right to talk to her about her feelings for Stoney?

Violet began to run—run as fast as she could. It was harder to run in her boots. She told herself she would have to remove her boots before the footrace at the picnic if she were to have any hope of winning.

She was standing beneath the old cottonwood tree, even before she realized where her mind had led her. She looked up into the gnarly limbs blanketed with green leaves. Dropping to her knees, Violet let her fingers trace the weathered carved heart—Stoney's and her own initials marked in its center.

She'd been a child when she'd known Stoney Wrenn, when she'd left him. She couldn't have fallen in love with him over the course of ten years—while she was in Albany and he was in Rattler Rock! It was impossible.

Still, her heart cried out, silently confessing it wanted nothing but to belong to Stoney Wrenn, no matter what her sensible mind professed.

Desperate for respite, for some sort of tranquility of mind, Violet sat down in the grass and unlaced her boots. Pulling her boots off and tossing them into the taller grasses nearby, she stripped off her stockings and discarded them as well. Reaching up, she pulled the pins from her hair, combed her long, auburn locks with her fingers, and looked up into the tree once more.

Violet took hold of a lower limb, braced one foot against the tree's trunk, and began to climb. Her mother hadn't let her climb trees once the family had left Rattler Rock for the more sophisticated life of Albany. Violet had resented the fact most vigorously. She loved climbing trees. She thought about the way she and Stoney would climb into the branches of the old cottonwood and talk for hours. Sometimes they wouldn't talk—simply eavesdrop on other folks who might happen by and pause beneath the old tree either to talk or to engage in other "goings-on." Whatever presented itself beneath the old cottonwood, Violet had adored lingering in its branches. She wondered now if she might find a trace of the same respite she knew then.

Settling herself in the crook of a large branch, she sighed. She looked down, realizing she'd climbed up much farther than she realized. Yet she didn't care, for she suddenly felt freer than she'd felt in years. This was a place meant for finding peace, for deep contemplation—a place where worries could be put to rest and solutions to problems presented.

But Violet's respite was brief, for she'd been resting in the tree branches for only a short time when she heard voices. Her heart began to hammer with brutal force in her bosom as she heard Stoney's voice wafting to her on the breeze—Stoney's voice and that of a woman.

"You didn't have to walk all the way out here, Layla," Stoney said.

Violet held her breath as she looked down through the branches to see Stoney Wrenn and Layla Asbury stop beneath the tree. She was instantly furious. The tree was her and Stoney's secret place! He had no right to bring another girl to it.

"You coulda asked me tomorrow at the picnic," he said.

"I know that," Layla said. "But there's something else I wanted to talk to ya about."

"It ain't proper for you to be out here with me . . . without somebody else here too, Layla. Yer pa would be mighty disappointed knowin' you'd come out here. I don't exactly have the best reputation where women are concerned."

"I know that," Layla said. "And that's one reason I wanted to talk to you privately."

Violet frowned, careless of the impropriety of eavesdropping. She was far too intrigued, curious, and jealous to worry about good manners.

"Are you ever gonna ask my daddy permission to court me proper, Stoney Wrenn?" Layla asked. "I-I thought you would. For weeks I've been waitin'. I even told Daddy to refuse Coby Fisher permission to court me . . . 'cause I thought you were gonna ask."

"I know," Stoney said. "Believe me, I know you tossed Coby's heart in the crick . . . and I didn't mind gettin' blamed for it 'cause I thought you just didn't like him. But, Layla, I—"

"I know yer used to havin' yer way with women, Stoney," the young woman said. "I know it must be difficult for you to see me, be in my company, want me the way you do, and know you can't have me like ya have other women. But I wanted to assure ya that you can have me anytime ya want, Stoney Wrenn. You can kiss me right now, while nobody's near to see. That way, I keep my good reputation . . . and yer bad one doesn't matter."

Violet was seething. From her perch in the arms of the old cottonwood, she considered swooping down like a crow, burying her hands in Layla Asbury's ebony hair, and yanking it out by the roots. Furthermore, she swore to herself that if Stoney Wrenn did kiss Layla she'd peck his eyes out.

"Well, that's real sweet, Layla," Stoney said.

209

"I feel really honored that you would consider lettin' me have my way with you. But there's two things yer either forgettin' . . . or that ya don't already know."

"And what are those two things, Stoney Wrenn?" Layla cooed, moving closer to Stoney, reaching up, and caressing his cheek with the back of her hand.

"Well, first off, I hate to disappoint, but I ain't the womanizer folks make me out to be," Stoney said. "And second—"

"You are gonna ask Daddy, aren't you?" Layla interrupted. "You are gonna ask him to come courtin' . . . aren't ya?"

"You need to get on home, Layla," Stoney said. "If anyone finds you out here alone with me, it won't matter what I'm fixin' to do . . . 'cause yer daddy will skin me alive."

"Just kiss me once, Stoney," Layla said.

Violet held her breath as Layla moved closer to Stoney and pressed her body against his.

"Kiss me once, and I promise you . . . you'll be beggin' my daddy to court me."

"No, no, no, no, no!" Violet whispered. She clamped one hand over her mouth when she saw Stoney glance behind him, as if he'd heard something.

"You need to run on home, Layla," Stoney said. "This ain't proper. You wouldn't want us to make a mistake that kept us apart for sure, would ya?"

Violet heard Layla's delighted giggle. "I guess yer right, Stoney. We don't want my daddy havin' any reason to refuse you when ya ask him for permission to court me after supper on Sunday." Violet watched as Layla stepped back from Stoney. "You are a gentleman, Stoney Wrenn," Layla said.

"Are ya so surprised?" Stoney asked.

"Not at all," Layla said. "Just disappointed."

Violet watched as Layla turned and walked away. Stoney exhaled a heavy sigh. He removed his hat and ran his fingers through his hair. Violet watched as he strode from beneath the tree.

He was gone; she was certain he was. Still, she looked at the locket clock she wore about her neck, waiting ten more minutes before deciding it was safe for her to climb down from her perch in the tree.

As she began to climb, Violet mumbled to herself. "Who does she think she is? I could just tear her hair out!"

So focused on her anger and jealousy, Violet wasn't careful in her descent. Her foot missed a branch, and she tried to wrap her arms around the tree's trunk to keep herself from falling. Instead, she landed with a painful thud on her bottom in the grass beneath the tree. Looking down to the front of her shirtwaist, she winced. The bark of the old cottonwood had torn the delicate lace and cotton of the shirtwaist—shredded it. The entire front of the shirtwaist was gone, and both sleeves fell away from her arms, too. Her camisole was completely exposed. How would she ever get back to her house without being seen?

"I seem to remember you bein' just a bit more graceful when climbin' down from a tree, Miss Fynne."

Violet closed her eyes and held her breath. It was Stoney Wrenn's voice.

"Shame on you!" he scolded.

Violet opened her eyes to see him standing before her, one hand outstretched in an offering of assistance.

"You oughta be ashamed of yerself, eaves-droppin' on folks' private conversations like that."

"I had a good teacher," she said, accepting his hand. He helped her to her feet, his opaline eyes shimmering with amusement.

"And you can't go back to town with yer skin showin' either," he said. Violet watched as Stoney began to unbutton his shirt.

"What are you doing?" she asked as he stripped the shirt from his body—revealing a chiseled torso, muscular and bronzed from hours in the sun.

"Keepin' you a reputable woman," he said, offering the shirt to her. Violet glanced down as Stoney pointed at her stomach. Violet gasped—blushed pure crimson when she looked down to see her camisole was torn as well. She hadn't noticed it before, but the tree bark had left several large tears in her camisole, leaving most of her stomach fully revealed.

Snatching the shirt from Stoney, she quickly put it on over her shredded shirtwaist and camisole. Irritated, she brushed her long hair back from her face as she fumbled with the buttons of the shirt.

"Now," Stoney began, "what were you doin' sittin' up there spyin' on me?"

"I wasn't spying on you," she said, combing one hand through her hair to brush it back. "I was out for a walk and decided to climb the old tree."

Stoney just stared at her, obviously expectant of further explanation.

"What was I supposed to do when you two came along? Just swing down and say hello?"

Stoney struggled to keep from reaching out and pulling Violet into his arms. As she began to twist a long strand of auburn hair, he nearly weakened—nearly reached out, determined to have her, no matter the consequences. She was so adorable, even more adorable than she had been as a child. Furthermore, except for the fact she was a beautiful woman instead of a beautiful little girl, little else had changed in Violet Fynne since she'd been taken from Rattler Rock so many years before.

He studied her quickly from head to toe. What

a sight she'd be to the folks in Rattler Rock just now. He almost laughed as she stood before him, hair wild and free, barefoot, wearing his shirt. She looked about as far from being Rattler Rock's prim little schoolteacher as she could, and he allowed himself to delight in it.

When he didn't say anything, Violet began to fume. How could he flirt so with Layla Asbury? How could he be alone with Layla beneath the old cottonwood—beneath their tree, hers and Stoney's?

"I'm just glad you knew I was up there somehow," she said. "For a moment I was afraid I'd have to be witness to you . . . to you—how did you say it?—having your way with Layla Asbury."

"I wasn't gonna have my way with her," he growled. "And besides, I didn't know you were there. I just heard somethin' while we were talkin', and when I started to leave, I saw yer boots over there in the grass. Yer boots and these," he said. Reaching around to his back pocket, he produced Violet's stockings. "You sure do wear fancy stockin's for a schoolteacher."

"Give me those!" Violet exclaimed, feeling the heated blush on her cheeks. She reached out to grab the stockings, but Stoney chuckled and moved them out of her reach. "Stoney Wrenn! You give those stockings to me this instant!"

"If the parents of the children at the Rattler Rock schoolhouse could see you now, Miss Fynne!" he laughed.

Violet was angry, embarrassed, and absolutely out of countenance. Furious, frustrated, and somehow brokenhearted, her educated woman's mind could think of nothing in response to his teasing. Therefore, she'd done what she'd often done when Stoney Wrenn had teased her as a child: she stuck her tongue out at him.

Instantly after doing so, however, she remembered the usual consequences. Clamping a hand over her mouth, she felt her eyes widen as Stoney's eyebrows arched over his green-blue eyes.

"Really, Viola?" he said. "We're back to you stickin' yer tongue out at me?"

Violet shook her head as Stoney threw her stockings to the ground and began to advance upon her. Pure indignation flamed in his eyes—mischievous indignation.

"I didn't mean it!" Violet exclaimed as he strode toward her. "I swear I didn't mean it! I-it just . . . I-I couldn't help it!"

She squealed as she stumbled on a fallen branch and landed hard on her rump. She looked up to see Stoney had not slowed his advance, and in the next moment she squealed again as she found herself flat on her back with Stoney Wrenn straddling her and sitting down hard on her legs as he held her hands at the side of her head.

"You remember what Bud used to say stickin' yer tongue out meant?" he asked.

His eyes were smoldering with mischief; any anger or irritation was gone. Still, Violet's heart hammered so hard within her bosom she thought it might burst right out of her chest.

"Y-you provoked me, Stoney," she panted.

"*I* provoked *you?*" he asked, smiling a deliciously alluring smile. "You were the one eavesdroppin' on me, Viola. Remember?"

"Stoney," she began, "I swear . . . I did not climb up in that tree with the intention of—"

"I'm sorry, Viola," he said, "but Buddy was right. Stickin' out yer tongue at folks is a bad habit. Somebody's gotta teach you some manners."

Violet was rendered breathless—completely breathless and covered in the bliss of erupting goose bumps—as Stoney's mouth pressed moist and warm to her neck. He kissed her neck just below her right ear, and a pleasurable shiver raced through her. She had meant to struggle—to attempt to free herself from his restraint—but as his lips slowly traveled along the length of her jaw, she forgot.

He kissed the hollow of her throat, and she trembled when she felt his tongue lightly taste her flesh there. He kissed her chin—her cheek—

the corner of her mouth. Violet struggled for a moment—tried to free her arms so she might wrap them around his neck, pull him closer to her. Yet Stoney held her wrists tightly pinned to the ground, so she ceased her endeavors to fulfill her desire to embrace him.

He paused in placing tender kisses to her cheeks and chin. Violet gazed into the fascination of his eyes, her mouth watering for want of knowing his kiss pressed to it.

"That's just a terrible habit, Viola," he said, his voice low, enthralling, as alluring as temptation itself. "Somebody has got to teach you a lesson. I guess it might as well be me."

"I guess so," Violet breathed.

She didn't move, didn't struggle as he pushed her hands up over her head, pinning her wrists with one hand as he cradled her chin in the other.

She gasped, sighed, and allowed euphoria to overwhelm her as his mouth crushed to hers. His heated kiss demanded response, and any remaining sense of propriety Violet owned a moment before was lost as she met its demand. Though he yet sat on her legs—his torso hovering above hers—she could feel the warmth of his body, sense the scent of his skin. His rough whiskers chafed the tender flesh about her mouth, but she didn't care. If only he would release her, allow her to hold him as every thread of her being silently begged to hold him. How desperately she wanted to lose her fingers in the softness of his hair, feel the warmth of his flesh beneath her palms. Yet he held her wrists pinned fast as he continued to instruct her mouth to meeting his in a passionate, flavorful melding.

Impish thoughts began to intrude upon her mind—thoughts and wishes that Layla Asbury would return to the old cottonwood and find Violet overcome by Stoney Wrenn. She thought she would do anything he asked of her in that moment, follow him anywhere he chose to go. How desperately she loved him! How entirely, how eternally, how utterly unconditional was her love for him. She would never be separated from him again—never!

All these thoughts were Violet's as she bathed in the bliss of Stoney Wrenn's kiss.

Stoney tightened his hold on Violet's wrists. He feared his grip was too strong—that he might bruise her tender hands—yet he could not allow her to touch him. Were she to struggle free, were he to feel her hand on his face, his shoulder, his chest—were Violet Fynne to touch him in any way—he would lose any shred of self-restraint he had left. She tasted like the nectar of heaven itself, and he feared he would never quench his thirst for her enough to release her.

He crushed his mouth to hers, devouring her

passion, drawing vigor from the sense she was meeting his demands with a driven fervor of her own. For a moment, he wondered if she loved him—truly loved him—was in love with him. Surely this response, the passion he could feel flowing through her, surely it was not simply bred of the guilt she'd borne for so many years—the guilt of having left him behind. Surely it was more than that—more than guilt—but in the next instant, doubt owned Stoney Wrenn.

Violet gasped as Stoney suddenly broke the seal of their lips. She gasped again as he stood, pulling her to her feet.

"Have ya learned yer lesson this time, Viola?" he asked.

Violet stared at him. He seemed unaffected, as if nothing had happened, as if it had merely been a conversation they'd shared and not flaming passion.

"Y-yes," she stammered in a whisper.

"Then let's get you home before someone finds us out here and thinks . . ." His voice trailed off as he began to lead her, not toward the road but to the creekbed. Violet followed as he held her hand, pulling her along as he followed the creek toward town.

They didn't speak—just walked. Soon the back of the little house was visible. The sun was beginning to set as Stoney turned to Violet.

"Yer gonna whip that Webster boy for me tomorrow, aren't ya?" he asked.

"I . . . I'll try," Violet said.

"Good," he said, nodding. Without another word, Stoney Wrenn turned and walked away.

Violet watched him go—marveled as the muscles in his arms and back moved as he walked. When he'd disappeared behind a grove of young cottonwoods, she turned. She'd locked the back door of the house when she'd first arrived. As she slipped around to the front of the house, she determined to unlock the back door once in a while. She peeked around the corner to see no one in the road. She looked toward town—no one in sight. Quickly she ran up the steps and into the house.

Once inside she looked out the front window. No one was in the street. It seemed she'd made it back to her house wearing Stoney Wrenn's shirt without being seen. She thought of her stockings and boots, still lying in the grass at the foot of the old cottonwood. She hoped no one would find them, or Stoney's reputation as a womanizer would be set in stone.

Still gazing out the window, she glanced down at the porch, to the abandoned plate of cookies. She thought of Jimmy Ritter and of what he told her—that she could turn Stoney's head. Was it true? Could she win Stoney's heart? It seemed too dreamlike to be real, too much to hope for.

Later, Violet decided not to wear her nightdress. Instead she lay in her bed swathed in Stoney Wrenn's shirt. The scent of him still clung to it, bathing her in a sense of serene security. Come what may, Jimmy Ritter had been correct. There, snuggled in her bed, clothed in Stoney's shirt, Violet allowed herself to admit that Jimmy Ritter had been right. She'd returned to Rattler Rock for one reason: she'd returned to find Stoney Wrenn and keep him.

# CHAPTER NINE

"Are ya worried about the race, Violet?" Maya asked.

"I'm more worried about what the folks in Rattler Rock are gonna think when I hitch up my skirt to start running than whether or not I'm going to lose," Violet answered.

She paused, as did Maya, their attention returned to the contest taking place before them.

"Stoney Wrenn will win this one easy," Maya said.

"He will?" Violet asked, as the repeat of a rifle echoed in her ears.

"Oh, sure! Everybody knows he's the best shot in the county. I don't know why Sheriff Fisher even tries."

"Well, Coby did shoot better than everybody else, the same as Stoney," Violet reminded her friend. Still, she was anxious. She wanted Stoney to beat Coby in the shooting contest. So far Stoney had hit every target dead center.

Maya giggled.

"What?" Violet asked. She looked to Maya, who wore an expression of delighted amusement.

"A couple of years back, a bunch of the younger kids in town came up with the notion that Stoney was a gunman . . . a real outlaw. You should've seen them scatter whenever he walked into town," she explained. "Of course the rest of us knew it wasn't true." She paused and smiled at Violet. "He used to give me butterscotch when I was little. I always felt special. He'd give me two pieces, but he'd only ever give Layla one. He used to whisper in my ear, 'Because yer sweeter than yer sister.' I think that's why I always liked Stoney Wrenn so much, no matter what folks said about him. I used to dream I'd grow up and marry him one day. Of course, that was before he hired Jimmy. Once I saw Jimmy Ritter, I didn't care how many pieces of butterscotch Stoney Wrenn had in his pockets. I was gonna marry Jimmy."

Violet giggled as Maya gasped and clamped a hand over her mouth. "Oh no!" she breathed. "I can't believe I said all that! Please don't tell anyone, Violet! I . . . I . . ."

"Of course I won't tell anyone," Violet said. "Anyway, I already knew that you and Jimmy were sweethearts."

Maya paused, and Violet watched as Coby Fisher hit every target Stoney had, with as much accuracy. Two men were now lining bottles up on a fence a ways out. Five bottles stood on the fence. Coby Fisher would try first.

Silently Violet began to wish bad luck on him—inwardly chanting the word *miss*. Coby took aim—careful aim—took his time. The rifle repeated, and the first bottle shattered. Everyone cheered and applauded. Again Coby took slow aim—steady aim. Another bottle shattered.

"What'll happen if they both hit all the bottles?" Violet whispered to Maya.

Maya shrugged. "I don't know. Nobody has ever gotten this far against Stoney."

Violet looked to Stoney. He was standing nearby, casually leaning up against an old tree stump. He seemed as calm as a summer's day as Coby Fisher hit the next bottle.

Violet watched, anxious. She wanted Stoney to triumph, and it looked like he might not. After quite some time, time spent on gauging a steady aim, Coby Fisher hit the third bottle. The fourth bottle fell and then the fifth.

"Nobody's ever gotten that far before," Maya said. "It usually ends long before this. Sheriff Fisher's been practicin'."

Violet watched as Coby Fisher inhaled deeply and nodded his thanks to the crowd of onlookers.

"You'll have to hit every bottle, Stoney," Mr. Deavers said as Stoney stepped forward. "Even if ya do hit 'em all, we'll have to think of somethin' else . . . or just call it even."

Stoney smiled and patted Mr. Deavers on the back. "Don't worry, Alex," he said.

Violet held her breath as Stoney leveled his Winchester.

"He'd better take his time," Maya whispered.

Before the words had entirely escaped Maya's mouth, however, Violet startled as a shot rang out. The shattered pieces of the first bottle hadn't even hit the ground before Stoney had cocked his gun and the next bottle shattered—then the next—the next—the last. It had taken Coby Fisher several minutes to do what Stoney Wrenn had done in a matter of seconds.

The crowd cheered, and even Coby Fisher smiled as Stoney Wrenn lowered his rifle.

Violet smiled, entirely delighted. She applauded with everyone else in town as Mr. Deavers handed Stoney a blue ribbon.

"Hmmm," she mumbled aloud.

"What is it?" Maya asked.

"How can a man who shoots like that shoot at a trespasser and miss?"

"Maybe he don't see too good in the dark," Maya giggled.

"Oh, Stoney! That was wonderful!" Layla Asbury chimed, taking Stoney's arm.

"Thank you," he replied.

Instantly, Violet's temper was pricked. She thought of the way Stoney had kissed her the day before—thought of the way he hadn't kissed Layla when she'd wanted him to. She wished she could just run up to him, throw her arms around his neck, and kiss him square on the mouth in front of Layla and everyone else in Rattler Rock. Still, though she'd shared the most impassioned kisses she could ever have dreamt with Stoney Wrenn, kisses were all they shared—kisses and a connection to the past. She had no claim on him, and he'd made no claim on her.

Violet tried to remember everything Jimmy Ritter had said to her. She tried to imagine that the young man had been right—that Stoney truly cared for her and she could win him. Still, as she watched Layla shamelessly flirting with Stoney, her stomach churned.

"Layla thinks that tomorrow, when Stoney comes for supper, that he's gonna ask Daddy if he can come courtin' her . . . officially," Maya whispered.

Violet didn't respond. Her stomach was too wound into knots for her to speak.

"Do you think Stoney Wrenn has ever kissed Layla?" Maya asked.

"What?" Violet gasped.

Maya smiled, and Violet noted a certain mischief in her eyes.

"I don't think he has," Maya whispered. "But I bet he's kissed you. Hasn't he?"

"Wh-whyever would you think something like that, Maya?" Violet stammered.

"Well, for one thing, yer as red as a beet right now," Maya giggled. "And for another thing . . . well . . . I want to ask ya somethin' . . . about Jimmy . . . about me and Jimmy."

Violet glanced around, wondering if anyone

had been standing close enough to her and Maya to have heard their conversation. No one seemed to wear an aghast expression of surprise or disapproval, however. Her heart was madly pounding, both from fear of being overheard and from the memories of Stoney's kiss.

"I want to know if ya think I should let Jimmy kiss me if he tries," Maya whispered. "I mean, I want him to . . . but I know Layla wouldn't approve and—"

"Layla?" Violet exclaimed in a whisper. "You're worried about what Layla would think?"

Violet couldn't believe Maya was worried about what her sister would think. Layla? The same Layla that had fairly offered herself to Stoney Wrenn the day before?

"Layla's the last person on the face of the earth that you should worry about," Violet said. She glanced to where Layla stood talking to Stoney, still holding to his arm. Why couldn't she just walk up and take his arm? After all, didn't she have as much right to touch him as Layla did?

"Shh!" Maya scolded. She took Violet by one arm and pulled her farther away from the center of the crowd. "She'll hear you!"

"I'm sorry, Maya," Violet began. "It's just that . . . and I don't even know if you should be asking me. I'm not sure I should give you my opinion. It might not be what your parents would—"

"What would you do if you were me, Violet?" Maya asked. "If you loved Jimmy so much it hurt, and he wanted to kiss you, what would you do? Tell me the truth."

Violet looked at Maya—looked past the fact she was sixteen and her pupil. In those moments, she saw only her good friend—a kindred spirit and sister in the world of loving a man so much it was painful.

"Of course you should let him kiss you," she answered in a whisper. "And you should kiss him back. Don't leave yourself open for a life-long, very painful regret . . . just because you're worried about what Layla might think."

Maya smiled. "That's what I was thinkin'," she said. "I only just needed you to—"

"Come on," Stoney Wrenn said, taking hold of Violet's arm from behind. "The footrace is startin' in a few minutes . . . and I got money bet on you."

"What?" Violet asked, looking up to Stoney as he rather pushed her along. Layla was at his other side, hurrying to keep up.

"I think my Stoney has lost his sense," she said. "He's bet fifty dollars on you to win this silly race, Miss Fynne!"

"What?" Violet gasped. "Have you gone mad?"

Maya caught up to them. "Don't worry, Layla," she said. "If Mr. Wrenn thinks Miss Fynne can win the race, then I'm sure she can."

"Fifty dollars?" Violet asked Stoney. "What were you thinking?"

"I was thinking that Tony Asbury is too big for his britches," he grumbled.

"My daddy says you shouldn't even be runnin' in the race, Miss Fynne," Layla explained. "He says it ain't proper . . . and that no woman can run as fast as a boy anyway."

Violet stopped, yanked her arm from Stoney's grasp, and glared at Layla Asbury. "Is that so?" she nearly growled. She looked up to Stoney— saw the grin spreading across his face, the daring twinkle in his eyes.

"Yes, it is," Layla said. "And I must say, Miss Fynne . . . I agree with him entirely."

"Do you?" Violet asked, seething with indignation.

"Oh, she's mad now," Stoney chuckled.

"You get out of my way, Miss Layla Asbury," Violet said. "And tell your daddy he may as well hand Stoney that fifty dollars right now."

"I'll wait for ya at the finish line," Stoney chuckled.

"You do that, Stoney Wrenn," Violet said as she leaned over to pull the back of her skirt forward—upward to tuck it in at her waist. "And be ready to make good on what you promised me."

"What did you promise her?" Layla asked. "What is she talkin' about, Stoney?"

Violet stepped up to Layla. Placing her hands on her hips and staring Layla Asbury right in the eye, she said, "Never you mind. You just run along and tell your daddy to get his money ready."

She stormed off then, toward the place where everyone was lining up for the race. She ignored the gasps of several women as she passed by with her skirt hitched and her ankles showing.

*Let them think what they want,* she thought. "Let them think that Stoney Wrenn's a womanizing son of a gun and that I'd be better off working as a saloon girl than teaching at the schoolhouse," she mumbled.

Violet was angry. The fact was she couldn't remember the last time she was so angry. She loathed Layla Asbury—loathed her for too many reasons to count! She wondered how it could be that Maya could be Layla's sister—how two people from the same family could be so opposite.

"You sure you want to do this, Miss Fynne?" Mr. Deavers asked as Violet took a place next to Hagen Webster.

"There are four other girls in this race, Mr. Deavers, aren't there?" she asked.

"Well, yes . . . but . . ." he stammered.

"I'll be fine," she said, forcing a smile and patting his arm with reassurance.

"All right," he said. He walked to the starting line, shaking his head with uncertainty.

"Yer a real fun teacher, Miss Fynne," Hagen Webster said. He chuckled as he studied her from head to toe. "We ain't never had a teacher like you before."

"Why, thank you, Hagen," Violet said. She let her smile broaden and leaned toward him. "How would you like to make a little wager with me?" she asked.

"You mean like a bet on who wins?" he asked. She could see the confidence, the pure vanity in his eyes.

"Exactly," she said.

"Name it!" he exclaimed.

Violet studied him for a moment. He was a cocky, conceited little cuss. She'd never liked him much.

"If you win, you don't have to take your turn cleaning the outhouse at the school for the rest of the year. I'll do it whenever your day comes around," she said. Hagen's smile broadened, and his eyes lit up like stars in a night sky. "But if I win," she continued, "then you quit treating girls like they're just something for you play with. You consider their feelings and tender hearts. You only kiss a girl when you truly, truly care for her. What do you say?"

Hagen's smile vanished. He looked like a child caught stealing candy from Mr. Deavers's store.

"Well?" she prodded.

"I don't know what yer talkin' about, Miss Fynne," he mumbled.

"Of course you do, Hagen," she said. "I'm talking about all the girls you've coaxed into sparking with you out by the old Chisolm place. Do we have an agreement?"

He frowned—nodded—but frowned.

"Good," Violet said.

"Hey there, Miss Fynne," Jimmy Ritter said, taking his place on the other side of Violet.

Violet smiled. "Hello, Jimmy."

"Mind if I give a go at tryin' to outrun ya?" he asked.

"Not at all," she giggled.

"Stoney says I won't. He says nobody will. But I ain't opposed to second place," Jimmy chuckled.

Violet smiled at the boy and made certain her skirt was tucked tight into its waistband at her stomach as Mr. Deavers raised his pistol and said, "Ready . . . set . . ."

A gunshot pierced the air, and Violet was off. She'd worn her old boots, the ones that were so worn they were nearly flat-soled. She'd also worn her muslin petticoat and lightest skirt. She heard the crowd hollering and cheering—could hear the other runners behind her—close behind her. She was out front, but barely.

All at once she saw him—Stoney—there on the

other side of the finish ribbon. She saw him put his hands to his mouth—heard his voice, distinct among all the others—heard him shouting, "Come on, Viola! Come on!" Her heart began to pound furiously, and she didn't know whether it pounded for the exertion of running or from the sight of Stoney Wrenn waiting for her at the finish.

Out of the corner of her left eye, she saw Hagen Webster. He was fast and matching her stride. Jimmy Ritter was to her right, also matching her stride. She couldn't lose the race! She wouldn't! With every ounce of determination and strength left in her, she forced herself to run faster. Her feet felt sure, and she was amazed at how little her clothing restricted her. She thought of what a sight she must look to the spectators—the prim little schoolteacher in her lacy shirtwaist and skirt, matching strides with the young men and children in the race.

She saw Stoney smile and begin to laugh. She kept staring at him, as if he were the prize for the winner of the race. He took off his hat, whipping it around over his head as she drew nearer. She could still hear Hagen and Jimmy—hear their mad pace. Yet she could no longer see either of them from the corners of her eyes.

"Come on, darlin'! You whip that little cuss!" she heard Stoney holler.

Her lungs were burning with exertion, and her

legs were beginning to feel weak, but she didn't slow her pace. She saw Stoney still standing on the other side of the finish ribbon. She smiled, knowing that if he didn't move and she managed to cross the finish line first, she'd run smack into him. This realization only spurred her on, and Violet pushed herself—ran harder than she could ever remember running.

"You got 'em! You got 'em!" Stoney shouted.

In the next moment, Violet felt the finish ribbon across her chest. Her momentum made it impossible for her to stop short, and she plowed into Stoney Wrenn, knocking him to the ground and tumbling down with him. He didn't pause—simply got to his feet and helped her to hers.

Instantly Violet was surrounded by a crowd of well-wishers. Everyone in Rattler Rock seemed delighted she had beaten the boys, not upset or disgusted—everyone except Mr. Asbury and his daughter Layla, who stood to one side with expressions of pure annoyance.

"Miss Fynne! Miss Fynne!" Susan Gribbs giggled. "You were so fast! I never seen nothin' like that!"

"Thank you, Susan," Violet panted.

"I never seen a woman run like that, Miss Fynne," Jimmy Ritter said, offering his hand. "Not in all my life!"

"Thank you, Jimmy," Violet said.

"Violet Fynne," Mr. Deavers chuckled as he

approached, shaking his head with disbelief. "I hereby declare you the winner of the Rattler Rock Founders' Day Picnic footrace!"

Everyone applauded and cheered as Mr. Deavers handed Violet a blue ribbon.

"Thank you," Violet said, watching as Mr. Deavers handed a red second-place ribbon to Jimmy Ritter and a white third-place ribbon to Hagen Webster. Something in her secretly delighted in the knowledge that Jimmy had beaten Hagen too.

"You cost me a bit of money," Tony Asbury said, walking up to stand next to Violet.

Violet looked to him and forced a smile. "I'm sorry, Mr. Asbury," she began. "But you wouldn't want someone teaching the children of Rattler Rock who wasn't going to teach them a lesson or two about the pitfalls of gambling, now would you?"

His face softened; he even grinned. Nodding, he handed Stoney Wrenn a handful of paper money. "I guess it ain't only the children who learned that lesson today, is it, Miss Fynne?" Mr. Asbury said. He touched the brim of his hat and turned to walk away. Layla, however, remained.

"I can't begin to tell you how improper that was, Miss Fynne," Layla said.

Violet felt her eyes narrow. Layla Asbury was going to accuse Violet of impropriety when the girl had offered herself to a man just the day before? "Well, I think we all have our moments . . . don't we, Miss Asbury?" Violet asked.

Layla's cheeks pinked, her indignation rising.

"Can I see the ribbon, Miss Fynne?" Phelps Pierson asked. "Just let me hold it for a minute . . . will ya?"

"Of course," Violet giggled, handing the ribbon to Phelps. She smiled when she looked up to see Maya holding Jimmy's red ribbon.

"I'm only second place," she heard Jimmy say.

Maya glanced to Jimmy and whispered, "Not to me."

Violet smiled and looked to Stoney as he shook his head and rolled his eyes.

"Hey, Rattler Rock!" Sam Capshaw hollered. Everyone looked to where Sam stood next to his mother near the long table laden with food. "Let's eat!"

As everyone began to move toward the food tables, Stoney caught hold of Violet's arm, staying her. "I knew you could whip that little son of a . . . gun," he said when she turned to face him.

"Well, I'm glad you were so certain," Violet sighed. "I still can't believe you talked me into it." She looked down to the blue ribbon Phelps had handed back to her before running off.

She pulled the hem of her skirt from her waistband and wiggled a little to help it fall back in place.

• • •

Stoney smiled; he couldn't help but smile. He figured he'd smiled more in the past two weeks than he had in ten years. He watched Violet smooth the loose strands of hair back from her face—watched her tug at her sleeves to straighten them. He thought of her temper, the way Layla Asbury had fanned Violet's normally dormant indignation. He knew it had helped her to win— the fact he'd bet money on her, the fact Layla had chewed on her a little.

He'd spent most of the night scolding himself for kissing her the way he had the day before. He'd lost his reason out there under that old cottonwood. If Violet Fynne needed anything to prove Stoney was the womanizer everyone thought he was, he figured she had it in her pocket now. Still, he hoped she understood he didn't kiss every girl the way he'd kissed her— hoped she somehow understood he didn't kiss every girl anyhow.

Truth was he was barrelful of confusion, desire, and fear. Oh, he couldn't let on, of course— couldn't let Violet know she could lead him like a lovesick puppy. After all, she'd been away for ten years—been a kid when she left. Kids didn't know what love was, and she'd only been back for two weeks. Fact was, Stoney was wondering if he actually was becoming the womanizer folks named him to be. Still, he thought being a womanizer meant a fellow had a herd of women he wanted to hold, kiss, and keep—not just one.

"Well?" Stoney asked.

"Well, what?" Violet asked in return. Everyone was over near the food tables now—everyone but her and Stoney.

"I made ya a promise," he began, "and I figure now's as good a time as any to make good on it."

"You're really going to let me go inside?" Violet asked in an excited whisper.

"I promised, didn't I?"

"Right now?"

Stoney glanced to where everyone in town was gathered at the food tables.

"I figure, with everybody else so busy eatin' and enjoyin' themselves, won't nobody be around to see me playin' favorites and lettin' you in Bud's old place," he said.

"Then let's go!" Violet exclaimed, taking Stoney's hand. "We can go the back way—cut through the north pasture. It's faster than going all the way around. Remember?"

Stoney chuckled. "Of course."

Violet couldn't believe she was finally going to step foot in the old haunted house—in the old Chisolm place. Ever since she'd first seen the light of the lovers' moon, she'd wanted to see inside. Ever since Buddy Chisolm himself told her the story of the rich man from New York City, she'd dreamt of crossing the threshold—of breathing the air of the past inside.

"I guess you really wanted to see in that old house," Stoney said as they walked. He shook his head and chuckled. "You shoulda seen the look on that Webster boy's face. I feared for a minute he might drop dead of the shock."

Violet giggled. "I wish I could've seen him too . . . though I'm wicked for feeling that way."

"No, yer not," Stoney said. "He had it comin'."

"You're very chivalrous, you know, Stoney Wrenn," Violet said. "Wanting to see Hagen Webster humbled because he's a little woman-izer."

"I ain't so chivalrous as you think, Viola," he said.

"Why not?" she asked. The grass was high and tickled her arms as she walked beside Stoney.

"'Cause I shoulda run the race myself—whipped up on the little rat myself—instead of sendin' you to do it."

"You sent me because you knew it wouldn't look so competitive then. You knew if you would have raced him, it would have just seemed like you were just wanting another blue ribbon. Hagen wouldn't have gotten the message the way he did when I raced him."

He smiled at her, and she knew she was right in her assumption of his reasoning.

"And besides," she began, "you might not have been able to beat him."

"What?" Stoney said, stopping dead in his tracks. "Are you sayin' I couldn't have beat that little bas . . . son of a gun?"

Violet shrugged. She'd always enjoyed teasing him to get his dander up. It was another thing between them that hadn't changed in ten years. "What do you think?" she teased.

"I think I could whip you right now," he said. He looked across the pasture. "I think I can beat you to the crick. From here to the crick. Winner gets yer pretty new blue ribbon."

"All right," Violet said. Giggling, she exclaimed, "Go!"

"What?" she heard him ask as she took out running across the pasture. She laughed, somehow liberated by the sense of the breeze in her hair as she ran, the dirt beneath her feet, the scent of summer. She knew full well that Stoney Wrenn couldn't beat her—not with the pure mass he'd added to his form and stature over the past decade. Certainly she knew she wasn't as fast without having her skirt hitched up, but she was still small and quick compared with Stoney.

She could see the old creek moving closer. Violet leapt over a small pile of rocks and giggled as the tall grass tickled her legs. There it was, just ahead—the creek, hers and Stoney's, the one they'd played in, fished in. For an instant, she thought perhaps she'd leapt the pile of rocks and landed in the past, for little looked or felt different.

Violet gasped as she felt his hand at her back—felt him fist the fabric of her shirtwaist in one strong hand and pull. Her feet flew out from under her as his arm encircled her waist from behind.

"Gotcha!" he said a moment before Violet found herself whirling through the air. Though Stoney softened her fall by placing his body between hers and the ground, the force of their landing still drove the air from her lungs. Violet gasped for breath as Stoney pushed her body from his and lay on his back panting for his own breath.

"I . . . I can't believe . . . I can't believe you caught me," Violet panted when she could breathe once more. "You're as big as an ox! You can't be faster than me."

Stoney smiled, coughed, and chuckled. Sitting up, he said, "But I've got longer legs now. What you still got in speed, I make up in stride."

Violet giggled and placed a hand over her bosom as she gazed up at the billowy clouds overhead. "I'm not as young as I used to be, that's for sure. And besides . . . I already ran one race today." She panted, "I feel like I'll never catch my breath."

Violet Fynne made a profound mistake then:

241

she glanced over to Stoney Wrenn. Her heart leapt at the expression on his handsome face! He'd lost his hat in their race. Resting one elbow on one knee, he raked strong fingers through his tousled hair. He smiled at her, and for just a moment—for just a breath—Violet could see the boy she once knew. As his opaline eyes shone with delight, she could see the boy yet lingering in him.

"I thought you were gonna get away from me there for a minute," he said, still smiling at her.

"I almost did," she said, still staring at him. He was so attractive—alluringly so!

He chuckled again. "This is the first time I ever beat you, ain't it?" he asked. "When we were kids, I only won when ya let me . . . didn't I?"

"Maybe," Violet giggled.

"Why did ya let me win sometimes?" he asked. A slight frown puckered his brow, though his smile remained. "Just to make me feel better, I suppose."

Violet shrugged. "Maybe." She smiled at him and added, "Or maybe I just liked for you to catch me."

His frown softened, as did his smile. His fascinating eyes narrowed as he looked at her. Violet knew he wasn't certain whether to believe her. She sat up, placing her hands behind her and leaning back.

"I know that look," she giggled. "You're not sure if I'm teasing or not."

"I think yer teasin'," he mumbled.

Violet leaned toward him and whispered, "Well, I'm not."

Her heart fluttered when he reached out and caught her face in one hand. Her mouth watered as his gaze lingered on her lips. His grip tightened; his thumb traveled slowly over her lower lip. He was considering kissing her—she knew he was—and her heart began to hammer brutally within her bosom at the thought.

"Go ahead," she whispered, gazing into the alluring quality of his eyes. "I want you to."

He winced, as if something had suddenly caused him pain. Yet Violet sighed—closed her eyes as he leaned forward, pressing a soft kiss to her mouth. His hand slid from her cheek to the back of her neck as he kissed her again. Another kiss—this time his lips were parted, coaxing her to meet him in a moist and warmer exchange.

It happened then—the same thing that had happened the day before under the cottonwood tree. Passion erupted like dynamite going off! All at once her mouth burned, flooded with moisture as Stoney forged a kiss of such heated bliss as to render her arms and legs entirely numb. Driven and insistent, moist and savory, Stoney Wrenn's mouth owned hers—bewitched her entire being.

As before, his kiss demanded response—set a fire to blazing within her! Violet trembled as the flavor of his mouth bathed her in pleasure. She marveled at how naturally she met his instruction—at how it seemed she had been made to kiss him, as if their mouths were meant to fit together, to blend in flawless union.

She was dizzied by his kiss—breathless—and she reached out, placing a hand to his chest to steady herself. Instantly he gasped, breaking the seal of their mouths and pulling back from her. His hand left her neck, and he ran trembling fingers through his hair.

"I lost my damn hat," he grumbled. He nearly leapt to his feet, inhaled deeply, and, without looking back to Violet, offered her his hand as assistance.

Violet accepted his help, but he dropped her hand as soon as she was standing. She wanted to throw herself against him, feel his arms around her, beg his forgiveness in abandoning him so many years before. She wanted to soothe his worries, smooth the frown from his brow, taste the flavor of his mouth every minute. She wanted to gaze into his eyes forever—weave her fingers through his soft, brown hair—lay warm in his bed at night—awake in his arms each morning. She wanted to love him!

"We better get on with it if ya wanna look around before the sun starts settin'," he said.

"All right," Violet said, brushing the grass off the seat of her skirt. She was confused—couldn't figure why he'd broken from her so instantly. Surely it couldn't have been because she touched him. Yet she wondered if it was. She thought of the other times he'd kissed her—the way he'd held her face in his hand, as if intentionally directing his attention to only her mouth. Even yesterday under the cottonwood, he'd trapped her by sitting firmly on her legs and holding her wrists. It was as if he was making certain she couldn't touch him in response. Why didn't he want her to touch him?

"There's somethin' else, Viola," he said as he picked up his hat and placed it back on his head. Violet felt the hair on the back of her neck prickle. "There's somethin' else I need to tell you . . . a truth I've been keepin' from ya since ya come back."

Violet felt tears well in her eyes. Her heart began to hammer brutally within her bosom. "Wh-what is it?" she asked.

He looked at her, his beautiful eyes filled with guilt and some deep sort of sorrow. "I'll tell ya when we're there . . . when I'm sure I'm ready," he said.

She felt ill, as if she might vomit. What did he mean to tell her? Was he truly in love with Layla Asbury? Is that why he had refused the raven-haired beauty when she'd offered herself to him under the old cottonwood—because he loved and respected her? Was he truly a womanizer, quenching his thirst for passion with Violet because he couldn't yet quench it with the woman he loved?

"You still comin'?" he asked as he started down the creekbed toward the old Chisolm place.

"Y-yes," she stammered. She would follow him—no matter where he led her, no matter what heartache waited for her at Buddy Chisolm's old place.

# CHAPTER TEN

The old Chisolm place never appeared quite as ominous in the light of day. Even as a child, Violet had always thought the old house looked lonesome and harmless when the sun was shining. As she stood before it now—gazing at the white columns, the empty windows, the long porch where perhaps folks once sat sipping buttermilk and listening to the cicada song—she thought it looked more sad than frightening.

"It's not nearly as menacing in the sunshine as it is at midnight during a full moon," Violet mumbled.

"Nope," Stoney said. He pulled an iron key from his pocket and slid it into the keyhole of the looming door before him.

Violet tried to swallow, but her mouth was so dry. She trembled—not from fear of the house or the ghosts who might be lurking within but from the knowledge Stoney Wrenn had something to tell her, something she feared would break her heart. She couldn't wait! She had to know. What was the "truth" he'd kept from her?

"How many others have you let inside the house since Mr. Chisolm left it to you?" she asked. She thought, *Have you taken Layla inside?*

"Just one other person," he said. "That's what I want to talk to you about."

Violet swallowed the lump in her throat and choked back the tears gathering in her eyes. She watched as Stoney turned the massive door's latch, pushed the door of the old Chisolm house open, and motioned that she should step over the threshold before him.

She gulped as goose bumps sprouted over her arms, as the hair at the back of her neck stood near on end. Cautiously she stepped into the house—stepped into the old Chisolm house, the place that had so captivated her imagination for as long as she could remember.

The air was heavy and old. Violet shivered as the scent of age filled her lungs. Yet it did not smell bad—just closed up, as if the house had not breathed fresh air for a long, long time. She startled as the door closed behind her.

"Wait!" she said, whirling around to face Stoney. "I'm a bigger coward than I thought," she whispered. "I don't know if I can—"

She heard it then—a low murmur, a quiet howl, whispering.

"Stoney!" she cried in a whisper. "I hear them! I can't stay here!"

But Stoney smiled. Reaching out, he clasped her hand in his and said, "Come with me. There's somethin' I need to show you."

"Oh, no! No, no, no!" Violet breathed. "I can't.

I don't want to see anything . . . anyone that might be dead and wandering."

"Trust me," he said. "Come on."

Violet nodded—tried to keep her legs from disobeying Stoney and running for the door.

"Come on," he said again, tugging on her hand. "Up to the attic."

"What?" Violet exclaimed. The sound of her own voice echoing through the old house startled her, and she jumped. Placing one hand at her bosom to try and settle the mad beating of her heart, she took one step with him, then another.

"Look around," Stoney said. "Ain't it somethin'?"

"Look around?" Violet breathed. "I can hardly stand, and you want me to look around?"

Yet she did glance about the room as Stoney led her toward a large staircase. There were paintings on the wall. Some were lovely landscapes; some were portraits. A large fireplace stood on one wall. On its mantle stood several small, framed photographs surrounding a line of old books. There were chairs and a sofa, lamp tables, and even a tea table set with china. A grand piano stood in one corner and in an opposing corner a desk, an inkwell, and an open ledger on its surface, as if someone had been working figures and just stepped out of the room. Drapery still adorned the windows—blue velvet draperies. Most astonishing of all was the neat condition of the room. There were no cobwebs—no dust. The house was perfectly clean, as if some sort of ghost maid had been forever going about her duties.

"It's as if—" Violet whispered.

"As if someone still lives here?" Stoney asked.

Another shiver traveled down Violet's spine, and she could not help but move closer to Stoney, wrapping her arms around one of his strong ones. He chuckled, and she said, "It's not funny, Stoney Wrenn."

"I know," he said.

They reached the foot of the staircase, and Stoney stepped onto the first stair.

"I-I don't want to go to the attic . . . do I?" she asked. She was trembling—afraid of who or what might be waiting for them at the top of the stairs.

"Come on," he said. "There's nothin' to be afraid of. I promise."

Violet swallowed, nodded, and followed, clinging to him as they ascended. The flight of stairs led to the second story, and again Violet was struck with the fine furnishings there. Yet they did not linger long, for Stoney led her to a second staircase. This set of stairs was hidden in an alcove, narrow and perhaps only ten steps high. At the top of the staircase was a small door—a closed door.

"Stoney Wrenn," she began in a whisper, "if you're thinking I'm going in there—"

"You are," he said as he began to climb the stairs.

"I can't!" she breathed, pausing. She'd heard the whispering again—the quiet mumbling. The terrifying noise was coming from beyond the little door at the top of the stairs.

"I'm here," he said. "And there's nothin' to be afraid of. I promise, Viola," he said.

Violet trembled—fairly shook as she watched Stoney's hand reach out and turn the latch.

"Stoney?" she breathed.

"Shh," he said. "Listen."

A quiet squeak of terror escaped Violet's throat as he pushed the door open. Instantly the whispering grew louder, exactly as if ghosts were sitting in the attic simply conversing among themselves.

"I can't," she whispered.

"It's only the breeze," he said as he pulled her into the room. "It's the breeze whistling through the fireplace flue and a hole in the chimney."

"What?" Violet asked, frowning.

"Come and see," he said.

Violet glanced about the attic. It was filled with trunks, old paintings, empty wooden crates, and several chairs. A bed stood in one corner, a night table with a washbasin and pitcher nearby.

Violet squealed and startled as the whispering

sound suddenly grew louder, as if someone were scolding them for intruding. "Stoney Wrenn! I'm going to die of fright!" she whispered.

Stoney chuckled. "No, you ain't. Here . . . listen." He led her to the fireplace.

Violet frowned as she drew nearer to it, for the whispering sound—the sound of mumbled voices echoing through the room—grew louder. As she drew nearer and nearer to the fireplace, she realized the voices were indeed coming from the hearth.

"I can feel the breeze coming in," she whispered.

"Yep," he said. "It's only the wind . . . though there was a family of bats living in the rafters when I first moved in. They made quite a noise comin' in and out, and they were devils to get rid of."

"So . . . so that's what was making the noises all these years?" Violet asked. "The wind through the flue and bats?"

Stoney nodded. "That's what I want to tell ya, Viola," he began. "I know I shoulda told you right off. I don't even know why I didn't . . . but I shoulda." He smiled at her—chuckled a little. "There ain't no ghosts," he said. "Not two ghosts . . . not even one."

"What?" she asked. "But what about the light? This explains the noises," she said, pointing to the fireplace. "But what about the light?"

"Come back downstairs with me," he said, "and I'll tell you everything."

Violet nodded and followed Stoney. As they descended the small attic staircase to the second floor, she was surprised by the sense of disappointment her heart and mind were experiencing. How odd that she should be disappointed to learn that there were no lingering spirits haunting the old Chisolm place.

Stoney led her to a large bedroom. She gasped as she entered, awed by the beautiful high-posted bed, the richly varnished floors, the intricately woven rugs that embellished them. There was a lovely chest of drawers, and again Violet noticed the framed photographs adorning its dustless surface.

"This was their room," Stoney said. "This is where they slept . . . together."

"Who?" Violet asked.

"The rich young man from New York and the wife he loved so much—the pretty girl from Rattler Rock."

Violet again felt goose bumps racing over her limbs. She glanced around the room. Her heart knew an odd sort of melancholy, for there she stood, in the very house the rich young man from New York City had built, in the very room where he'd held his pretty wife through the dark nights.

She shook her head, confused. "I don't understand," she said. "How can there be a light in the windows yet no ghosts?"

"It was Buddy," he said. "The light was just Buddy's way of keepin' folks away from the house."

Violet frowned. "Buddy Chisolm? He used to come out here every full moon and run around inside this house with a candle? Just so folks would think the house was haunted and stay away?"

"A small lamp," Stoney said. "The candles always blew out, so he took to using a small lamp."

Violet sighed—nodded as full understanding washed over her. "And when he passed away, you came. You wandered about in the house during a full moon . . . so the story of the light of the lovers' moon would continue to keep everyone away."

Stoney nodded. "Buddy asked me to," he said.

Violet frowned. "But . . . but I was with you . . . that night we saw the light together. You couldn't have carried the lamp."

Stoney shrugged. "It was Jimmy," he said. "When I started findin' signs of trespassin' . . . well, one of us needed to watch the outside of the house. So I had Jimmy start carryin' the light. He's the only other person I've ever let in this house . . . or told the truth to."

"Jimmy?" Violet breathed, aware of the smile

of relief and joy spreading across her face. "Jimmy . . . not Layla Asbury?"

"Layla Asbury?" Stoney exclaimed. "I wouldn't tell Layla Asbury the name of a dog I didn't like, let alone the truth about the light of the lovers' moon!" He smiled, and Violet's stomach fluttered at the sight of his handsome dimples.

"So . . . so you're not going to ask her father if you can court her when you go to the Asbury's house for supper tomorrow night?" Violet asked.

"Oh, hell no!" he grumbled, scowling. "I only give that family any attention at all 'cause I feel guilty about the whole mess with Coby Fisher, even though it wasn't my fault. I never did anything to encourage Layla Asbury to think I was gonna ask to court her—at least not when Coby was so sweet on her. I suppose . . . I suppose I ain't handled it all too well since then. I just felt so guilty I figured I better make good on whatever she had in mind. That is, I figured on doin' that 'til you came back and knocked some sense into me."

Violet smiled. "So it was Layla Asbury that had you and the sheriff swapping fists?"

Stoney nodded. "Tony Asbury's a horse's hind end . . . in case ya haven't noticed," he began, "and he was fool enough to believe Layla when she told him she thought I wanted to court her. So she tells her daddy to refuse Coby's offer, and bein' that Tony Asbury's a horse's hind end, he went on and told Coby that I was wantin' to court Layla and that Layla preferred me. Naturally, Coby blamed me instead of that ignorant girl and her father. He comes up to me after Mr. Asbury turned him down, throws a fist at my jaw, and—well, I'm sorry, Viola—but he tickled my temper, and I laid it back to him. We were both purty bloodied up." He paused, smiled, and added, "But I wiped up the street with him."

"Then you felt guilty and . . ." she prodded.

Stoney shrugged. "I did feel guilty. Folks already had me named as a womanizer. I figured if I didn't start acceptin' Mrs. Asbury's supper invitations, it would only get worse. I couldn't leave Rattler Rock, not after the promises I made to ol' Buddy." He paused and added, "And not 'til I was sure . . . not 'til I was sure . . ."

"Not 'til you were sure of what?" she asked. He was still hiding something from her; she sensed it with every thread of her being.

"Not 'til I was sure Jimmy was ready to leave . . . to set out on his own life," he said.

"So you soothed Layla by having supper with her family," Violet said.

"Yeah," he admitted. "I thought she'd get tired of me after a while and settle her affections back on Coby. But that was over six months ago, and she ain't got sick of me yet."

"I'm sure she never will," Violet said. "You're not the kind of man a girl gets over."

256

He didn't say anything—only stared at her, green-blue opaline eyes smoldering.

"So when you started suspecting trespassers, Jimmy became the guardian of the light," Violet said. She caressed one beautifully carved bedpost. It felt warm, solid, and somehow safe.

"At first I thought it was just Coby," he said. "He was angry. He knew I didn't want nobody around this house. But now I'm not so certain."

"Why not?" Violet asked. After all, it did make sense—that Coby would try to make Stoney's life difficult.

"Someone got in, the night I got bullet-grazed," he explained. "Me and Jimmy heard 'em inside the house . . . saw a light. They got into the ground floor. We scared 'em off, and whoever it was took a shot at me. But . . . but when I seen that all the cupboard doors were open in the kitchen—they'd rummaged through an old trunk in the downstairs storage room. They were lookin' for somethin', and now I think I know what they were lookin' for . . . though I can't figure how they'd come by knowin' about it."

"What?" Violet asked. "What do you think they were looking for?"

"Treasure," Stoney said. "Buddy Chisolm's treasure."

Violet's mind whirled. Treasure? Old Buddy Chisolm had treasure?

"Treasure?" she asked. "What kind of treasure?"

"Well, that's just it," Stoney said. "Buddy called it his treasure, but as far as I ever knew, I was the only one he told about it. I got to rememberin' later though—just recently, when Buddy was ailin', just before he died, he'd get in these fits of fever. Whenever he was like that, he'd start rattlin' things off, goin' on about his treasure, how I had to keep it safe. Well, I knew all about it. He'd told me about it many times 'fore he took ill. Still, if someone woulda heard him goin' on during one of his fits, they might well have come lookin' for it."

"But you were the only one who was with him," Violet said.

"That's right—except for once, once right before Buddy passed, just a day or two before he went. I come home from fixin' a fence, and Coby Fisher was in the house with Buddy. Buddy was still livin' in that same ol' shack he lived in when we were kids, and I walked in, and Coby Fisher was talkin' to him. Buddy was upset—goin' on about the past, lippin' off things he woulda never wanted to tell nobody—and Coby Fisher was listenin'."

"You think it's Sheriff Fisher out here trespassing, looking for Buddy Chisolm's treasure," she said.

"He's angry with me, jealous about Layla, even though there ain't nothin' to be jealous about. Maybe he thinks wealth would win her over. Maybe he thinks if he could find Buddy's treasure, he'd win Layla back."

"But who wants to be loved for their money?" Violet asked.

"Not me," Stoney said.

Violet looked around the room, even still amazed at how clean and perfect it looked. "You say Buddy told you where the treasure was?" Violet asked.

"More like he told me what it was—asked me to keep it safe," he said.

Violet smiled at him. "Just like the stories he used to tell to us," she said. "Remember the one about the boy who meets up with the pirate and the pirate tells him where the treasure is . . . asks him to keep it safe? In end, the boy opens the treasure chest to find only a letter—a letter telling him that the pirate's greatest treasure was his son—that the boy was his son." Violet sighed. "You're Buddy Chisolm's treasure, aren't you, Stoney? He loved you like a son, even when we were children. I remember how his eyes would light up when you'd come around."

"He did love me like a son," Stoney said. "He told me that more'n once. But as far as the treasure we're talkin' about here . . . it ain't what Coby Fisher thinks."

Violet frowned—watched Stoney as he strode to the chest of drawers and lifted one of the framed photographs. She followed him and took the photograph when he offered it to her.

"It's the rich young man from New York City," he said. "And the pretty girl from Rattler Rock."

Violet gazed at the photograph—a wedding photograph. The young woman was beautiful! Her light hair and wide eyes gave her the look of one who lived life wholeheartedly. The young man next to her was handsome—dark-haired, strong-jawed.

"He was handsome, the rich young man from New York City," Violet whispered.

"He was Buddy Chisolm," Stoney said.

"What?" Violet gasped in disbelief.

"That there's Buddy," Stoney said, pointing to the man in the photograph. "On his weddin' day—the day he married Sanora Lester, the pretty girl from Rattler Rock."

Violet looked at the photograph more closely. She could see it then, the resemblance the young man in the photograph owned to the weathered old man she'd known as a child—to Buddy Chisolm.

"He's buried right next to her, out in the old graveyard south of town," Stoney said. He chuckled. "And you and me thought we were so smart. It never once occurred to me to go readin' headstones out there."

"We roamed that graveyard for hours on end," Violet giggled. "She was there all the time?"

"Yep. 'Sanora Chisolm. Loving wife, loving

mother.' Their children are out there too. Don't know how we missed four headstones with the name Chisolm carved on them. If we were smarter, we woulda put ol' Bud's story together long before he had to tell me the truth. He musta had a real good laugh or two over our not havin' the sense of a toad."

Violet smiled. Suddenly she understood, and she gasped as the full weight of understanding washed through her mind.

"It's this house!" Violet exclaimed. "This house is Buddy Chisolm's treasure! Not because it's worth so much as money goes, but because it's where he was happiest, where he held his wife in his arms at night, watched his children play. This house is the treasure. This house is what he asked you to protect and keep safe. Isn't it?"

Stoney laughed. "You always were just as smart as ya looked, Viola Fynne," he said.

Violet laughed and spun around with delight. "Oh, I love it all the more now!" She sighed, looking around the room again. "I used to always imagine the sad, heartbroken man from New York City, the one who built this house, lost his wife and family. I used to imagine him wandering the world, weeping and moaning in despair, returning to the house with every full moon to carry the light in and out of the rooms in searching for his lost lover. It made me so sad. But not anymore," she said. "Because Buddy Chisolm—and broken as his heart must've been—he was happy when we knew him. Wasn't he? He wasn't dead and wandering the house in misery. He was alive, and we used to make him laugh like I've never seen anybody else laugh in my life. The rich young man from New York City who built this house—Buddy Chisolm. I can't believe it."

Violet gasped as another thought came to her. "How do you find the time, Stoney?" she asked. "There's not a speck of dust anywhere in this house! And with only you and Jimmy to care for it—"

"Well, yer here now, ain't ya?" he chuckled. "I figure you can pitch in. And I'll admit it's a job. It only looks so good right now 'cause I had Jimmy spend the whole of yesterday gettin' it ready for you to visit."

Violet giggled and took hold of Stoney's hand. "May I be the light sometimes?" she asked. "Oh, please say I can, Stoney! On the next full moon, may I come with you to carry the lamp through the house? I want to carry the light of the lovers' moon. Please, Stoney!"

Stoney laughed, charmed by the excitement on Violet's pretty face. In that moment, she reminded him so much of the little girl he'd once known that he felt he could almost touch the past—almost feel the joy he'd known in her company before her father had taken her away.

Still, the joy he'd begun to know since her return—he knew if she would just stay with him, if she'd promise never to leave again, he'd know more happiness than he could ever before have imagined.

Yet he doubted himself—of course he did. She seemed so glad to be in his company—seemed to enjoy kissing him as much as he bathed in the wonder of kissing her. He could imagine then—as he had many times before—imagine the pain Buddy had endured at losing his wife. Stoney mused he would die himself if anything ever happened to Violet. He loved her—and if he wanted to keep her, it was time for him to trust her once more. After all, she had promised to return to him, and she had. She'd kept the promise she'd made as a young girl. Even though it had taken her ten years to find a way to return, she had returned—and he was beginning to believe she loved him enough to stay.

"Of course you can carry the light, Viola," he said. "When did I ever refuse you anything?"

"You didn't let me poke the stick into the dead cow over in the pasture that time," she giggled.

"That's 'cause I didn't want you to get sprayed with guts," he said. "You know that."

"But you will let me carry the light?" she asked.

He smiled, and Violet's body trembled with

delight at the smoldering mischief in his eyes, at the dimples in his strong cheeks.

"On one condition," he said, moving closer to her.

"What condition?" she asked.

"That you come on back to my house with me and . . ." He paused, taking her chin in one hand as his head descended toward hers.

"Come back to your house with you . . . and . . . and what?" Violet breathed. Her mouth was watering for want of his kiss, her body aching to be held in his arms.

"Come back to my house with me . . . come with me into my bedroom and let me . . ." he mumbled.

Violet was breathless! What was he implying? Surely not what her mind was imagining.

"Come into my bedroom and let me . . ." he repeated as Violet began to tremble, "get the letter out of my chest of drawers that Buddy Chisolm left for you."

"What?" Violet exclaimed, shoving his chest hard. "You are a scoundrel, Stoney Wrenn!" she scolded as he released her chin and began to laugh. "A scoundrel! I thought you meant to . . . to . . ."

"Are you gonna stand there hollerin' at me, or do you wanna know what Buddy Chisolm had to tell you just before he died?" he asked, still smiling, still chuckling.

"To tell me?" she whispered. "H-he had something to tell me before he died? He wrote a letter to me?"

"Yes," Stoney said. "The last thing Buddy said to me was, 'When Violet Fynne comes back to ya, boy, you give her this here letter. Tell her to read it to you where and when I say.' Then he told me he loved me like a son, that some big lawyer from Texas would be comin' to talk to me, and he passed."

"He left me a letter?" Violet asked, still stunned by Stoney's revelation. "He knew I'd come back to you?"

"He did," Stoney said. "Sometimes . . . sometimes I stopped hopin', thought there was no way you coulda remembered me all these years. I was too afraid to come lookin' for you, afraid I'd find you all settled in nice and snug up there in Albany. So I stayed here . . . hopin'. Ol' Buddy, he kept tellin' me you'd come back, and somehow I kept believin' it. It's why I never left Rattler Rock again, no matter what folks said about me, no matter what went on. You promised me you'd come back. And you did."

He reached out, brushing a strand of hair from her face.

"I missed you so much, Stoney Wrenn," she whispered. Violet reached out, pulling his hat from his head with one hand, running the fingers of her other hand through the soft brown of his hair. "I've loved you for as long as I can remember."

She was in his arms at once, pulled tight against his powerful body as his mouth crushed to hers. He was holding her at last! At last, she knew the bliss of being in his arms—the pure rapture of knowing his touch.

How lovingly and thoroughly he kissed her! She could not satisfy her thirst for his kiss. She marveled at the blissful sense of his mouth coaxing her own to a perfect melding. She would never stop kissing him. She couldn't! How could she possibly stop? Every thread of her mind and body—heart and soul—every grain of her being wanted nothing more than to stay in his arms forever, know the flavor of his demanding kiss. As her mouth mingled with his in shared passionate affection, she knew she could know no greater pleasure than the moist, heated flavor of his kiss.

Violet sighed—let her hands travel over Stoney's shoulders to the back of his neck—upward—weaving her fingers through the softness of his hair once more. Oh, how she loved him! With every shred of her soul, every thread of her being, she loved him.

Slowly he broke the seal of their mouths. He placed his cheek against hers—whispered, "I love you, Viola. Promise me you'll stay with me."

Violet kissed his neck, smiled, and said, "Promise me you won't ask Mr. Asbury if you can court his daughter tomorrow at supper."

He chuckled as he stared down at her. Violet felt goose bumps rippling over her body as she stared into the fiery green-blue opalescence of his gaze.

"Come on back to my house with me," he mumbled, cupping her chin in one hand. "We'll go in my bedroom . . ." He smiled a mischievous, playful smile. "And I'll have my way with you." He tipped his head to one side, frowned slightly, and said, "Or we can just get the letter out of the drawer where I've kept it all this time . . . along with my underwear."

"I'm glad you kept it in such a safe place," she giggled, caressing his cheek with the back of her fingers. He took hold of her hand, pressing her palm to his lips.

"Come on," he said. He ended their embrace yet held her hand as he led her out of the room. "I've been waitin' four years to see what ol' Buddy might have to say to you."

"If I were you, I'd be hoping you'd have to wait ten years to see what Layla Asbury might have to say to you," Violet teased.

Violet swallowed the lump in her throat—brushed a tear from her cheek.

"Don't worry, Viola," Stoney said. "I'm sure it

says somethin' real sweet. He thought you were about the best thing since them butterscotch candies he used carry around."

Violet smiled and held her hand out to Stoney.

He cleared his throat, reached into his pocket, and handed her a piece of butterscotch. Removing the paper the candy was wrapped in, she popped the confection into her mouth and considered the envelope in her hand.

*Violet Fynne* was written on the envelope in just about the worst penmanship she had ever seen. Drawing a courageous breath, Violet opened the envelope. Inside was not just a letter but a letter sealed within another envelope.

"To Violet Fynne," Violet read aloud. "This is Bud. I wrote this letter for nobody but you. So take it and Stoney to the old place. There's a room there that I like . . . it's my favorite. Stoney knows which one. Open this letter in my favorite room just before sunset."

"I don't understand," Violet mumbled.

She looked to see a deep frown furrowing Stoney's brow.

"He's up to somethin'," he said.

"Maybe he just wanted to make sure you let me see inside the house," Violet said. "He knew how badly I wanted to see inside."

"Maybe," Stoney said. He glanced up. "We got about an hour before sunset," he said. "I say we go back today. I want to know what that ol' coot wrote to you. It's been eatin' at me for years!"

Violet smiled and laughed.

"What's got you so tickled?"

Violet wrapped her arms around one of Stoney's strong ones. "I was just wondering if Layla Asbury has noticed that you're missing from the picnic."

"I wonder if she's noticed *yer* missing," he chuckled, drawing a moist, heated kiss from her lips as they walked.

The sun hung low in the sky as Violet climbed the front porch steps of the old Chisolm place with Stoney. She felt a little melancholy, a little disappointed in that moment to think that the old house was just an old house—that no ghostly lovers truly roamed about in it by the light of the full moon.

"I love Mr. Chisolm more than I ever did," Violet said as Stoney drew the iron key from his pocket and pushed it into the keyhole.

"Why?" he asked.

"Because of his treasure . . . of what it truly was."

"And just what might that be, Miss Fynne?"

Violet gasped as she turned to find herself facing the long barrel of a rifle. In truth, the rifle was leveled at Stoney, yet it may as well have been leveled at her own heart.

Tears sprang to Violet's eyes as she stared into the face of the man holding the gun.

"Well," Stoney began, "I guess I owe Coby Fisher an apology."

"I guess you do," Mr. Deavers said. "As much as I owe him my thanks on lettin' me in on ol' Bud Chisolm's secret."

# CHAPTER ELEVEN

"Now, Alex," Stoney began, "you don't need that rifle. Buddy Chisolm didn't really own any treasure."

Violet stood motionless—paralyzed by fear and by the shock of understanding it was Mr. Deavers who had been trespassing on Stoney's property.

Slowly Stoney stepped in front of Violet as Mr. Deavers said, "You just want it for yerself, Stoney, and I understand that. But my business ain't been too good, and since my wife passed—well, the Widow Wilson would sure rather keep company with a rich man than a poor one."

"There's no treasure, Alex," Stoney said. "I mean it. It's just the memories kept in this old house that Buddy held dear."

"Yer lyin', Stoney," Mr. Deavers said. "Coby Fisher told me different."

"Alex," Stoney argued, "I promise I ain't—"

"Remember that day in town, 'bout six months back?" Mr. Deavers interrupted. "Actually, it was night—the night Tony Asbury told ol' Coby he couldn't date that prissy little Layla of his. Tony, bein' the idiot that he is, he told Coby he and Layla was expectin' ol' Stoney Wrenn to come courtin'. He told Coby Layla preferred you to him. You remember that night, don't you?"

"Yes," Stoney said, "I do remember it, but—"

"Well, Coby was mad as an old rabid badger, and he come after you. Remember?"

Violet swallowed and moved closer to Stoney, taking hold of his arm.

"Stay behind me, Viola," Stoney said, pulling his arm from her grasp and gently pushing her to his back again.

"You and Coby, you went around a bit," Mr. Deavers said, "throwing fists and knees and what have you. The whole town saw it all. Still, it didn't take long for you to beat poor Coby down, now did it?"

"Alex, I—" Stoney began.

"Anyhow, ol' Coby, he headed straight for the saloon," Mr. Deavers said. "Of course, you probably knew that. Everyone in Rattler Rock knew he was in there drinkin'. What they didn't know was it was well past midnight 'fore he quit pourin' liquor down his gullet."

Violet held her breath as Stoney took a step toward Mr. Deavers.

Mr. Deavers shook his head, stared down the barrel of the rifle to take better aim, and said, "Hold on there, Stoney. I'm explainin' things to you."

"All right, Alex. All right," Stoney said.

"So there I was, workin' late in the store, when I heard somebody come stumblin' down the boardwalk," Mr. Deavers continued. "I looked out, and there was a beaten, bloodied Sheriff Coby Fisher, drunk as a happy huntin' hound and staggerin' off toward the jailhouse."

Violet was frightened. Tears were streaming down her face as she stared at the rifle Mr. Deavers had leveled at Stoney. What if he accidentally pulled the trigger? Alex Deavers didn't seem the sort to be too handy with a gun. What if he shot Stoney, accidentally or on purpose?

"Now you stop that weepin', Violet," Mr. Deavers said, glancing to Violet for a moment. "Everything will be just fine."

"Coby was mad at me about Layla?" Stoney asked, drawing Mr. Deavers's attention back to himself and away from Violet. "He was angry, so he told you about Buddy's treasure? All this time I thought it was Coby tryin' find it."

Alex shook his head. "Naw. He's a good boy, that Coby. He was just drunk and humiliated that night—and, yes, angry too. He told me he'd been with ol' Buddy shortly before he died, that ol' Bud had told him he had treasure hid out at this old place. Coby said he had half a mind to come out and burn the place to the ground. He said burnin' it would save himself a heap of trouble too. Said folks wouldn't be out here roamin' around lookin' for the light of the lovers' moon if there weren't no house for them damn ghosts to haunt."

"Believe me, Alex," Stoney began, "there really ain't no treasure out here. I suppose the house itself is worth something, and the furniture and all, but there really ain't no treasure."

Alex Deavers's eyes narrowed. He studied Stoney and looked to Violet.

"If there's no treasure, then why do you guard this ol' place like yer keepin' watch over a gold mine, Stoney?" he asked.

"Ol' Bud asked me to, Alex," Stoney explained. "It was Bud Chisolm who had this house built, lived in it with his wife and family 'til they died of the consumption right after the war. He made me promise I wouldn't let nobody harm it or disrespect his memories. I swear it. Now . . . put that gun down. You can blow a hole right through me if ya want, but I don't want ya missin' and hurtin' Violet."

"It's true, Mr. Deavers," Violet said. She brushed the tears from her cheeks. "And even if it wasn't, what in tarnation are you thinking?"

He was silent for a moment. Violet saw his eyes fill with tears. "I'm thinkin' I miss my wife, miss her company. Velma Wilson says she's already been married to one man who didn't have a dollar in his pocket. She says she won't make the same mistake twice."

"Then she isn't worth worrying over, Mr.

Deavers," Violet said. "Any woman who would put money over the love of a good man isn't worth a second look."

"I know yer lonesome, Alex," Stoney began. "Ol' Bud was lonesome too. But you've got friends . . . just like he had."

"You sure there ain't no treasure, Stoney?" Mr. Deavers asked as he lowered the rifle.

Stoney nodded. "Bud told me the house itself was his treasure—the memories of the happy life he lived here with his wife and children."

Mr. Deavers wiped a tear from the corner of his eyes. "I-I don't know what come over me," he choked. "All at once I feel like I just woke up from a bad dream. What was I thinkin'?" he said, dropping to his knees in the grass.

"You were grieving for your wife, Mr. Deavers. Lost in the pain of your grief," Violet said. Although she was still trembling from the fear of seeing a rifle pointed at Stoney—although she was furious with Mr. Deavers—suddenly she did understand where his madness had originated.

"I promise you, Alex," Stoney added. "Mrs. Velma Wilson would never have been able to fill that loneliness yer feelin' over losin' Mrs. Deavers."

"I can't believe I tried to rob ya, Stoney Wrenn," Alex mumbled, shaking his head in disbelief of his own actions.

"I can't believe you took a shot at me," Stoney said.

All at once Violet could not restrain the emotions she'd been holding in. Bursting into tears, she threw herself into Stoney's arms, clinging to him desperately.

"I was so frightened!" she whispered.

"It's all right, sugar," Stoney said, placing reassuring kisses in her hair.

"I'm a yeller-bellied coward, Stoney," Alex said. "I'll do whatever you and Coby Fisher decide I should do. But I never took a shot at you. This rifle ain't even loaded. It wasn't me that shot at you the other night, though I was here. I about dropped dead from thinkin' that whoever it was coulda shot me easy as anything."

"What?" Stoney asked.

Violet didn't want to let go of him; she wanted to stay safe in his embrace forever. Yet as she heard Alex Deavers step up onto the porch, Stoney released her to accept the rifle as Alex handed it to him.

Stoney checked the rifle.

"It ain't loaded," he said to Violet.

Violet looked to Mr. Deavers. He shrugged and said, "I noticed the two of you weren't at the picnic no more. I figured you were off somewhere together. I figured you were too all wrapped up in each other's arms somewhere private, that you'd be too distracted to be watchin' the house, Stoney."

Violet blushed. They had been wrapped up in each other's arms—she and Stoney—and it had been wonderful!

"I've seen Jimmy Ritter out here at night with ya, but he was at the picnic—him and that little Asbury girl makin' eyes at one another. I figured it was as good a time as any to come lookin' for Buddy Chisolm's treasure. I just brung the rifle in case I needed to look like I could shoot somebody . . . though I've always known I never could."

"But somebody took a shot at me last week. I got the graze on my shoulder to prove it," Stoney said.

Violet began to tremble. If it wasn't Mr. Deavers who shot at Stoney, then who did? Was he in danger still?

"I'm afraid that was me," Coby Fisher said, stepping out from behind a nearby cottonwood. "I was out here keepin' watch that night. Stoney had been naggin' me like an old woman," he said, smiling. He looked at Mr. Deavers and explained, "I seen you sneakin' around in the dark. Couldn't make out who you was, just knew you was tryin' to get inside this ol' house. You was comin' up behind Stoney, so I took a shot at you . . . but I missed and hit Stoney."

Stoney inhaled, an attempt at calming his

temper. Violet watched as his eyes narrowed at Coby Fisher.

"You shot me?" Stoney growled. "You told Alex about Buddy's treasure? I just gotta say it, Coby. You need to work on yer sheriffin' a bit."

"Don't I know it," Coby said. Coby looked to Mr. Deavers. "I always wondered how I found my way to my bed in the jailhouse that night, Alex," he said. "I don't even remember leavin' the saloon." He shook his head shamefully. Coby looked up at the old house. "So that's it? That's all? The treasure Buddy was talkin' about before he passed . . . was just this old house?"

"The real treasure is buried out in the graveyard with him," Stoney said. "He just didn't want anybody treatin' his memories bad."

Coby nodded and looked to Violet.

"I heard stories of a girl Stoney Wrenn used to run out with when he was a child," he said. "Buddy Chisolm said you two were purty near in each other's pockets all the livelong day. I guess that hasn't changed much."

"And it won't," Stoney said. He looked to Violet and smiled as he put an arm around her shoulders and pulled her against him.

Coby nodded—even smiled at Violet. "I knew it, that day you were talkin' to me and Stoney Wrenn waltzed up," he said to her. "You started into chokin' on that piece of butterscotch, and he whapped you on the back like he'd done it a hundred times before. Then he just put another piece of candy in your mouth without a word . . . and I knew, I knew all them stories Buddy Chisolm used to tell me about Stoney Wrenn and Violet Fynne were true . . . and that I might as well just step back." He chuckled and winked at Stoney, "I know how mean yer fists are when it's over a girl that you don't care a lick for. I wasn't about to go up against you over this one." He laughed, and Stoney chuckled. "Sorry about the bullet graze, boy," Coby added.

Stoney nodded and offered Coby a hand. "Let's call it even. I give you the beatin' of yer life, and you added to my collection of scars."

Coby laughed, accepted Stoney's hand, and shook it firmly.

"I guess I'm off to jail then," Mr. Deavers said. "I'm ready to go, Sheriff."

Stoney shook his head, and Violet wiped an empathetic tear from her cheek.

"I remember listening to ol' Bud tell me about his pain, that killin' pain he felt when he lost his wife," Stoney said. "He used to tell me he wished he woulda died along with her, that he done some right insane things just after she passed, that he was so lonely he could hardly breathe at times." He glanced at Violet; his eyes narrowed. "It was a pain I understood, a pain we shared," he said.

Violet smiled at him, letting her eyes convey her promise to never leave him again.

Stoney was quiet for a moment. Then, suddenly, he looked up, smiled, and said, "Let's just call this one even too, Alex. You just keep that butterscotch jar stocked full, and we'll just forget all about it. Nobody will ever have to know. The four of us will keep this a secret." He looked at Coby, adding, "All of this. We'll keep this whole mess to ourselves: Buddy's treasure, the drinkin', the trespassin'. Ain't that right, Sheriff?"

Coby chuckled. "Sounds good," he said.

"Alex?" Stoney asked.

"Yer . . . yer just gonna let me go, Stoney?" Mr. Deavers asked.

Stoney smiled and placed a reassuring hand on Mr. Deavers's shoulder. "You remember that time when I was, oh, about six years old?"

Mr. Deavers frowned as if struggling to remember.

"My daddy had just given me a good lickin', and I come into yer store cryin' and snifflin'. You gave me a hug, a pat on the head, and three lemon drops. 'Yer a good boy, Stoney Wrenn,' you told me. 'And you'll be a better man than yer pa—a good, kind man to be trusted and admired.' That's what you said to me, Alex. I'm guessin' you don't even remember that . . . but I do." Stoney gazed at Violet. "I got everything I want. Let's just call it good and get on with it."

He kissed her then—Stoney kissed Violet square on the mouth, right there in front of Mr.

Deavers and Sheriff Fisher. She wasn't bashful in accepting his kiss either—or in returning it. His lips were warm, his mouth so familiar.

He smiled at her, rested his chin on the top of her head, and whispered, "I love you."

"Sheriff . . . Mr. Deavers," Stoney said. "I promised Violet she could see the inside of the house again before nightfall. If you don't mind, we'll be about our business."

"Of course, Stoney," Mr. Deavers said. "Of course."

Coby Fisher winked at Violet. "Miss Fynne," he said, touching the brim of his hat. He looked to Stoney and added, "Stoney."

Stoney nodded, and Violet watched Mr. Deavers and Sheriff Fisher head off toward the road.

The sun sat very low on the horizon. Violet drew Buddy Chisolm's letter from her skirt pocket.

"Will we make it before sunset?" she asked. "I don't want to wait until tomorrow. The curiosity will drive me mad!"

Stoney chuckled, took her hand, and led her to the enormous front door of the old Chisolm place.

"What on earth would he have to say to you in there?" he said, nodding toward the letter as he led her into the house. "And why read it here? Is he plannin' on hauntin' us or something?"

281

"To Violet Fynne," Violet read aloud as she looked at the envelope once more. "This is Bud. I wrote this letter for nobody but you. So take it and Stoney to the old place. There's a room there that I like . . . it's my favorite. Stoney knows which one. Open this letter in my favorite room just before sunset."

Violet smiled at Stoney. "Which room was his favorite? He says you know."

Stoney smiled, his mesmerizing eyes burning with gladness.

"I do," he said. "It's the bedroom, his and Sanora's. He always said it was his favorite. He said they'd lie in their bed at night, gaze up at the stars, and talk about their children, the crops, just whatever they wanted to talk about."

"Well, let's hurry. The sun is beginning to set!" Violet exclaimed. Hitching up her skirt with one hand, she pulled Stoney toward the staircase. Quickly they climbed the stairs and hurried to the bedroom they'd stood in earlier in the day—the room where Stoney had told her all his secrets of the light of the lovers' moon, the room where he'd told her he loved her.

Warm light flooded the room—the soft, orange light of early sunset. Violet was astonished at how much sunlight the room captured. It glowed with a welcoming embrace somehow.

"Open it," Stoney said.

Violet nodded and tore one edge of the envelope away. She pulled out the letter, unfolded it, and began to read.

"Miss Violet Fynne," she began, "I know you'll be back for Stoney . . . 'cause I know you love Stoney Wrenn about more than anything, even if you wasn't full grown when you left Rattler Rock. I also know that the two of you was meant to be together . . . forever . . . just like me and my beloved Sanora. In knowing that, I've been wishing there was something I could leave to you . . . to you and Stoney . . . something that would forever remind you two of me, old Buddy Chisolm, who loved the two of you like you was his own children. I left my land and stock, even this old house, to Stoney. Tell him he can do whatever he wants with it after you get back to him. If he wants to he can sell it . . . or just let the varmints move in. But I'd like to see him living in it, know from my seat in heaven that this old place will be filled with love again. The choice is his, but I left something in the house for you, little Miss Violet. I left the most beautiful part of the house to you 'cause it reminds me of you, all sparkling with life and love. I left the stars for you, Violet Fynne. They belonged to my Sanora. Many were the nights me and my Sanora would lay in our bed, held warm in each other's arms, and gaze up at the stars. We'd point to one and name it for a memory we'd shared, then we'd point to another and name it for another memory. The biggest star we could see was the memory of the first moment we saw each other, the first moment we fell in love. Look for the star that shines the brightest. That's our love, mine and Sanora's, and it's yours too, yours and Stoney's. You and Stoney do whatever you want with Sanora's stars. I'm giving them to you 'cause she'd want you and Stoney to have them . . . and so do I. They're yours to dream under or scatter to the wind. You just remember old Buddy Chisolm knew you'd be back . . . and that you'd be lying safe in Stoney's arms under Sanora's stars one day. Remind Stoney he's my boy and I love him. Have him kiss your pretty face for me and tell you I love you too. Now, the two of you children, hop up on that old bed and wait for sunset. Count them stars and remember the old man who loved you."

Violet brushed the tears from her cheeks and looked to see the plentiful moisture gathered in Stoney's eyes.

"He wants you to live here," she whispered.

"He wants us to live here, Viola," he said. He reached out, brushing a strand of hair from her face.

Oh, how she loved him! How had she lived ten years without him? In that moment, she couldn't believe she had managed it.

"And he's giving me the stars," Violet squeaked, her throat tight with emotion. "How sweet, to give someone the stars. What a heavenly gift."

"Leave it to ol' Buddy to turn to romance on his deathbed," Stoney said, smiling at the memory of their dear, departed friend.

Violet glanced out the window. The sky was orange and pink and lavender. The sun had begun to set.

"It's setting," she said. She frowned. "Will we be able to see the stars through the window?"

"Maybe that's why he said we have to stretch out," Stoney said. "Maybe we gotta be lower or something." Stoney hunkered down for a moment. "A body can't see stars by the light of sunset anyway. I don't know what he was talkin' about."

He stood straight and glanced about the room. He chuckled, smiled at Violet, and took her hand. "Come on. I guess this'll be the first time we've shared a bed in long time."

Violet gasped and slapped his shoulder playfully. "We haven't ever shared a bed, Stoney Wrenn. My reputation is entirely unsoiled."

"What about that time you had that fever?" he said, leading her to the bed in the very center of the room. "Remember? I snuck in yer window and stayed the night with you . . . in your bed."

"I was seven years old!" Violet exclaimed.

"It still goes toward sharin' a bed," he said.

Violet watched as he rather flopped down onto the bed.

"Ahhh!" he sighed as he crossed his ankles and tucked one hand behind his head. "Come on now, Viola. Buddy said to hop up on the bed and gaze at the stars with me." He patted a spot next to him on the bed.

Violet bit her lip, completely enchanted. There wasn't any place she would rather be—couldn't imagine a more beautiful heaven than lying in Stoney Wrenn's arms every night forever. Violet lay down by him and kissed him sweetly on the cheek as the light in the room grew warmer.

"Well, ain't that something?" Stoney said.

Violet gasped as the light in the room seemed to intensify. Instead of growing dimmer, it was almost as if the room had been built to capture the last, most radiant sunlight of the day.

Violet glanced toward the window. The brilliant rays of the setting sun danced through the room, the sky outside a perfect gold woven with deep scarlet clouds.

"I still don't see any stars," Violet said.

"Oh my hell," Stoney swore in a whisper. "That ol' son of a gun!"

"What?" Violet said, looking to Stoney. His eyes were wide with astonishment as he stared at the ceiling. Stoney began to chuckle, and Violet followed his gaze—gasped as she saw the ceiling, the twinkling stars imbedded overhead. The ceiling of the room was painted a deep sapphire blue. A very detailed moon was painted there as well, and littering the portrait of a night sky were tiny flashes of light—stars—stars made of something that sparkled like the heavens.

"What is it?" Violet asked as Stoney rose from the bed, still staring at the ceiling.

He laughed. "It can't be," he whispered. "I-I always thought he was just tellin' tales."

"Tales about what?" Violet asked, rising from the bed herself. Stoney went to one corner of the room and picked up an old trunk. Returning to the bed, he sat it on the bed just at the foot. Violet watched as he stepped up onto the bed and then the trunk.

"Buddy Chisolm? That rich young man from New York City?" Stoney began, running his thumb over one of the stars in the ceiling. He chuckled and looked to Violet. "Ol' Buddy Chisolm made his fortune mining diamonds!"

He shook his head. "I always thought he was just feedin' me a trough of hogwash. But he wasn't. I think these are diamonds, Viola!"

"You're teasing me," she breathed. Stoney shook his head, however, and offered her his hand. Violet stepped up onto the bed and then the trunk. As Stoney helped her balance on the trunk, she looked more closely at the stars imbedded in the ceiling.

"Nope," Stoney said. "I remember now . . . what he told me once when I asked him what he done with all his diamonds. I didn't believe him—thought he was just tellin' tales again. But he said after he got rich off his diamond mine, he moved out west, built this old house . . ." Stoney paused to laugh. "He said, 'After I found Sanora, I didn't want them diamonds no more. They didn't sparkle as purty as Sanora did.' Buddy told me he threw 'em out. 'Tossed 'em up to the heavens. That's where the stars come from, Stoney,' he said. 'The stars in the sky are all that's left of them ol' diamonds.' "

Violet laughed as Stoney's dimples deepened—as his opalescent, jeweled eyes sparkled with amusement. She thought then that she knew what old Buddy Chisolm meant, about the diamonds not owning the beauty Sanora did, for nothing in the world was as beautiful to Violet Fynne as the light of pure joy in Stoney Wrenn's opaline eyes.

"Diamonds," Stoney whispered as he helped

Violet down from the trunk and bed. "That sneaky ol' devil."

Violet stared up at the ceiling. As the sun continued to set, the sparkle of the diamond stars in the ceiling dulled until only the painted moon was still bright.

Stoney opened a drawer in the little table by the side of the bed. He pulled out a match and lit the lamp sitting there.

"Well, what are you going to do with them, Stoney?" Violet asked.

But Stoney shook his head and chuckled, "Oh, no you don't, Viola. Buddy gave the diamonds to you. That's yer choice, not mine."

"But you own the house," she said. Suddenly, the responsibility of hidden wealth caused Violet a great discomfort. She didn't want wealth; she had Stoney. What need did she have for diamonds?

"It don't matter," Stoney said. "The diamonds are yers." He smiled at her, his eyes smoldering in the lamp light.

"Then I choose to leave them where they are," Violet said, smiling as she slid her arms around his waist and kissed him tenderly on his strong chin. "For as long as this house stands with you as the owner, I think they should stay—Sanora's stars."

Stoney smiled. "Maybe you could let me have just one," he whispered. "Let me take just one of Sanora's stars so that I can have a real purty weddin' ring made for you. And every time you look at it, you'll think of ol' Buddy . . . how he loved Sanora . . . how much I love you. That way we'll always carry a piece of ol' Buddy Chisolm with us, not just in our hearts, but really carry it with us."

Violet felt tears trickle down her face. "Wedding ring?" she breathed. "Are you—"

"Proposin' marriage?" he interrupted. "Of course! I been practicin' since I was twelve, though it didn't come out quite like I'd planned all this time."

Violet wiped a tear from one cheek. Stoney bent and kissed the tears on her other. "Will you marry me, Violet Fynne?" he whispered. "I've been waiting so long to love you. Will you stay with me forever? Will you live in this house with me, let me hold you in my arms every night, kiss you every mornin'?"

Violet trembled, her body quivering with joy. "Only if you'll promise not to ask Mr. Asbury for permission to court Layla when you go to supper tomorrow night," she teased.

Stoney chuckled. "I promise," he said.

"Then I will marry you, Stoney Wrenn," Violet whispered. "I've been planning to marry you for a long, long time."

"How long?" Stoney asked, kissing the corner of her mouth.

"Since I was five years old and you gave me that daffodil on Easter," she said.

"That is a long time," he whispered.

Violet gasped, and Stoney looked to the window. It was dark out, but Violet was certain she'd heard something: laughter.

"That didn't sound like Coby Fisher or Mr. Deavers," he said.

"Sounded like a girl," Violet whispered.

"You don't think that no-good Hagen Webster is out here sparkin' some poor filly again, do you?" Stoney asked.

Violet shrugged as Stoney lifted the lamp.

"Come on," he said. Taking Violet's hand, he led her out of the room and down the stairs.

"I think I see something," Violet said as they peered out through a downstairs window. Stoney turned the lamplight low, set the lamp on the floor, and followed Violet's gaze.

She heard him chuckle, and as her own eyes adjusted to the darkness, she smiled as well. She gazed through the window to where Jimmy Ritter and Maya Asbury stood in the moonlight. Jimmy seemed to say something, and Maya nodded. Violet felt her heart flutter as Jimmy took Maya's face between his hands then, kissing her ever so softly on the mouth.

"Maybe it wouldn't hurt to take two stars from Sanora's sky upstairs," Violet whispered. "Just two. One for my wedding ring—"

"And one for Maya Asbury's?" Stoney asked.

Violet nodded. "But that's all. Just two. I want to lie in your arms and gaze at Sanora's stars the way Buddy and Sanora did. I want to name our memories by them . . . name them after our children."

"There are hundreds of diamonds in the ceiling, Viola. How many children you plannin' on us havin'?" he teased.

Suddenly, Violet's eyes filled with tears once more. She reached up, running her fingers through the softness of his hair—caressed his whiskery cheek with the back of her hand.

"Ten years," she whispered. "Ten years . . . stolen from us."

Stoney brushed a hair from her cheek. "It doesn't matter," he said. "All that matters is now. We're together now."

Violet nodded. He was right, and her heart was at peace. He was there—Stoney Wrenn—standing before her, holding her in his arms, and nothing would separate them again. Her very soul knew it.

"Do you want to go down to the creek? We could cool our feet in the water and talk," Violet suggested.

Stoney smiled, and Violet's entire body was suddenly alive with mad fluttering. He bent, placing a moist, lingering kiss to her throat.

"How 'bout we go down to the crick and kiss 'til the sun comes up?" he whispered.

Violet giggled, her entire body rippling with goose bumps.

"Then we can run in to town first thing in the mornin' and have the minister marry us. What do ya say?"

"I say I love you, Stoney Wrenn," Violet breathed as he pressed his mouth to hers. "But I do wish it was tomorrow already."

He chuckled, his opaline eyes gleaming in the lamplight. "Oh, don't you worry, Viola," he whispered. "Between the crick coolin' yer feet and me warmin' up yer mouth, tomorrow will be here before ya know it."

"Promise?" she asked, lovingly kissing his chin.

"I promise," he whispered. "I promise."

Violet melted against Stoney. Lost in his arms, lost in the pure pleasure of passion's kiss, Violet felt as if Stoney embraced her very soul. Stoney Wrenn—her friend—her lover. When the sun rose, he would be her husband, and they would spend their days together—and their nights. Oh, such nights they would spend in loving, in naming memories, and in gazing at the painted moon and Sanora's diamond stars.

Books are produced
in the United States
using U.S.-based
materials

Books are printed
using a revolutionary
new process called
THINKtech™ that
lowers energy usage
by 70% and increases
overall quality

Books are durable
and flexible because
of smythe-sewing

Paper is sourced
using environmentally
responsible foresting
methods and the
paper is acid-free

# ABOUT THE AUTHOR

Marcia Lynn McClure's intoxicating succession of novels, novellas, and e-books—including *The Visions of Ransom Lake*, *A Crimson Frost*, *The Rogue Knight*, and most recently *The Pirate Ruse*—has established her as one of the most favored and engaging authors of true romance. Her unprecedented forte in weaving captivating stories of western, medieval, regency, and contemporary amour void of brusque intimacy has earned her the title "The Queen of Kissing."

Marcia, who was born in Albuquerque, New Mexico, has spent her life intrigued with people, history, love, and romance. A wife, mother, grandmother, family historian, poet, and author, Marcia Lynn McClure spins her tales of splendor for the sake of offering respite through the beauty, mirth, and delight of a worthwhile and wonderful story.

**Center Point Large Print**
600 Brooks Road / PO Box 1
Thorndike, ME 04986-0001 USA

(207) 568-3717

US & Canada:
1 800 929-9108
www.centerpointlargeprint.com